D0056562

PRAISE FOR BJ MAYO AND *ALFIE CARTER*

"In his debut novel, *Alfie Carter*, BJ Mayo has crafted extraordinarily original and real characters that will encircle your heart and camp out with you long after you've read the last page. Join Jackaleena and Alfie in their amazing journeys from Africa to Texas in a delightfully original and harrowing path of survival, growth, courage, and faith that showcases grace in its purest form. You will not be disappointed."
>—**Marian P. Merritt**, author of *The Moon Has No Light*

"From the war torn jungles of the African coast to the dusty hills of West Texas, *Alfie Carter* is an incredible story of courage, faith and love."
>—**Robert C. Martinez**, PE, president and CEO,
>Titan Rock Exploration & Production

"A wonderful story masterfully written. The storylines were presented and woven together to make a fascinating read—easy to follow with proper attention given to detail. Highly recommended."
>—**Rory Pendleton**, Texas A&M class of '78

"Bob Mayo is a good storyteller whose attention to detail draws the reader into this wonderful story of hope, perseverance, and faith. A very enjoyable read."
>—**Tommy Knowles**, retired oil and gas executive

ALFIE CARTER

ALFIE CARTER

A NOVEL

BJ MAYO

Skyhorse Publishing

Skyhorse Publishing books may be purchased in bulk at special discounts for sales promotion, corporate gifts, fund-raising, or educational purposes. Special editions can also be created to specifications. For details, contact the Special Sales Department, Skyhorse Publishing, 307 West 36th Street, 11th Floor, New York, NY 10018 or info@skyhorsepublishing.com.

Skyhorse® and Skyhorse Publishing® are registered trademarks of Skyhorse Publishing, Inc.®, a Delaware corporation.

Visit our website at www.skyhorsepublishing.com.

10 9 8 7 6 5 4 3 2 1

Library of Congress Cataloging-in-Publication Data is available on file.

Cover design by Daniel Brount
Cover photo credit: Shutterstock

Print ISBN: 978-1-5107-6425-5
Ebook ISBN: 978-1-5107-6426-2

Printed in the United States of America

There is something about a stream that calms the spirit.
A calm spirit cleanses the soul.

CHAPTER ONE

"Ms. Carter . . . Counselor, please approach the bench," said a seemingly exasperated Judge Ivis Parker. "Defense counselor, you too." His tremendous, pepper-colored, and generously woolly eyebrows narrowed to a gray V, as they always did when he was not happy. The bushy black and gray twigs melded together at the seam above his nose. Normally unflappable, his tone denoted no further tolerance.

"Judge, I am so sorry," Jackie said, barely above an audible whisper, "I was merely in deep thought. Again, I am deeply sorry."

"Okay, okay, please proceed, counselor, and let's please try to stay focused on our task at hand. This is the second time in today's proceeding that you seemed to fade off, and I sincerely hope it is the last."

"It will be, Judge," Jackie replied.

Jackie Carter, County Prosecutor for Spring, Texas, was more than deeply troubled by the case at hand. The alleged rape of a ten-year-old girl by two local seventeen-year-old boys was going fairly well for the prosecution, until the girl and her parents agreed to allow her to testify in front of the jury. There she sat on the witness stand, barely below the age of puberty, innocent and pure. The normally stoic prosecutor became overwhelmed with empathy, to the point of a near flood of tears just visualizing what had potentially happened to this young girl. Every time the girl was given a question, she spoke in halting, one-word answers, and Jackie's skin would crawl.

The defense attorney was merciless. His line of questioning seemed to tilt the guilt in the little girl's direction. Jackie interrupted him time and again, as he put forth questions that made it look as if she had provoked the attack by the two young men. As Jackie thought of the brutality of the event, she could not gain full control of her emotions and began to weep.

Judge Parker immediately summoned her to the bench. His gravelly voice barely above a whisper, he said, "Ms. Carter, may I ask what in the wretched sam hill is wrong with you today? I have seen you handle some of the roughest cases ever to come across my bench without so much as a flinch, always prepared, always professional, and might I say, somewhat like stone at times. What is so different about this one? The first time I can forgive, the second is questionable. But crying publicly, counselor, and in front of the jury, for all to see? Are you trying to elicit sympathy for the plaintiff, disgrace for the defendants? If you want to wreck this case, keep on doing what you are doing, but I will highly advise you to dry it up, and I mean now. Do you understand me? I want no more of what I have seen, do I make myself clear?"

Jackie faltered, bringing her tissue to her very red eyes. "Judge, I do not think I can continue today," she said in a whisper. Her head was pounding, sinuses draining uncontrollably. Her tissue, wadded up in her clinched hand, was no longer of use. It was saturated. "If you can bear with me, I would like to see you in your chambers."

"Very well, counselor, but it better be good, and I mean damn good. Look at the cost of the court," he said in his low, rumbling voice. He never spoke loud enough for anyone else to hear. "Remember, our docket is very loaded for the next three months and this only adds to that business by another day. Why can't people control their emotions? I mean, I understand that some folks' feelings are subject to change on a whim, but this is pure nonsense. This is not you."

Judge Parker gaveled the day's proceedings to a close and rescheduled for 9:00 a.m. the following day.

"Counselor, I will see you in my chambers. Defense counselor, I will call you later this evening," he said as he waved his hand that there would be no further questions from anyone. Jackie knew he was more than fair, but his hackles were clearly up. It was speculative as to what was going to happen in his chambers. When his hackles got raised, he was a quite a bone to be chewed.

She sat quietly in Judge Parker's chambers, awaiting his dreaded arrival. *I guess he deserves the truth, as he is a good man*, she thought. She had never known him to be unfair in her years as county prosecutor of Spring. For the most part, he always kept himself tempered and mindful, never letting his facial expressions betray his thoughts. However, on rare occasions this did not hold true, specifically when a man, being tried for the murder of his wife, actually jumped up and spit in the judge's direction. His complexion turned dark red and his great furrowed eyebrows narrowed. The skin between his eyebrows seemed to turn a dark red in a giant wrinkle. "Handcuff this man and gag him, if necessary," he said. "I will not tolerate rude behavior in my courtroom." It certainly got everyone's attention, and a further outburst did not occur.

The judge, at six feet five inches, was quite the specimen of a man's man. He weighed close to three hundred pounds, well-distributed on his massive frame. His giant arms were evident under his flowing black robe. He was always well-groomed, with the exception of the great bushy eyebrows, and always impeccable in his slim black tie. Courtroom witnesses and jury pools always seemed to be taken aback when the Honorable Judge Ivis Parker was brought in by the court bailiff and the courtroom called to order. Jackie always studied the members of the jury's reactions when he entered the courtroom. His no-nonsense persona was commanding in a calm way. Somehow the audience got the impression that justice just might prevail in a case with a judge like this. He was always a very attentive listener with attention to precise detail. With the exclusion of the man spitting in the judge's direction on one occasion, there had never been outward signs of animosity towards Judge Parker.

Judge Parker entered his chambers, removing his robe as he walked through the door. From the color of his cheeks she ascertained that he was probable quite angry, just as he had appeared to be in the courtroom. He hung his robe on the wooden peg next to a framed picture of him and his wife, Melissa.

"Judge . . . I need . . ." She stopped and grabbed the tissue again as tears streamed down her face. "I really need to talk to you if you will permit me a little bit of time. Will you allow me a few minutes?"

Judge Parker, ever the mind reader, sensing he was in for some kind of ride he did not prefer to go on, sighed deeply. "Jackie, please do proceed, take your time, I have only but time," waving his hand in a broad wave " . . . and I always like a good story. I am all but certain that yours is going to be a good one after what I saw today."

"My name, my name is . . . it is Jackaleena Karino N'Denga," she said haltingly.

Judge Parker's eyes narrowed with great surprise and interest when she spoke these words, knowing they were fixing to go off a cliff and he was being dragged along. The little crow's feet on his eyes crinkled up, and looked much like the topo maps of the Grand Canyon she had seen. That look struck fear in some areas of her mind, and affection in others. She sat transfixed, stammering for another second or two, just trying to read his face map.

"I am Cabindan. My mother, her name was Juliana, and my father's name, it is Mauricio. My little brother A'rao Olimpio died of malaria when he was very little. Maybe about four years old. At that time in our village, I did not know that mosquitos carried the illness. We had no window covering as we lived in a thatch hut. These were the members of my family. There are no others alive but I."

Judge Parker looked on in amazement. "Excuse me for my interruption, but may I ask how you got here? Cabinda is somewhere in Africa, is it not?" He spun the world globe on his desk. "Please show me where

Cabinda is on this thing. That had to have been a remarkable journey, to say the least. Please go on."

"Yes, Judge, it is indeed in Africa," as she placed her finger on the exact spot on the globe. "As I said, if you will allow me a few minutes, maybe I can explain exactly what twisted me off in court today. Please excuse me, as my head is pounding and my nose is running somewhat uncontrollably."

"Judge, do you have any aspirin in your chambers and a bottle of water?"

"Why yes," the judge said as he fumbled around in his desk. He produced a little tin of aspirin and handed it to Jackie. He went to his small refrigerator and pulled a cold bottle of water out.

She took two aspirin and swallowed them down. Her heart rate was beginning to slow as she began.

"I am of the Ovimbundu people. I am Cabindan. My tribal language is Umbundu. I lived in the village of B'Douro. I am fluent in Portuguese; my father taught me. I believe the year to be 1978 in which I was born. I say the year to be 1978 as I am not sure exactly when that day really was.

"I was born in our house, which I remember to be thatch, and our floor was dirt, as all other houses were in my village. My mother told me I was born there during the harvest of the crops.

"I remember well that my father worked the soil and grew crops. My father owned two cows and four goats. He raised corn on a small plot outside our village. He also helped with beekeeping and honey- and wax-gathering. Our village traded with the Portuguese. My mother cooked for our family. We enjoyed eating good for a while.

"One day, men came and took him away. That night, or the next day, I think, they took my mother. I never saw either of them again. I believe they were no longer of this earth shortly after the men came. Clairvoyance, I suppose. Anyway, I know they no longer walk with us. I was very young and remember most parts of my early life very well, while others are a little fuzzy. I no longer have the nightmares, or wake up in a cold sweat as before. Until today, I had never lost my public composure. For that, I deeply apologize."

CHAPTER TWO

Jackaleena sat quietly by the slow-moving stream. The peaceful birds called back to each other as they flew gracefully over the water. She wriggled her toes in the mud. She smiled as she noticed again that her toes were the same color as the mud. All of her people were colored like she. Some from the mountain regions were lighter in color. Maybe the night light in the sky made them lighter, as they were not shaded by as many trees as her people. They were not as well accepted within her tribe, but were tolerated, unless the witchy man Toto said no. They could purchase their purity with a few beautiful shells from the ocean, or, if it was his wish, with bloodletting from their veins and into his drinking cup mixed with cow's milk.

Her mother was not Milano and had the blood marks on her arms. She never told her why they were there. Jackaleena's father always told her she was as smart as the leopard and as pretty as the flowers. She always looked into the quiet pool at her face. She thought she did not look like a flower, but flowers were pretty. She guessed it to be true; she might be as pretty as a flower.

She knew leopards were smart animals. She knew she could sometimes perceive what most people were thinking about saying before they spoke their words. She guessed her father was right. A leopard always seemed to know the hunter's next move, she had heard many times by the communal fire when the men were talking. They always feared the leopard, and rarely saw one, much less killed one. She always loved to sit close to the communal man's fire and listen to their bush stories, especially the stories of the hunts.

She would sit for hours at the stream, until mother whistled her special bird call and she was to come quickly to the house. Most days, Jackaleena was out when the sun was two fingers flat above the land, exploring the areas of the stream. The giant tree by the stream always induced exploring, with its gaping root bundle and secret entrance. It was narrow to get into but large on the inside. She would wiggle through the roots and into the big "room" in the middle. It was big enough for her to sprawl her legs out. She could stand up straight and peer out her eyeholes. Rarely had she seen anyone pass, other than people from her village and the animals. She would sit quietly and watch the animals come by, some very close, and until now they never knew she was there. Some would pause, bolt, and run, seeming to know something was not right. Others, like the great band of monkeys, moved through quickly, always ready to scurry up the great trees at a moment's notice if the predator alarm was sounded. Once the call was sounded, loud barking and screeching rained down from the safety of the treetops.

It was here she first saw the three young boys in soldier caps walk in from the sunny side of the jungle. They seemed to appear out of nowhere. She did not dare to breathe loudly when she heard them, and squatted low among the roots of her tree. Her heart was pounding wildly as she struggled to remain calm and quiet. The boys were not much older than she, and were cursing and smoking with guns on their shoulders. Their camouflage shirts and breeches blended closely with the jungle.

One of the village elders had a gun he had found in the jungle. He told the other men it had special powers, even though he had no ammunition. Each of the boys had an ammunition belt around their waist, with many bullets. They had soldier hats on and appeared nervous, gesturing and pointing back toward the sun. The cigarettes they were smoking seemed to make them look older, but their vulgar talk showed they were just young boys, possibly from the spirit world.

She called on Toto, the village witchy man, to come remove her on wings from her hideout. She touched her hands together twice, very quietly. She had been taught that if you were truly looked upon well by Toto, clapping your hands twice after a fervent request, it would be honored. Jackaleena was scared, and wondered if they could hear her heart beating. It sounded like it was going to come out of her chest. She needed to relieve her water maker badly, but dared not. The burning sensation was overwhelming, but she forced herself to remain motionless.

"We will go into the B'Douro camp today and kill many for Unita," blustered the tallest of the group. He acted crazy, his hat cocked on his head. "We will crawl through the brush and wait until their fires are low and the huts are quiet. Then we will each go into the first hut we find and kill them all. Captain Mingas said he wants all of the young girls if we find them. I say, to hell with him, and take the girls for ourselves and kill his rooster."

"You do and you will be dead if he finds out," said the squat one with narrow eyes.

"Hell, I say Mingas is too old to catch me if I decide to run."

"You decide to run and he will kill us all. You know how he gets when he smokes the brown-brown."

All shook their heads in agreement. He was a mean and merciless killer when he smoked the brown-brown, and most of the time was just merciless. He always kept his prize rooster with him, day and night. Mingas kept the rooster in a small wooden cage a short distance from his sleeping area. If anyone approached within 100 meters, the rooster would let loose with nonstop crowing. All of the men and boys in his command were made to sleep 150 meters away. There he kept four more roosters in cages, placed a short distance from where they slept. Any disturbance caused nonstop crowing and squawking from the outside roosters. If this was before daybreak, they all knew trouble was close.

This alarm system worked very well for Mingas. Some soldier boys felt he treated his beloved roosters better and fed them better than they. They were made to catch grasshoppers for all of the roosters on a daily basis.

The boys knelt and drank at the stream, cupping their hands and bringing the water to their mouths. Jackaleena remembered her father talking at the communal fire about Unita. They were a guerilla group that wanted to take over the country. She heard her father say they captured young boys from villages and made them kill people for the guerilla fighters' army. These must have been some of those boys. She wondered how they came to be in the band, and the villages they may have come from. They were only a few meters from where Jackaleena always sat and wriggled her toes in the bank mud. She hoped they did not see her footprints, as they would lead them to her tree.

They slaked their thirst and stood facing away from her. The oldest one lit another cigarette and motioned the others to head west towards the tall trees. They quietly melted into the jungle. She could smell the aroma of the cigarette. It was sweet and burned her nose.

Jackelena sat quietly for a long while, shaking and trembling. She had an ominous feeling. Maybe she should call on Toto the witchy man again for guidance. He had not taken her out on wings as she had requested. He must have been busy; after all, she was just a girl. The great Toto had bigger things to do, as he was protector of all, not just a scared little girl.

After the boys had been gone a long time, she inched out of the tree room, squatting outside to relieve the burning from her water maker. Afterwards, she set out for home, not wasting any time along the way, careful to conceal her presence. She must hurry and warn everyone in the village.

When she was a long stone's throw from her village, she heard screaming and then the shooting started. Her heart raced as she ran towards the village under the protection of the trees.

Hiding behind a great tree, Jackaleena held her hand over her mouth, lest she dare to make a squeak. There were several soldiers in the village.

All were in camouflage uniforms and carrying guns. Some were grown men, and some were boys, like she saw by the stream. While some stood outside, others would enter the huts with their guns. Some men were dragged out and beaten unmercifully, while others did not come out. She noticed some of the soldiers had blood on their hands and uniforms. Her heart pounded, and she tried to find her mother and father. She could not see them in the torrent of activity.

The unmistakable and sickening sounds of machetes against flesh could be heard, sounding like a machete when one of the men cut a tree branch in the forest. Loud and fearsome screams filled the air, as all in her village were being tortured and killed. Some of the older women were herded into a group, guarded by the three young boys from the stream. Jackaleena watched helplessly as the soldiers pulled two screaming girls out of one of the huts. She recognized them to be Arao Mvungo's only children. She played with them sometimes, always in the village but never at her secret place. The soldiers ripped the tunics off of the two girls. Two soldiers held each girls arms down while two others pulled their legs apart and held them to the ground. The girls screamed in agony as at least eight soldiers put their man parts into them, squealing like wild hogs as they humped up and down, throwing their heads back after a time. All of the other soldiers clapped when a new man got on, gleefully blowing smoke from their cigarettes, sometimes in the faces of the girls while they laughed and grunted.

After they were through, the only sounds to be heard were the weeping of the women and the quiet moaning of the two girls. She heard two men curse the girls for the blood they had on their man parts. They hit both girls with the backs of their hands and told them to quit screaming. The oldest boy soldier was summoned by the leader man, called Mingas. He said, "Come here, shit for brains, and kill these bloody-legged girls. They are no longer of use. They stink like gopher's shit and you have ruined them. Prove to us you are a man."

The young man approached, lighting a cigarette for comfort. "Go ahead, you goat penis, shoot them." The young man took a couple of smokes off of the cigarettes. His hands seemed to be trembling. He pulled his pistol from his belt and quickly shot both of them in the head. His hands trembled after their heads exploded. He shot them at such close range, Mingas screamed at him as some brain matter got on his boots. "Always aim your bullet the opposite direction from where I am standing, goat penis. Wipe this shit off of my boots." The young soldier knelt down in front of Mingas and wiped the brain matter off with his hat.

The soldiers erupted in a chorus of jubilation. Mingas erupted, saying, "You are no longer shit for brains, you are now cow shit, an elevated status. One more kill and you will no longer be shit and can be considered a person. Two or three more kills, and you'll be a real soldier. One thousand more, a Mingas." He bellowed with laughter, waving and shooting his gun in the air, crazy-eyed and mean.

She could hear a rooster crowing somewhere close to the camp. There were no chickens or roosters in her camp. He must be the one the boys spoke of at the stream. Jackaleena's heart raced. Her body began to convulse and she vomited. She stuck her mouth on the floor of the jungle and tried to keep from making any noise. She did not have much in her stomach, but the convulsions did not stop for a short time. She caught her breath slowly, wiping the dirt and twigs from her mouth with her finger.

She slowly stood up, trying to comprehend what she was witnessing. Maybe she was dreaming in the spirit world, as she sometimes did. She waited to wake up and see her mother and father, but she was awake. She scratched her face, to see if she felt pain, ensuring she was awake. Her face hurt where she scratched, and she reasoned that everything she was seeing was real.

Mothers wept, and old men quietly accepted their fates. She watched as the soldiers went to each man and made them kneel while the others watched. They hit them on their necks with their machetes. Some of the men's heads hung on by flesh and they fell over. The others' heads fell off on the first hit. They looked like forest birds with their heads pulled off.

Jackaleena ran as fast as her legs would take her, to the stream, to the tree, into the hole, and securely in the tree room. She gasped for air and vomited again. This time nothing came out at all. Tears streamed from her eyes as her small frame shook. She could not calculate what had just taken place. Her family was probably dead, even though she did not see her mother in the group. She did not see them take her father but knew that it was true. Maybe she should have asked the witchy man Toto to place a curse on the boys, but there was no time. It was over. Maybe her mother was still alive. She did not dare return to the village for a while.

Jackaleena caught frogs to eat and two grasshoppers. Her stomach was not ready for food. She placed the dead creatures on a log and looked at them. *Why do others have to die to feed me? Who made up these rules? But if I do not eat, I will die.* She pulled a handful of moss from the tree and tried to eat it. She finally ate the small frogs and grasshoppers. The brown juice from the grasshoppers dripped down her lips. She gagged but did not vomit this time. She reasoned that she would sneak back to the village in the dark, to see if there were any fire lights, and maybe see if her mother and father were still alive. She reasoned they were not. But the witchy man Toto may have protected them. He could fly and see all tribes at the same time. He had been known to stop a man from dying who had been bitten by the black snake that stands tall and moves fast. He had probably protected her mother and father, because Jackaleena had given thought to him when the men were using their machetes.

At the time when the sun meets the earth, she crept back through familiar trails to a stone's throw from the village. She stood quietly and listened. There were no fires, no sounds, except for sounds of the forest animals and night insects. She climbed a tree and sat perched in the second fork from the top through the night, watching and listening. Night animals did not scare her as badly as the soldiers did. She thought she heard the sound of the leopard roar. Maybe he was telling her he was there to protect her. Her father told her she was as smart as a leopard.

Daylight was long in coming as she stayed in her perch. Her body ached all over. She listened carefully, unable to sleep. When the sun was two fingers from the earth, she crept down from the tree. She slipped along the ground until she was half a stone's throw from the huts. She waited under the brush until the sun was three fingers flat from the earth, and slipped up to the camp.

She entered her empty hut. The floor was saturated with blood, with signs of a struggle. There were many machete cuts on the thatch wall and great spurts of blood. What little clothes they had were strewn on the floor. Mother's teapot, her only cherished possession, lay broken on the floor. Jackaleena lay there and wept.

After a time, she began to make her way around the camp. There were many dead men with no heads. The soldiers had placed their heads on sharp sticks around the communal campfire rock ring. There were still some smoldering coals in the ring. Some of the men's heads had eyes wide open, frozen in fear, dried blood staining their faces. All had swollen tongues and dried blood and grass stuck to their ghostly faces. Some of them had their man parts cut off and were stuffed in their mouths. One man had one of his ears stuck in his mouth. Others' eyes were closed.

She recognized Arao Mvungo's head on one of the poles. He must have tried to fight as they were putting their man parts into his daughters. His head was nearly completely flat on one side. Maybe they hit him with a rifle butt or a tree limb . . . maybe a big rock, before they cut his head off. She recognized the animal bones he wore in his ears. He was the only one in the village that had the "membe bat" leg bones adorning a hole in his ears. He was never without them. He had climbed high into the trees to catch one on their perch. The story was told many times in the village, because the tree was four fingers tall from the ground, as Arao Mvungo told it. It was said that the membe bat carried special powers in his wings, and that the person who caught one would be able to fly. She never knew Arao Mvungo to fly, and now his membe bat bones drenched in blood did nothing to protect him, letting him fly away from the soldiers.

How could the witchy man Toto allow this? He was supposed to be the guardian of the village. These were his people. Where was he? She screamed, "Witchy man Toto, this is Jackaleena." She clapped her hands twice. "I call on you to end this spirit dream now. I call on you to produce my mother and father and all the people of my village. I call on you to kill the soldiers. Do it now." She clapped her hands twice. She listened quietly and only heard jungle sounds. Maybe Toto was busy with worse problems, though she could not think of anything he needed to be doing but answering her request. In fact, if he was a good witchy man, he would not have allowed it to happen.

She hoped he could not think the same thoughts she was thinking, as he might become angry with her. He might put a curse on her and cause her hair to turn white and her skin to turn yellow. He had been known to place this curse on a whole village. The old ones spoke of it at the communal camp fire. They were called the "parrot village." Other tribes were forbidden from traveling to the parrot village or talking to the villagers. Toto said he was the only witchy man who knew how to find the parrot village. He would not let any other tribes make contact with the parrot village until the signs were right. She guessed the signs had not been right up until now, because no one had ever been there. But she believed it.

CHAPTER THREE

I cannot say how genuinely ticked off I was as I made my way down county road NM 2105 to the bend in the river. Beatrice's parting comment nearly stopped me in my tracks as I left home, but I did not let on. Stopping only for gas, fourteen hours of travel were beginning to muddle my brain. Birdie, my '68 Ford truck, was feeling the stress of the rutted-out road, but continued to putt along at my command. As in the past, a small pat of gratitude on the dash seemed to keep her going. Even with the carburetor job I did on her, she was still not running like her old self, probably the timing was off just a smidge.

I was never great at setting the points under the distributor cap. I always had trouble filing the tits off flat. "Atta girl, Birdie," I said as I patted her blue, cracked dash. We trailed out at the stand of cottonwoods, ancient and fiery yellow and orange in their November beauty.

Slamming Birdie to a stop, I stepped out, not bothering to close the door. The river ahead was flowing quietly in front of me. Slow forward steps, drinking in the smell of the mountain country, I made my way to the edge and sat. My brain felt like it was going to burst for the first few minutes, but the tension began to ebb the longer I sat and looked at the water. The river was low and flowing at a moderate rate, but still offered the same peace it had given me on my yearly visits, about twenty of them, now. I always like to study the smooth rocks on the bottom of the stream, worn smooth by relentless flow. Kind of like most people: starting out strong and resilient, but somewhat worn down over time with the relentless flow of life. Hell, I was one of those rocks.

The sounds and smells absorbed me, and the stresses of the past year seemed to take a reluctant back seat for a time. Looking to the northwest, I could see Old Hatchet Rock and the hazy blue features of Sacatonee Ridge. My eyes tightening, blocking out the setting sun, I strained to see if there was a snowcap above the aspens on White Water Baldy. After my eye surgery four years prior, the syrupy brown floaters seem to travel across my left eye at the most inopportune moments. In younger times, I could make it out with my bare eyes, but not so today.

To Birdie I went, to fetch my binoculars. Sure enough, snow it was, just above tree line. I don't know why Texas folks always get excited when they see snow, but it always gave me a bit of a tingle. As the sun began to drop below the horizon, I glanced at my watch: 5:20 p.m. NM time. I was in no hurry to set up camp, but the mid-November evening was cooling down rapidly. I grabbed as much quick firewood as was to be had, and in short order had a nice campfire going.

I set up my small tent with Birdie's headlights. My old Coleman lantern still held the mantles I installed on my last trip. It was somewhat amazing that they were still intact, in my rush to leave and get that witch behind me. After pumping the handle for a couple of minutes, careful to keep my thumb over the hole, I realized there would be no pressure without oiling the stem. All I had was a can of engine oil in my truck tool box.

I opened the plastic container and immediately had a mess with oil on my hands and jeans. Flaring with post-travel anger, I threw the container into the fire and cursed. I could feel the heat on my face, as I did when rage was upon me. I was quite sure the light V birthmark on my forehead was turning purple.

My heart rate began to slow and the heat began to dissipate. I then began to methodically retrace my steps to Birdie, and retrieve another quart of oil, feeling as always quite childish in not controlling my temper, especially over something I had created.

My head was splitting, as it always seemed to after a long trip. Anyway, this time I was successful, and upon lighting the lantern, the scary night was transformed into something I could deal with. No critters would come into my camp as long as I had a fire and a lantern burning, I told myself.

I pulled off my boots and let the fire warm my feet. The hole in the heel of my right sock was getting bigger, but I simply could not throw them away. I remembered my first pair of cowboy boots when I was ten. A neighbor boy gave them to me. They were a size ten; I wore an eight. They were already several years old, probably his stepdad's. I kept them for at least ten years. Like old friends, they helped me identify with the rodeo cowboy white trash crowd I lived with in our run-down country neighborhood. I guess they let me be part of their inner sanctum because I had a pair of boots and chewed tobacco. No matter that it made me sick, just the fact that I chewed it in front of them elicited a certain amount of poor boy toughness that they seemed to like. They knew I could not afford a pair of boots, but it did not seem to matter.

The fire began to dwindle. I pulled up one dead stump and hoisted it onto the fire as my nighttime log, and moved the lantern into the tent, careful to hang it at the highest point, to allow the fumes to travel upward and out the vent holes.

I propped my head against my pillow. It had been a long day and, as always, a long drive. I pulled out the picture I had secretly borrowed from Mr. Couch's trailer. The young lady in the picture was quite striking in her pep squad uniform. The black and yellow colors indicated she was local, as the newspaper said. My research thus far had my blood boiling in the most unprofessional way. Being an officer of the law, I was to be above the fray and the politics of any case I was assigned. "Just the facts" was my motto; let them take you where they may. It seemed when I knew that there was much unpleasantness ahead, I always rushed to the only place that offered solace in a turbulent world, my Gila mountain country. It was wild Apache country back in the day, and was still wild, yet without the Apaches. Even though it was several hundred long miles away, it was always worth the trip to straighten out my mind. The mystical qualities of her remote primitive areas, where humans seldom abide, allured me like a great mountain whore, there for the beholding. She always seemed to give me more than I took from her.

While here, my biggest fear was being eaten by a mountain lion or maybe a pair of Spanish wolves. The eerie womanlike scream of a mountain lion at night had turned me yellow on a previous trip. I ran into my tent and grabbed my pistol, ready at the helm if it came into my camp, even though it was night.

I trembled for a long while on that occasion. If worse came to worse, I could always sprint over to Birdie. Once inside, she would protect me. That really scared and unnerved me. What would I do if he came into my camp? I heard they always hit from behind, and on the back of the neck, just like they kill a deer. I still get chills, thinking about it.

I peeked outside the tent at her silhouette in the cool November night sky. The moon was half-full and I could see Birdie's full outline. Even with her 236,000 miles and two overhauls she was still running strong, and she was one thing I could depend on, never once lying, spitting in my face, arguing, or hitting me back. She started when she was supposed to, and could be counted on to get sixteen miles to the gallon, uphill or down.

There was still that dark spot on the seat from the bleeding. I never could get it out. At least now you could not tell it was from blood. I never even thought about it much anymore. It was just part of Birdie now. Stepping out into the night air, I quickly relieved myself a short distance from my tent. The cold night air invigorated me. The sky was brilliant with stars, and the Milky Way was there for the touching. Before turning in, I quietly thumbed through the daily *Desert Plains* I had purchased before I left Spring many hours before. My old habit of studying the obituary columns would not show me relief tonight. I was drawn like a moth to a flame. As I studied what was written about each person, I would parlay that against my own existence and see if I measured up to them, or, if they were poor enough, see how they measured against me. Some of the older folks would have long writeups, following their entire family tree and every detail of their lives. I guess back then they called everyone by their first and middle names. I would typically rank myself well below someone if they grew up in an affluent family, particularly a well-bred ranching family that sent all of their kids to college, or if they were a family of the military. I could somehow see the older ones laid out in their caskets at the funeral home, other oldies passing by, saying how good they looked dead. How peaceful and content they looked. And younger, too, I heard them say. I might go see one, but I'll be crap if I will say how good they look dead. Never could stand those funerals.

After carefully reading about the four dead folks in the obit column, I quickly conducted my comparative analysis and figured I was ahead of two of them, mainly because they were south of I-30. A clear separation point for the uppity and white trash like me. But that gave me the upper hand, because I was still alive and they were dead. The other two were military guys who fought on D-Day, so I fell in behind them. Knowing how I ranked on this night, which was clearly a 50/50 deal, I was able to drift into a somewhat peaceful sleep. Other nights, when I was less than 50 percent of the deal, I could easily spend hours backtracking on my history, and wishing I had been born an affluent person from a college family, or maybe been the son of an army captain instead of the son of an alcoholic roughneck. I would examine every detail and crossroads from the time I could remember until the present day. It was always an exhausting exercise, but trying to stop or control it seemed futile. It was like my brain could not turn off this kind of activity.

No living person knew about this particular piece of my identity. Not even Beatrice. I always hoped I could shake it before anyone ever found out because of the sheer foolishness of it all. Why in the world would anyone think like this? If anyone ever found it out, they might reason that I was crazy and not in charge of my faculties. An officer of the law might not be one very long if they found out.

* * *

I awoke the next morning to the howls of coyotes, at approximately 5:00 a.m. Such eerie yet beautiful, wild sounds were rarely heard inside the city. I stepped outside the tent and could hear the slow movement of the stream. It always sounded like there were thirty or forty of the coyotes. They howled for a good ten minutes and then went quiet as a mouse. Maybe they were doing some type of clan roll call. It had been said they roll-called nightly. When certain members did not answer, the others assumed they were dead. The females, it was said, would go into heat and therefore produce sufficient offspring to perpetuate the species. Maybe that is true, because there is never a shortage of coyotes, it seems.

My nighttime log was now a smoldering ember. I added wood to the fire. I filled an empty orange juice can with lantern fluid and tossed it on the fire. The volatility of the liquid always amazed me. The explosion of the liquid when hit by a lit match was impressive. Out in our country, everyone burned their trash in barrels. No one had the money to take their trash to the county dump. That cost two dollars per load, plus the gas to get you there. Most poor folks figured that was money badly spent. Some of the oil field hands, like my father, would steal empty drums from the oil field leases and bring them home. A good chisel and hammer could take the top out. Then you punched holes in the sides for air flow. Two small pieces of metal rod wired to the lid, and you had an instant burning barrel. Sometimes Mama's empty cheap hairspray cans would blow up and blow the lid off. Prowling cats were always looking for food in the barrels. Sometimes you could sneak up on the barrel with a baseball bat and hit the side loudly. The cat came out like a quail.

All of us learned at a young age to use gasoline to start the fire. Of course we always used more than was required. Sometimes it blew the lighted trash out of the barrel like a Roman candle—particularly danger-ous in fall and winter, with dead grass and all. That's how Mr. Reddy's chicken house burned down, with all the chickens in it. Nubbin, his son, told him that a neighbor kid shot a bottle rocket over the fence and caught it on fire. We used to shoot them at each other all the time during firework season, so it was a little feasible. I guess he believed him.

Normally, he would have beaten him for just about any reason. I saw him beat Nubbin with a water hose until I thought he was dead. And I ain't just talking on the ass, he hit him all over. Even a couple of times in the face. Nubbin had cussed him over him beating his mama.

I seldom saw him when he was not drunk, and when he was drunk he was violent and mean. I never knew of anyone named Nubbin in my whole life except Nubbin. I think his real name was Travis. His mama told me that his daddy called him Never Nothing, because he figured he would never amount to nothing. His father made him repeat the name he had given him, one night when he was drunk. Over and over he tried to make the boy say "Nothing," laughing and gee-hawing when he would mispronounce the word. He could not say it correctly and kept saying Nubbin instead. "What did you say your name was, boy?" "My name is Nubbin." They old man would laugh until tears came down his face. "Whatever you say, Nothing," he would proclaim. "Go get yourself a sugar-tit and go to bed. Mama," he would proclaim, "get some sugar in a sock and give it to Little Nubbin so he can get to bed." I guess they were the only family I knew that was poorer than we were growing up, with maybe the exception of the Pattersons, who lived at the end of Creek Road. They had seven kids and a father that ran out on them. Their mama worked as manager at the Silver Dollar to support them. There was no sheet rock on their walls, and sometimes they ate only cucumbers for supper. I always thought deep down that maybe Nubbin was somehow responsible for the dead dogs I found hanged by our old swimming hole. There were four of them, and they were all hanged from the neck with baling wire on cross tie posts on the fence line. Later, about two years after high school, Nubbin beat his father to death with a baseball bat, shortly after witnessing his father beat Nubbin's mama within an inch of her life. All for spending an extra fifteen dollars on groceries. She was only allowed thirty-five dollars a week. He went to the federal pen. I guess he became something more than a "Nothing," he became a killer. I was surprised he hadn't done it sooner.

I drank three cups of camp coffee and shoveled dirt over the fire. It was an automatic fine from the ranger if you left live coals and got caught. I had heard that for twenty years, but had only seen one ranger. Being a law officer and all, I had to err on the side of caution. I could always envision the *Desert Plains* headline: "Alfie Carter, Law Officer, Leaves Campfire Unattended in Gila Wilderness." Responsible for ten-thousand-acre forest fire. Currently being held by Silver City, New Mexico, authorities awaiting trial.

Birdie fired right up and we began to head toward the high country to the north. She never sputtered once while we were making our way up the treacherous switchbacks on the mule trail to Dead Tree Ridge.

The stubble on my chin was beginning to irritate my face. Even though it felt good being off-duty and not bound to the drab dress code I religiously followed, the red hair on my face itched beyond belief. Maybe it made me look like a real person in the real world, rather than a rank-and-file squeaky clean officer of the law.

As a matter of fact, I had decided to not change underwear for the entirety of my trip, or at least not until the last day before heading home. With only four days remaining off, that would be a stretch. That's how the real men did it. I would throw them away at the first KOA campground I came to. Beatrice would never know. Hell, she probably would not even care. She did seem to know which kind of underwear I preferred, as if it was any of her business. "Alfie, why do you keep shoving that blue pair of Fruit of the Looms to the bottom of the pile? I thought you liked blue." Hell, I like black, not blue, not gray, not green—just plain old black. But I never said a word. She was like a bad rash sometimes. Men's underwear are not supposed to be every color of the rainbow.

We topped out at Oz's camp and I stopped to sniff around a little. Having spent many an hour sprawled out around a campfire on this very ridge at this very camp site, I smiled to myself, remembering my surprise at seeing men with pistols on their hips when I first rode my horse into their camp. They asked me what kind of saddle gun I had. I said my old faithful .30-30. "Hell, boy, we use those for crutches up here. We shoot 7mm. We shoot mountain-to-mountain guns." Now that pissed me off. That .30-30 had killed many a white tail in Texas. The smell of the mountain cedar in their campfire that day is still etched in my memory. I listened to them argue over dominos, boo-ray, and whores. It seems like a lifetime ago, even though it has only been eighteen years.

I decided to drive the last short section of trail out of Oz's camp to the northwest and park at the trailhead. I hid Birdie as best I could behind two large mountain cedars and took out my poke bag, and was careful to load my flashlight. Since I was in mountain lion country, I always took my .44 mag pistol along, just in case I needed it. That witch would knock a bear's ass down in a pinch and definitely a mountain lion if I saw him first. I passed the same discarded plastic Pennzoil can that was at the trailhead. I stopped to inspect it years ago, and here it still lay. Amazing how long it takes nature to degrade plastic. I suppose it will be there for the next generation or two, if they happen by this way. However, I never picked it up and carried it away, as it was a good trail marker for me.

I hiked approximately one mile to the top of the ridge, and peered down into the gorge below. It was here I had happened upon when I was lost, trying to return to camp during my first mountain trip years ago. It was here I lay for hours under stands of pines, listening to nothing but the wind. It was here I could look down to the south and see the Arizona border, with no signs of humanity as far as the eye could see. It was also here that I did my best reflecting. It seemed the reflecting always turned to growing up in that sorry place with my worthless father and my poor mother who had to put up with him.

My watch said 10:00 a.m. I had already been sitting for nearly three hours, and was completely lost in the beauty and majesty of the mountains. Chipmunks scampered from log to log, and there was almost imperceptible movement below, in the brush at the bottom of the gorge. Probably an elk or a mule deer. Navajo messenger crows cawed back and forth. They had disrupted many a hunt for me in past years, with their relentless cawing at the precise moment a muley stepped into my sights. I had seen them flying with pieces of paper or shiny tinfoil in their beaks. Maybe they were messengers, as the Navajo said, but messengers to other animals was my thinking, because every time their sorry asses were around, there were no mule deer in the area. I swear they called down and warned them.

I remember Beatrice's narrowed gaze when I told her of my plans to go to the mountains for a few days. She gave me her black widow stare. From immature mama's girl at eighteen years of age when we married twenty-some-odd ago, to a strong, independent, no-bluff kind of girl at forty-three. No longer could I get by with much of anything out of line without immediate and strong rebuttal. Although she was one of my strongest private defenders, especially as far as my cases were concerned, the woman was mean as a one-eyed snake. I thought about her often when I was here. I thought about things here that we never discussed at home.

Somehow it seemed okay, here in the mountains, to think about our daughter who only lived for a few short hours after birth. Beatrice could not attend the simple graveside service, as she was still in the hospital. It was nearly unbearable to go it alone at the funeral, with only her parents and mine present. My roughneck father did not even wear a suit, and had his standard pack of unfiltered Camels in his front pocket. It was surprising that he wore clean clothes and was sober.

Everyone's hopes and dreams lay before us, or at least mine and Beatrice's. Their tearful eyes watching me kneel beside the small, white casket. I was in a little too much shock to really give a shit about how anyone else felt. How could a loving and caring God take our daughter? It changed my thinking on whether or not He really exists, to have let that happen. I never went back to church, from that day. I never missed those hypocritical assholes. Kind of like my pa, going to church on Sunday after an all-night drinking binge on Saturday. Hell, he beat Mama sometimes when he came in, and then stood beside her in church on Sunday, singing, "Bringing in the Sheaves," like nothing ever happened. Most folks did not stare as much as they could have, looking at the puffy side of Ma's face. She once covered up the black eye he gave her with makeup, but you could still tell. It looked like she had a broken vein in her eye. Anyway, he mostly did not hit her in the face, because he didn't want folks to see. He was a sorry and mean son of a bitch. I would just run and hide and cry for my mama. He was too big for me to take on.

Her name was Patricia Jean Carter. The doctor and the preacher said she had jet-black hair, like her mama. She was so premature, so little, I guess she didn't even have a chance. After all of these years, her name is still not spoken, nor is the event referenced in any form or fashion. If Beatrice has visited the grave, she has done it privately, without me being there to hold her hand.

Hell, I bet she has been there. The fact is, I never returned to the grave. Time has eased but not erased the pain. Beatrice's mama tries to talk about it from time to time, and I just walk out on her talkative loud-mouth ass. She'll say Patrica Jean would be about eighteen now. Do you ever think about her, Alfie? As if that is any of her nosy-ass insensitive business. I just get up and walk out. She seems to take great satisfaction in dragging it out of the closet.

Tears streamed down my face. The fall sun warmed it as it made its way steadily upward, above the line of trees. I guess it is okay to cry, as long as it is not in public, as my father used to say. Don't be a sissy boy, he would say. Sissies don't make it in this world, dry up that crying.

It was a release to shed tears. I guess that is why women do it so much, and men stay tied up in a knot. Such a dispassionate shithead he was.

I am usually with steadfast gaze and my emotions in check, giving the appearance of an oak tree. However, up here it was more like a willow. I always seemed to hold it in for at least a year and somehow could react emotionally while sitting on this mountain. Up here, I had to let it all drain out. Empty the till. Drain the piggy bank. Or, as my pa would say, shovel the shit out of the barn. And my barn was always full when I got here.

Beatrice's parting comment about maybe thinking about adopting a kid someday angered me beyond imagination. I did not respond. I jumped into an already packed Birdie and left her standing at the door. How dare she bring up adoption at this time in our lives? Hell, she had probably never been to the gravesite of our daughter and paid her respects. We were forty-three years old, for goodness's sake. What a foolish, stupid and irrational notion. We were trying to run a farm while I was busy being an officer of the law. And a detective with investigations to handle, for crying out loud. We damn sure did not have time for kids. Especially an adopted one.

I figure if God wanted us to have our own, He would have given us Patricia. Our animals, those goats and horses, were our kids. And besides, she had never dared to speak Patricia Jean's name to me after she died. She keeps bringing up maybe wanting to adopt a child. The woman has never even reconciled herself to the death of our daughter.

Who would put such a foolish notion into her mind? I bet it was her preacher. Ever since she started going to church a couple of years ago, she has been acting strange. Some kind of do-gooder / voodoo crusader.

The further I stayed away from the church and its hypocrites, the better I liked it. All they want is your money, and they damn sure can't bring back a little one.

I stayed pissed all the way to my campsite with fourteen hours to build as I traveled down the interstate and backroads, into the heart of the mountains. And another thing, why would Beatrice's "God" let another girl live over my girl? I guess Beatrice wanted to save the world or something. I know God don't have no use for me—well, brother, it goes the same way here. If He don't need me, I don't need Him.

CHAPTER FOUR

I pulled the picture of the young lady out of my pocket and studied it for some time. Her family had long lived in the county. Her father was Jerald Couch, refinery worker, and her mama Irene was said to be an athletic tennis player with an affinity for men other than her husband from time to time, as it was told down at Merle's Café by Merle himself, which means it probably was not true. His gossipy ass was always listening to other folks' conversations.

His version of events did not always align with what he overheard. I did not know them personally, only what the investigation was lending. Her grandpa, or Pap, as they called him, lived in an old dilapidated travel trailer in back of their two-acre place on the Houghton County line. It was about two miles north of Spring, and easy to find down a one-lane dirt road. The family lived in a fairly well-kept mobile home. It was underpinned with white tin and anchored down. There were tires on top of it due to high south winds that would ripple the roof like a washboard if something was not placed on top to hold it down.

Unfortunately, in this case, ten or fifteen old tires were giving the home the appearance of "poor white trailer trash," as the locals liked to call them. There was no one at home when I stopped in to visit them after Captain Burris assigned me the case. Jenna Couch, Jerald and Irene's daughter, was found dead two days before I left to come to the mountains. Her lifeless body was found by the lake keeper, hanging at the lake house at Moore's Lake approximately twelve miles northeast of town. The Moores' lake house was donated for community use by the Aubrey Moore III family in Spring. Aubrey was satisfied with the large sign outside the lake house declaring it Aubrey Moore III Lake House. "Welcome General Public."

There was a four-legged stool lying on the wooden floor. The rope she used to hang herself with was a red-and-black pleated lead rope with a two-inch brass spring clasp on the end. They sold these in the horse tack section at Rose's feed store in Spring. Rose was an old out-of-prime barrel racer who opened her store to be close to the cowboys that came in for horse feed. I don't know whether to believe that or not, but she always had on way too much perfume and had her shirt unbuttoned too many buttons to allow cleavage to show. She always seemed to have to bend over to pick up a receipt or something when I came in. Rose may have done extracurriculars on the side, but the law left her alone. She could sweet-talk the fat off of a pig. Back in the day, when she was in her prime, she commanded a lot of rodeo cowboys' attentions.

Dissecting the motive for such a senseless and selfish act was my job. I was called to the scene as soon as she was found. Blond-haired and blue-eyed, attractive and with her mama's same athletic build, it seemed such a tragic waste as I looked into her horrified blank stare and purple face. Her nearly black tongue stuck out grotesquely.

I took a thorough inventory of the dimensions of the building, careful not to disturb anything on the flagged-off scene of death, which was now a possible crime scene. She was dressed in blue jeans and a white, button-up blouse, regular school wear, even if it might be homemade. I am sure her mama did not shop at LaVelle's in town to buy her things. She had on silver earrings with a little makeup on. There was one ring on her pinky finger on her left hand with the letter "E" on it. On her feet, black, flat-soled tennis shoes, old with white shoelaces. No belt. Her britches were stained with urine and feces, from when her muscles relaxed, as they all do. The rafters in the lake house were approximately ten feet tall, all 2 x 6, not hardly bowing under her slight weight, which I guessed at 105 pounds. She appeared to have some type of burn mark on top of her left hand and her left calf, maybe from a cigarette. There was no sign of cigarette butts on the floor or on her person. Her hands did not smell as if she had held one in her hand. Time of death was estimated at two to three hours earlier, and rig had not set in. I wrote down my usual detailed notes and photographed relentlessly, as was my custom. It was not easy to tune out my feelings, looking at the dead young girl.

Spring's local JP, Cotton Banks, was onsite shortly before I arrived, and eyed me casually as I smelled both of Jenna's hands and proceeded to lift her feet out and away, one at a time, to look at the bottoms of her soles. He and I had worked many cases together, and we continued on without much comment. On the bottom of her left sole was a small piece of some type of material stuck on what appeared to be gum. I scraped it off with my clean pocketknife blade into an evidence baggie and carefully marked the date, location, and time of removal. Precious little evidence, but it was all I could find. The coroner would make his ruling within a couple of weeks, and maybe we would know more.

I made a little small talk with Cotton on how dry it was this time of year, and how puny the lake looked. He always appeared to me to look like an old English bulldog. Cotton's jowls hung about an inch on each side. He moved his head up and down when he spoke, and they seemed to fairly swing, just like an old bulldog. He was a dutiful family man, and he and Maude had been married for over thirty-five years with two sons. Both boys were cotton farmers. He had won the JP slot every year he ran, and was going on his twenty-fourth year. He hung his head down when he spoke as we prepared to exit the building.

"Alfie, this don't make no sense. This girl was a junior in high school. Far as I know, she ain't never been in no kind of trouble. My grandson knows her. She certainly ain't part of the doper/druggie group." Tears welled in his haggard face. "I hate to see someone so young taking their own life. What could have been so bad in her life to make her do that, you reckon? I ain't doing this job no more when my term is up."

Of course, he said this every time I was been around him on a teenage death case. This made number eleven in twenty-three years. Some were traffic fatalities, some drugs, and only one other suicide. He got torn up when the young Turner boy fell off the hood of the car, coming down Booger Hill. There were four teenagers in the Chevelle 396 SS turning ninety miles per hour when they came off the top of the hill and headed down, turning off their lights. The Turner boy was riding on the hood, trying to hang on, when he fell in front of the car. Cotton was on the scene to pronounce him dead. He cried like a baby.

I shook my head in agreement and we eased out the door. Walking up the small path to our vehicles, I spotted a couple of cigarette butts, barely visible in the crushed limestone. I took out my tweezers and separate evidence baggies and gathered both of them.

Daylight was fading fast. I had Cotton take out his little pocket light and keep it focused on the ground as I picked the first one up. He followed it up with the light as I put it in the baggie. It appeared to be a Marlboro, and had a sign of maybe dark lipstick on it with yellow flecks. Our girl did not have any lipstick on, for sure.

Cotton followed me down again as I bent back down for the other one. This one was chewed on the end and was a Camel brand. I carefully put it in the bag. There were no signs of lipstick on it. A lot of the young boys like to smoke unfiltered Camels. Only the sissy boys smoked the filtered cigarettes.

The paramedics awaited our motion and moved in, lifting her down gently. I told them to be sure and use gloves with the rope and to give it to me when they got it off her. They delivered it to me once they put her in the ambulance. I placed it in a large evidence baggie. It looked just like the lead ropes sold at Rose's Feed Store. She sold red-and-black ones like this and braided blue and yellow. I would definitely have to pay her a visit and sniff around a little.

I did not watch the paramedic team take her down. I put a little Merle on my eight-track and listened quietly in my unmarked vehicle. I watched as they rolled her out, strapped down in a black body bag. It seemed odd that her total being was wrapped up in that black bag. Anything she ever wanted to be, or that her parents wanted for her, was now beyond reach. They loaded her up and took her into Spring. Cotton pulled out before me, dabbing his eyes as he passed me with a wave. Sometimes life does not play fair. What a chickenshit way to go.

The next day I visited the Couch place. The family was not at home, nor was "Pap" in the small trailer in back of the place. Cotton knew Pap in passing from years gone by. He was an old cowboy, working nearly all the local ranches, day-working cattle, line riding, and whatever else he could pick up. He was said to be quite the horseman in the day.

I rapped on the old metal door with no answer. There was the heavy and sweet aroma of cigars, pungent in the air. It was evident that Pap smoked a lot in this trailer. A box of White Owls lay open on the small table with wrappers dropped on the floor around his easy chair. Cigar ashes had thumped inadvertently on the floor around the chair. Several dried chicken bones were lying beneath the table. A matching set of red salt and pepper shakers sat on a plastic table cloth. Faded, ruffled curtains hung over the west-end window. Yellowed from the sun and unwashed, they seem stiff and brittle to the touch. On the wooden shelf above the table were several pictures, none in frames, two or three arrowheads, and two small jars of Mentholatum. One picture was a cowboy on a palomino horse, rearing up. The rider had his hat off and was whooping it in the air. I assumed it to be Pap in his younger years. The hat he had on in the photograph was hung on the wall next to the picture. It was beat up pretty bad on the edges and stained with sweat beyond the hatband. He sported a yellow mustache in the photograph and smiled broadly.

The other photo was of an attractive young lady sitting under a fruitless mulberry tree outside Pap's trailer. I believed this one to be Jenna. Certainly attractive and athletic, not like the girl we found hanged.

I slipped it into my shirt pocket. What were they going to do, arrest me? Hell, I'm the law. They could kiss my mockingbird ass. I had every intention of returning it when I visited the family again, discreetly of course.

I moved to the end of the camper and viewed the unmade bed, unchanged linens, and slobber-stained pillow case. Cigar ashes were piled thickly on the floor by the bed, as well, with uncountable burn marks on the carpet. Amazing he had not burnt the place down. He had an old transistor radio on the headboard and a small twelve-inch television on a shelf at the end of the bed, with a set of rabbit ears on top of it with foil wrapped around each one. In the tiny bathroom were a wooden-framed mirror, toilet, and small sink. The fake wood toilet seat was not centered on the pot, probably from him sliding over when he wiped his butt. His shaving kit was propped against the edge of the sink. There was an old black coffee cup with water in it by the faucet. False teeth receptacle, I assumed. It was filled with water that had not been emptied for some time.

Nothing else piqued my interest, and I eased out the door. Captain Burris knew I had vacation scheduled when he assigned me the case, and he knew I wanted to leave today. However, even though I normally worked freelance when on a case, he asked me personally to pay a little visit to the Couch place and do a little nosing around with the parents if I could.

So I nosed around. He didn't have to know I had a picture of the deceased in my pocket. After making out my official report, I went home to finish packing. Of course I left out the part about the picture. The full-blown investigation would begin in earnest when I returned.

* * *

Beatrice watched me pack with a wary eye. She knew me far better than I cared to admit, and had gotten way too close to my business of late. Her questions penetrated me like knives. Everything she said seemed like a steady drip of water, irritating to the core.

I did not want to go into detail. I did not want to share. I damn sure did not want to talk, to articulate, to visit about it. I just wanted to get the hell out of Dodge and leave her in the rearview mirror. Could she not see that I would much rather deal with the worries of the day on my own? She knew all too well the intensity with which I took on a case. "The Bulldog," as Captain Burris had called me years before, was something she would not let me forget. "Alfie, why can't you just back off a little and not take everything so personal? Quit being so serious. When you are on a case, you go into your bulldog mode and you don't come up for air until you are finished. I am your wife and I would like to see you sometime during the daylight hours. There is more to life than solving some case. It's like your life depends on it. There are other detectives in the department. Why can't the captain stick someone else on them from time to time? You always seem to get the bad ones, and we never seem to have enough time for us."

Why in the world would I want to make time for "us," I almost said aloud. "We've had our time," I muttered below my breath.

As usual with Beatrice, I kept fairly quiet, knowing if I lost my temper it might be a week or two before things settled back to normal. With one last joust she reminded me that our wedding anniversary was coming up, and she would like to do something special. I had the date written in my logbook, but in the midst of some case I had forgotten at least twice. Her feelings were hurt beyond measure. In fact, I did not know I had forgotten until a couple of days after the fact.

She pulled me to her and kissed me gently on the lips before I left. "Is everything all right?" she asked. It was more of a peck than a kiss. She used to put a lip lock on me in our younger days.

I told her everything was fine. She said, "I wish I meant as much to you as the mountains and your trips do. I cannot compete with your mistress. Not only are you hardheaded, you are the most selfish person I know. And sometimes you are a downright asshole." It always shocked me when she said a bad word.

"When I brought up maybe adopting, it's like you turned off a switch or something. Just leave, please." She was crying as she closed the door.

She could kiss my mockingbird ass. Why would she even think about adoption? I never could stand for her to cry. I knew I was an asshole, and she was a better person than me. I just simply could never get the courage to tell her that.

Damn right I am an asshole.

I put the picture back in my pocket, not knowing where the investigation would lead me when I returned. A suicide is never pretty, and usually there is blame to go around, and it is a death that goes on punishing those left behind. Hopefully, when I returned, the coroner would have the results of the autopsy. In the meantime, I planned to indulge in my "mountain mistress," as Beatrice said, and partake of her wonderful charms.

Maybe Beatrice was right. I hope she keeps my horses and goats fed while I'm away. Maybe that will keep her mind off of adoption. Damn, what a goofy-ass notion. Hell, if we adopted a kid, we would be in our mid-sixties when they went to college, if they went to college.

CHAPTER FIVE

All of my schooling took place in Spring, Texas, in Houghton County, the heart of Texas. Our county was split by I-30 and sat squarely between the heart of Texas and Mexico. The small town was a unique blend of 30 percent blacks, 40 percent Mexicans, and the rest a tight lineage of white folks. Of the 30 percent of white folks, about 10 percent of those we considered well-off, and most lived south of the I-30. I was not one of them. I lived close to Apple on the Creek Road about four miles north of town, among working stiffs, none with an education past high school, unless they were smart and lucky. We had a bread man that woke up at 3:00 every morning to deliver Frostie Bread, an alcoholic who raised catfish and sold bait, oil field workers, an ag teacher, and—known only to a few folks around—a pimp at the local whorehouse. None of our folks knew he was a pimp, they just carried on about how clean and pretty his yard was. Little did they know he was a sex trafficker of women, men, and, we heard, some children the older adults wanted.

We were not very educated in social graces. I guess we did not really know we were poor, and thought it normal to ride the school bus from the country into the school in town. When we got to high school in the ninth grade, a lot of the boys from south of I-30 wore double-breasted sweaters and nice-looking shoes. We had Montgomery Ward rough-out cowboy boots, buck stitched belts with rodeo belt buckles. Well, I had rough-out boots, everyone else had wingtips, but we did not have enough money to buy them Tony Lamas at forty-five dollars a pair.

Even though we were poor, I was able to run fast and tried out for the ninth-grade track team. Coach told me I made the team and put me to running hurdles. He said I might be able to compete in the 1,320-yard relay, which back then was a precursor to the mile relay they ran beginning sophomore year. When tryouts for the 1,320 relay were announced, I went over to see who else was going to try out. There were nine boys my age standing around the 110 mark of the track field, waiting on Coach Bettis to show up. It was said he was a state champion in the 880-yard run in his high school days, but I dared not ask him about it. He instructed us to warm up and stretch for thirty minutes and meet him back at the 110 mark of the track.

We jogged one mile as a group, with no one talking but two of the boys in front. They had fresh haircuts and did not come from our neighborhood. I had never seen any of these boys before. They were laughing and cutting up about going to the show with their girlfriends on Friday night and making out during the show. The one in the lead said he did not even remember what the show was about.

I was careful not to finish in the rear of the pack, even though we were only jogging. We all sat as a group and begin to stretch our legs like Coach Bettis had instructed us to. The two talkative boys who led the mile run begin to talk about their girlfriends again. They were talking about how good they looked in their cheerleader uniforms with short skirts. They were talking pretty nasty when coach came up and told us to pair up into three groups and put three boys in the last group. He said each group would run a timed 330-yard dash, which is equivalent to one leg of a 1,320-yard relay. He said the best four times would qualify for the team, with the fifth-fastest time as the alternate.

The first group was the two boys who had led the mile run. The coach had a little starting gun, and another coach at the finish line had his stopwatch. He took us to the end of the first 110-yard mark and we got ready to go. The first two boys crouched and prepared to run, with the coach holding the gun in the air. They certainly looked more mature than I did, with my white, spindly legs and uncut hair. They both had sideburns and a lot of hair on their tanned legs. How in the world could your legs be that dark and covered with that much hair? To my surprise, these two guys were very fast and burned a trail around the track to the finish line. The coach on the finish line recorded their times. I watched them high-five each other and nearly got sick.

My turn came, and the boy I was running with had thick glasses, tall and lean. He looked somewhat like a parrot with the glasses on his face. He was a little knock-kneed and did not wear socks with his track spikes. His hair was blondish red and we were quite a sight, as my hair was flaming red. Coach said, "Okay, little red and big red, take your marks."

The other boys laughed. He shot the gun and, to my surprise, big red could run like a deer. I stuck with him through the 300-yard mark and then pulled slightly in front of him. We were giving it all we had when we crossed the finish line with him tipping me out at the end. I thought I was going to throw up but managed to hold it in because no one else was puking. When the other boys had finished, we all gathered around the timekeeper coach to hear the results. He announced that he thought we had the makings of a 1,320-yard relay team and called out the times in order of best to worst. He began: "Tillman 39.50, Faulkner 39.70, Carter 39.72, and Brazille 40.14. Alternate will be Burris at 41.50."

I was ecstatic I was on the team. The top time was Efron Tillman, number two was the boy that looked like a parrot with his thick glasses, Robin Faulkner. Then me and Brazille. "Congratulations," Coach said. "You will work out together throughout the school year. That will include you, Mr. Burris. One of these guys could break a leg, and then we will need a fill-in."

We all shook hands and introduced ourselves. We found out Mr. Burris was actually Billy Burris. Robin and I hit it off and paired up immediately. He told me he lived on Sycamore Street downtown. His father was a truck driver and his mama stayed at home. I told him my dad was a roughneck and my mama stayed at home as well, and did a little ironing on the side. He did not know what a roughneck was, so I explained it to him. It was a fella that worked on a drilling rig in the oilfield.

Efren and Teo seemed okay that we were part of the team as long as we remembered our places. I think both of these boys were rich or something, because when their parents came and picked them up, they were driving fancy pickup trucks. These looked like the big kind you pull cattle or horse trailers with. Certainly a far cry from the 1963 used Ford Falcon my dad picked me up in. I always thought it was pretty cool, because it had an SMU sticker on the back window.

Efron did lend me the courtesy of telling me goodbye before he got into his parents' vehicle. He rolled his window down and said, "See you tomorrow, Little Red." And with that, the name stuck like mortar to a brick. The other boys waiting for their folks laughed and began calling me Lil Red and Robin Big Red.

I looked forward to the daily practices, to the point that it was difficult to focus on my schoolwork. I still hadn't figured out how I was going to continue my weekend yard-mowing and cow sale–sorting jobs, with track meets being on the weekends. I would haul my father's old Montgomery Ward lawnmower around our country neighborhood with a gallon of gas and knock on doors to see if someone would hire me to mow their grass. Sometimes I would make up to fifteen dollars a weekend mowing, and pick up another eight dollars or so if I was one of the first four boys picked to work at the Saturday cattle sale. If you were picked, they gave you a wooden cane or a hot shot, and your job was to move cattle from alley to pen as the auction went on. You had to have a social security number and beat the other boys to the mark to get hired at the sale.

Anyway, I always gave Mama at least half and sometimes three-fourths of what I made, to help with groceries. She did not like taking my hard-earned money, but it was money enough to help buy a chuck roast or a couple of chickens at the store.

Dad tended to drink up most of what he brought in from roughneck-ing. He never seemed to question where she got the money to buy a few extra groceries. I guess he thought the money fell off of trees.

She took in ironing from time to time, to help ends meet, but it was never enough, especially when it came to buying clothes for herself and me. Dad was making $7.50 an hour and working well over eighty hours a week, but we never seemed to have enough to eat. He would disappear on Friday night, if he even came home, and we did not see him until Saturday evening. He would sleep it off and haul us to church on Sunday morning, saying amen to just about everything the preacher said, sitting all dignified with his clip-on red tie and black suit. I don't guess anyone in the church knew what a sot he really was but me and Ma.

I thought about trying to find something after track practice, maybe pumping gas at a filling station, but you probably had to be sixteen to do that. I was fifteen and would not turn sixteen until the summer. I was pretty good at finding places to make money, especially the poor-boy kind.

It became quickly evident that we had the makings of something special with our newly formed 1,320-yard relay squad. Even with the evidence of some quirky personalities, everybody had lungs and legs, even if mine were skinny and white with little hair. I was starting to get a little hair on them, but not nearly as much as Efron and Teo. Coach quickly adopted our nicknames, which somehow seem to stick for life. He never called me Alfie, only Lil Red. Robin was to become "Big Red," Efron became "Effie," and Teo became "Tea-Cup." Coach was the only one that could get away with penning the new nicknames on Efron and Tea-Cup. One thing was for sure: it kind of made you feel like you were in some-thing special, because you had a nickname. Even if we were poor, I was part of something.

Coach Bettis seemed to be getting a little excited as the squad pre-pared over the course of the next three weeks. Once we truly started get-ting our legs and lungs, we started to bond as a team. Even the alternate, Billy Burris, seemed to enjoy the camaraderie, but never seemed to truly fit into one of the "four," as we liked to think of ourselves. In fact, we became somewhat inseparable while at school, particularly on a meet day. Our times were good enough to place us in the top two or so in most meets.

We began to win nearly every meet we went to. Everyone's time was trimmed down nicely to the 38.5 to 38.8 range. Having four guys that could run in the 38s was fairly unheard of back in the mid-seventies, but by gosh there we were. We won the city track meet my ninth-grade year, and had much to look forward to going into high school as sophomores. There, we would be competing for a leg on the mile relay team, which was often filled by seniors. We all took a vow that we were going to stick together and take all four spots on the mile relay. Pretty cocky for four freshmen.

Effie's mom invited the squad to the Tillman Ranch, south of Spring, for an end-of-school get-together. I did not have a ride out to the ranch, and was not going to be able to attend, until Big Red's mom volunteered to come to our place and pick me up. Mama gave me permission to go, and made me promise I would be home before dark. The get-together was on a Friday afternoon after school, and if Pa held up to his normal tradition, he would not be home anyway. Mama would not have to explain where I was. He never found the time to come to any of my meets, and did not take much notice of the medals and ribbons I had pinned on my bedroom wall. His only competition was probably who could drink a beer the fastest at the bar. He was sure to win that.

* * *

Big Red's mom came by our house at 4:00 on the afternoon of the Tillman get-together, and did not act like we were poor folks. She was polite when she came to the door and met my mama. We drove what seemed like an hour, and arrived at the beautiful entrance to the Tillman Ranch. The entrance to the ranch was a huge white rock archway, with the words Tillman Ranch embedded in the native rock. It had a cattle guard in the middle of it, and was really beautiful. I could see what appeared to be

Black Angus cattle on both sides of the road. They had one thousand or so of them. *These folks must really be rich*, I thought. I knew a little about cows from working on Saturday mornings in the summer at the livestock sale. I listened to the auctioneer when he called them out.

Running parallel with the main road to the ranch was a runway running north and south. There was an orange windsock on the south end and a large, white tin airplane hangar. Sitting outside the hanger were two small aircraft. I did not know anyone that had their own private runway and planes. They must really be rich people.

Big Red's mom was nervous, with all of the cattle around, and was driving slowly. It was two miles or so to the main ranch house. I could see the Tillman brand on some of their cattle. It was a single "T" with a single line underneath it. The bulls we saw with the cows were massive and looked like they weighed a lot. They were not skinny cows, like the ones around our road. Their fences were made out of wire, straight and tight, not like the pallet fences down the road from my house, where Mr. Linch kept a few mixed-breed cows.

I always daydreamed about being a cowboy with lots of land and cows. I loved working at the livestock auction; all you had to have was a social security number and get there early, and they would put you to work. They even wrote you a check at the end of the sale, with your name on it. We sometimes had to fight to keep our places, because there other boys would try to take our spots if they could.

We finally arrived at the main ranch house, and to be truthful, I had never seen anything like it. Big Red's eyes looked big through his thick glasses, so I couldn't tell much about what he was thinking. But he had to be impressed. Our little oilfield shotgun house came off of a company lease and cost $2,200. Pa moved it in and set it down on cinderblocks. I think I heard him say that it had 868 square feet in it.

The Tillman house was about twenty times as big as our house. It was built like a giant Spanish hacienda. White stucco with red Spanish tile roof. The front yard was about five acres of beautiful, carefully mowed and trimmed grass, with desert palms lining the driveway up to the house.

The house was two stories and had a four-car garage built to match. There were two new vehicles under the roof, one Ford 4 x 4 Bronco, and one Chevrolet 4 x 4 Blazer. I did not know much about vehicle prices, but I guessed I was looking at over $50,000 dollars' worth of them in one garage.

Big Red's mom slowed their car to a stop at the main house. Effie's mom came out to greet us and invited us in. I had met her at our first track meet, and she and Effie's dad came to every meet, whether it was in or out of town. They were both rampant supporters of the squad. They always had on fancy clothes that didn't come from Montgomery Ward. I don't know where they bought those kind of clothes, but they were fancy.

She said that Effie and Tea-Cup were upstairs in the game room, playing pool. Big Red and I ran upstairs and into the game room. "Big Rade, Lil Rade, what it is?" hollered Effie, when we came through the door. "What's up, cats?" He never said Big Red or Lil Red, he always put an -ade on it, making it sound like the -ade in Gatorade. Little Rade and Big Rade. Anyway, it didn't sound so bad coming from Effie, in fact it kind of made me feel special, having a nickname. I sure did not know any other Big Reds or Little Reds. We shot a couple games of pool, and then went outside so Effie could show us the barns.

There were four big barns to the east of the main ranch house. I guess with the prevailing south wind, the smell from the barn would not filter down to the house. There was a large set of cattle-working pens on the west end of the barns, with two large cattle-loading chutes for loading cattle trucks. It was quite an operation. There was an entrance made of large telephone poles, with one lain across the top. The wooden sign beneath it said "House Pens." There was a large-horned cattle skull on each vertical post. I laughed to myself, thinking about my money-making cattle skulls.

Mama was looking pretty teary-eyed, one Monday morning before I went to school. When I asked her what was wrong, she would not answer. I knew it was money. It was always money, or should I say, the lack of money. I made my mind up that I was going to find her some. When I came in from school, she was scouring the newspaper for ironing work, and laid the paper down to go fix us some soup. I picked up the paper, went and sat on the front steps, and began to look through the wanted ads.

I tore off to the cotton field next to our house. I ran down the east turn row until I reached the mesquite grove next to the cow pasture. On the other side of the fence was the old, dead cow that had been there for the last two summers, bleached white by the sun, with a little black hair still on it. I climbed through the barbed wire fence and latched onto the head. It still had both horns on it. I chunked it over the fence and climbed back through. I grabbed it up and hurried back home. I lay it by the front porch and went in to wash up and eat.

Mama said, "Where did you go in such a hurry?"

"Nowhere in particular," I said and smiled to myself.

I ate my soup quickly and asked to be excused. Mama excused me but had a confused look on her face. I sneaked into the hallway, where the phone was, and called the number of the man buying cattle skulls in the paper. That same number was posted on a telephone pole near the cattle auction barns. I told him I had a really good cow skull, with both horns on, and he agreed to come out before dark and look at it. I hung the phone up and went outside, to pick a little hair off of the skull.

The man arrived in an old Chevrolet truck about 6:00. There I was, standing there, holding the skull when he drove up. He saw the skull and offered me seventeen dollars for it.

I took it as fast as he offered it. He said he used them to put turquoise and other pretty rocks on and sell at shows. He left and I walked into the house and gave Mama the money. She cried and tousled my hair. She called me her little man, kissed me on my cheek, and dabbed at her eyes with her apron. She hugged me for the longest time, and then held my face with her hands. It was not fun watching Mama cry and made me feel bad. Anyway, she could buy some good soup, baloney, bread, and pinto beans with it. We would get fat for a while.

* * *

We prowled around the barns for a long time. It was there we saw Efron's brother hunkered over a gasoline can with a sack. He face was red. He was breathing in and out real deep. Efron slapped him on the back, hard, and said, "Get your ass away from that gasoline, you dopehead."

The boy looked up with eyes that did not seem to recognize who was talking to him, and went back to huffing on the bag. I had never seen anyone sniff vapors off of a gas can until then. It kind of scared me that someone would want to do that. They nearly made me sick when I was filling Pa's lawnmower on my lawnmowing runs around the neighborhood.

Efron said, "Hell, he's hooked on that damn gas can like a calf to a tittie. He is a gasoline tittie boy. Ain't that right, tittie boy?"

He walked away laughing, but I wasn't. We climbed up a ladder to the hay loft and jumped down to the hay-covered floor. It was piled up, ten feet deep and soft. This took my mind away from the huffing boy and was really fun. Big Red did a gainer off the top and landed on his back. Walking back to the main house, I had a sense of terrible foreboding about this place.

Effie's mom fed us at the main house. Big Red's mama picked me up right before dark, and we made the journey to our little house. I really felt poor. At least we weren't sniffing gasoline, like the rich folks were.

CHAPTER SIX

Beatrice sat quietly in her loveseat by the bay window. Tears moistened her dark eyes. She grieved quietly and often this time of year. Two days forward brought the anniversary of Patricia Jean's death. It was always like an ocean wave approaching. She alone was never attended to by Alfie. In fact, she wanted it that way. It was always better if things were left unsaid and untouched. The long years passed by. Now, even after all these years, the old wounds began to open, and those distant memories resurrected themselves too routinely for what seemed like months. It was like a sprinkling of salt in an unhealed wound.

Finally, just like her usual hard monthly, after a while the pain would dissipate. She knew that menopause would probably be very hard on her, if her monthly was any indication. She could envision tremendous hot flashes lasting for days.

Here she was, alone again. Alfie taking off to the mountains like clockwork. He simply could not deal with it. Never could, and as far as she could tell, never would. He certainly never would talk about it or share his feelings. He simply held it all inside and said nothing. She knew that was the real reason he went to the mountains.

Of course, most men she knew were much the same way, except for the few she knew who were less coarse by nature. She remembered one she played hopscotch with when she was a child. He was a lot of fun. He was more like her than most of her girlfriends. They would hopscotch for hours in the summers.

Beatrice often wondered what became of her friend Butch. She often wondered why Alfie turned out like he did. He was mostly raised by his mama, but he was a man. She loved him with all her heart, and had no greater respect for any man, but he was the hardest person she had ever known.

Maybe he found some secret place and got drunk or found a woman. Maybe, perhaps, he had a secret woman in the area that she never knew about. For all she knew, he had fathered children with other women and went to see them every year.

He never said. He just left, always returning in a week, sometimes two if he had enough vacation time built up. He never gave her his off-time. Maybe she didn't deserve it. Who could blame him? She alone had deprived him of being a daddy. He certainly did not owe her anything.

Every year, the same pattern prevailed, leading up to, during, and after the date of Patricia Jean's death. The counseling she sought, at Dr. Lynn's advice, never occurred. Alfie simply refused. "I am not a headcase. People lose babies all the time. Why in the hell would I want to pay money for some SOB to tell me I lost a child? I know I lost a child. I know it hurt like hell. I know we have gone on living. She ain't here; we are. What else is there to know? I know we will never try to have one again. End of story, and don't bring it up again," most times storming out of the room. He would not speak for days until his pain receded, and then only speaking in short, tart phrases. It seemed like he never returned to his normal self until a week or so later.

* * *

It seemed like yesterday that Alfie carried her bleeding to his truck and rushed her into the Spring Memorial emergency room. Seven and a half months had come and gone, radiantly pregnant up until that moment, and she knew that something was drastically wrong when the bright red blood appeared on the toilet tissue. She could feel the beginnings of contractions.

Nearly passing out on the toilet, she screamed for Alfie, who rushed in to find her near hysteria. "I think I am going into labor. My baby is not due for another six weeks." Alfie made no comment as he grabbed her housecoat and was able to get it around her and buttoned up. He grabbed a handful of toilet paper, placing it on her vaginal area, and told her to hold it until he got the truck. He ran out the door.

He came back and she saw the fear in his eyes when he saw the blood now soaking her housecoat. He gently picked her up and managed to get her outside the door of the house and into the seat of the pickup. Alfie raced through stop signs and red lights to get to the hospital. When he came to a stop at the outside emergency room exit, he ran inside with bloody hands, screaming that his wife was trying to have a baby early and bleeding real bad.

The nurses, taking control, had Alfie wash his hands and had him sit in the waiting room, shaking uncontrollably.

Beatrice's instincts told her that the situation was somewhat dire, and she was more than a little comforted when Dr. Lynn, her obstetrician, strolled through the door. He quietly comforted her and put her feet in the stirrups of the examination table. Nurses applied absorbent cloth beneath her pelvis as he gently probed. He said, "Beatrice, your water has broken and this baby is coming. You are bleeding bright red blood and there is the possibility that you are hemorrhaging due to a tear in the vaginal wall."

The contractions were now coming at short intervals and were extreme. Dr. Lynn summoned a rolling gurney and had the nurses rush her up to the operating room. Beatrice was starting to hemorrhage severely. If immediate action was not taken, there was a strong possibility they would lose her and the baby.

* * *

When Beatrice awakened, she was in a hospital room. Still groggy, she searched the room for Alfie. She could see him looking out the window. His far-off stare was unsettling.

She tried to sit up, but IVs would not allow it. "Alfie, where is my baby?" she said.

He did not turn around for a while. Heavy tears dropped from his face as he turned to face her. "Girly, we lost her. She didn't make it. It was a little girl," he sobbed, wiping the curtains against his ruddy face.

Beatrice, blinking through tears, put her arms out to him. He fell on her chest, heaving. She held him for a long while, until his sobbing subsided, much like a mother would hold her son. Instinctively, she caressed his hair as he let it all on her hospital gown, crying a bucketful of tears.

She never recalled seeing him cry before. She held him tight for a long while. He quietly stood up, holding both of her hands in his. His eyes were hollow from no sleep. His whole complexion had changed overnight. The man she knew yesterday was not in the room. He looked like he did not want to be there. He looked like he wanted to run out the door.

"Damn, Bea, why us? I wanted that baby girl real bad. I mean, I was already planning her first birthday party and shit, even her first fishing trip and a . . . a doll house. I was going to buy her that little tricycle down at Millburn's department store that we saw a while back. Everything was going to be perfect. Me and her were going to spend a lot of time together. You know, get her a horse and all. Teach her to ride. Go to her sporting events. My dad never spent no time with me. All that has changed now. There's a hell of a lot of people that don't want kids that have 'em and don't take care of 'em. Why did God take ours away? Am I not good enough?"

Beatrice did not speak.

"Why did he take her away?" he began shouting. "Them preachers keeps preaching how wonderful God is, well, tell me how wonderful he is now! All of them do-gooders in your church are nothing but a bunch of assholes trying to feel better about themselves. Set in the front seat, Baptists saying amen, and acting a whole lot different when they ain't there. Hell, even those people have kids. I ain't believing none of it no more."

She only listened and looked into his eyes. Tears filled her eyes. He never spoke much about his feelings. Maybe it was best to let him try and get it out.

"I don't believe a true, loving God would do this. He loves children, don't He? Why in the hell did He take mine?"

Beatrice calmed him a little with her smile. "Alfie, we will try again. Life is not over."

"Shit no, and I mean shit no, girly, we will never try again. I am done. I ain't going through this shit again. This is not what it was cracked up to be. This is a total pile of shit. Maybe God thought I wouldn't be a good daddy. Maybe He's punishing me. To hell with ever trying again. He is not going to do this to me again. I am not sure He even exists. If He does, He sure don't care about me. I ain't never going to church again. Why would I waste my time?" he exclaimed. "Why didn't He—why didn't He just kill me instead of her?"

He was becoming irrational and uncontrollable, sobbing in great heaves.

Dr. Lynn came in. His quiet demeanor was comforting but not reassuring. "How's my girl?"

He checked Alfie with his eyes. Alfie stood and quickly turned to the window. Beatrice shrugged meekly: "Okay, I guess." He checked her vitals and checked for bleeding before facing them. "Your daughter lived about thirty minutes after we delivered her. Her lungs were not quite ready for this world. Your water sack broke early, and you went into premature labor. You did nothing wrong to endanger your baby, it just happened. My advice is that once you two have a little time behind you, you might both consider getting a counselor that specializes in grief counseling, together. I recommend that you stay in the hospital for at least three days, so we can keep a close eye on you. You lost a tremendous amount of blood. We ended up giving you four pints. Hopefully, you will start to have a little energy, going forward. I am truly sorry about your loss. I really am.

"I will check on you again, my next round. Call me immediately if you need anything." He paused at the door. "You are both still very young. Don't give up."

Alfie turned and continued his long gaze out the window with nothing betraying his thoughts. Beatrice looked at him with tears in her eyes. "Alfie, I am so sorry."

He turned slowly, approaching the bed. He gently touched her hand with his, bent, and gave her a gentle kiss. "I've got a few things to take care of. I'll talk to you later."

"Alfie, don't leave, I need you."

"Beatrice, I said I have things to take care of."

"What things?" she asked.

"Dr. Lynn is preparing the death certificate. I have to pick it up. Then I have to go to the funeral home."

Alfie turned and walked away, leaving her alone. The grim realities of the last twenty-four hours began to implode her brain. She dissected each day leading up to the miscarriage. She had religiously followed Dr. Lynn's orders and diet. She never knew she was in danger of miscarriage.

Her eyes clouded up again as she thought of Alfie. Her lovely, red-headed, blue-eyed fighter. Her track boy. Her detective. So determined to win. She admired his fighting spirit and she had just seen it go out the window. All of it was gone now. He had done something she never dreamed he would do. He gave up.

The few times he had joined her at church, he did a fairly good job of hiding his reluctance to join her. Only because of her insistent nagging did she prevail a few times. She presumed it was his father's influence that so turned him against any and all things religious.

Beatrice had seen Alfie's mom on occasion, during their high school days and during the first part of their marriage. The haggard face of premature aging. The worried eyes, but the fierce, determined look of a woman who would somehow survive it all. Bruised forearms and the slight appearance of a puffy black eye hidden by makeup. All of this Beatrice observed from behind a stack of canned goods on an aisle at the local Thrifty Way store in Spring. Alfie's mother was inspecting the sacks of potatoes in the produce aisle with great intensity, unaware of Bea. She would hold up each sack and inspect each potato, presumably to ensure there were no rotten ones—a strong indication of someone who had little money to waste on spoiled food. Her hair was neatly pulled back in a ponytail with a rubber band. Her jeans and denim shirt were clean and ironed, but showed signs of a lot of wear.

Then she thought of his father. Alfie never spoke much at all about him, only of his mama and how she did the best she could with what they had, and that his daddy drank up most of the money he brought home. He would take them to church on some Sundays, and say amen just about every time the preacher said something.

She knew that there was never any hope of Alfie going to church again. He might even leave her. What would a man want with a woman that could not carry his child to term? She knew that there would never be another chance, and so resigned herself to her fate that night. She tried to look at it from his view, but murkiness and mind fog prevailed.

She probably would not have been a good mother anyway, she reasoned. Otherwise, God would have let her have this baby.

* * *

Alfie entered Dr. Lynn's office. Dr. Lynn spoke quietly to the young man before him who was, only weeks before, jubilant. Now he was in utter despair.

"Alfie, I know words cannot—"

Alfie cut him off mid-sentence with a simple wave of the hand. "Doc, just give me the damn death certificate and let's get it over with."

Dr. Lynn said, "I have arranged to have it brought to the hospital, in the morning, to my office. Why don't you come in around mid-morning and pick it up? You will need it for various legal issues, including burial."

Burial had never crossed Alfie's mind. He did not own a burial plot, nor did he and Beatrice have enough money to buy one, he supposed. He did not know how much it even cost.

"Where do I go to see about getting her buried? Hell, how do you bury a child?"

Dr. Lynn said, "You will need to go out to the cemetery and talk to Mr. Baldwin. He owns the cemetery and can guide you on burial arrangements for your child. If there is anything I can do, let me know."

Alfie turned and walked out the door with his mind spinning, knowing they were fixing to go into debt. His plans were to get it over as soon as possible and tell no one. He would only tell his parents and her parents. He did not give a shit if either pair showed up at the funeral, if there was one.

Maybe he could have her buried privately with no one there but him. Maybe he did not have to be there because he never saw her. He certainly never got to hold her.

Maybe that was part of God's overall punishment for him, for some reason. Build his hopes for eight months and then, in one slam-dunk move, crush him to the ground and put him in debt at the same time with absolutely nothing to show for it. They had scrimped and saved to buy a baby bed and infant clothes. Bea had been careful, decorating the baby room, and had somehow only managed to spend a couple hundred dollars. She had done all of the painting herself, glowing and singing with every stroke of the paintbrush, happily pregnant.

Alfie entered the office at the graveyard stoically. The place was actually very peaceful and green. Ground squirrels scampered around headstones to their burrows, to escape the Texas heat. Water sprinklers gently watered the manicured grasses and trees.

"Can I help you?"

Alfie shook his gaze from the view, to see a short, bald man in a black suit. Hell, he even *looked* like an owner of a graveyard.

"Are you interested in a grave plot, or are you here to view a gravesite of a deceased love one?"

"I am here to see about—" Alfie fell short and started again. "I am here to see about, about seeing how to—about trying to bury my baby daughter. She just died."

He began to sob uncontrollably.

"Sir, I believe we can help you with that," Mr. Baldwin said, giving him a Kleenex and a moment to gather himself. "Would you be interested in a cup of coffee?"

Alfie nodded. Mr. Baldwin poured a cup of coffee into a paper cup.

"Were you interested in interment or cremation?"

"Cremation?" yelled Alfie. "Hell no, you ain't going to burn my baby."

"Sir, I was just asking. Some folks prefer that method over interment."

"Well, you sure as hell ain't going to burn her. How much does it cost to bury her?"

"Well let's take a look at our price listing in the Garden of Gethsemane. It is our exclusive children-only area of the facility. Looks like interment there will run around $700 for a child's plot."

Alfie's eyebrows raised. "$700? Damn, I just wanted to get her buried, not buy the place."

I am afraid that is what you are doing, sir. You are purchasing that plot forever."

"Well, how much is a casket?"

Mr. Baldwin stopped and extended his hand. "My name is Dave Baldwin, what is yours?"

"My name is Alfie, Alfie Carter," he said as he shook Mr. Baldwin's hand.

"Mr. Carter, you are a very young man and I am very sorry for your loss. Is your wife in your vehicle?"

"No, sir, she is in the hospital. She lost a lot of blood and is going to be there for a few days."

"When did you want to have the funeral?"

"Hell, I would like to do it today, if I can, but I don't have $700 to spare."

"That is okay, if your credit checks out we can set the whole thing on an installment plan. You can pay it out over forty-eight months, or even up to ten years, if necessary, with interest, of course."

"How much is a casket?" Alfie asked again.

Mr. Baldwin ran his bony finger up and down a list of prices for caskets. "A man in your position might be interested in a modest yet attractive wooden one, preferably white. We do have a small basket type as well, for very small infants."

"How much are the wooden ones and the basket types?"

"Well, let's see, the small wooden ones look like they will run around $250 or so, and the small basket types? Let's see, they look like they will run about—well, looks like they will run about seventy-five dollars."

"What other expenses are there?"

"Well, you have your plot, your casket or basket, whichever you prefer, and then there is a small charge for the grave digging, funeral tent, and permanent flowers. Also, Mr. Carter, have you given any thought to a headstone?"

"I ain't given no thought to none of this. Hell, I don't even know what questions to ask. I ain't never buried no baby before, you son of a bitch."

"Please calm down, Mr. Carter, I know you are under great stress and I certainly don't want to increase it. We here at Baldwin's Cemetery of Sacred Rest are sensitive to your needs in a time like this. We can arrange a package deal for $950 that will cover everything, including working with the funeral home and embalming."

That was exactly the wrong thing to say. Alfie had never considered the embalming of his little Patricia. His eyes felt like they were going to explode in his head. His veins in his forehead were protruding to the point of bursting. "I don't know nothing about no damn embalming.

Why in the hell am I having to handle this shit? I can't take it anymore."
He began to sob heavily. Thankfully, there were no other customers in the
office to see his grief.

"Mr. Carter, I will set up the entire thing for tomorrow at 9:00 a.m.,
with your permission. I will not worry about a credit check and will simply set up your account. If you agree, we will set the price at $900. There
will be no additional charge for the additional lettering, due to our new
engraving machine. It is less time-intensive."

"Mr. Baldwin, I don't give a shit about your new lettering machine."
Catching himself, Alfie apologized. "I am really sorry for behaving like
an asshole. I really am."

"Mr. Carter, I know. There is no need for apology. We are here to help.
Give me five minutes and I will have your document ready to sign."

Alfie studied the small man as he retreated to his office. He slowly
came to the conclusion that he was not the enemy, thinking, *Surely he was
a good man but said the wrong thing. He is one of those turd heads that knew
how and about everyone's grief. Why this one and that one died and how to
handle their damn embalming or cremating. What a sadistic life. Somebody
has to do it, but what a crap of a life. How could you get into the people-burying
business, anyway? How can the man sleep at night?*

CHAPTER SEVEN

Jackaleena studied the men's heads on the posts for some time. She wondered if Toto the witchy man would come by and take them away to the spirit world. She wondered if she should scrape a hole in the ground and pile the heads on top of each other, or maybe side by side, and cover them with dirt. At least, the animals would have to work to get to them.

If Toto came by, he might be angry with her if she buried the heads without the right body attached to them. She noted the sharp lines in which the heads were severed from the men's bodies, and the fine little sinews and pieces of muscle that were cut in half. The only sounds she heard were the birds and maybe a few monkeys talking through the treetops. She called out to Toto and asked him to come in and take them men's heads and bodies so they could be restored.

Clapping her hands twice, she decided to leave. She would forever make B'Douro the village of ghosts in her mind.

Jackaleena took stock of her situation. She would have to grieve for her parents while traveling, to where she did not know. Their bodies were not among the dead, but she knew in her heart they were with the spirits. She had only the tunic sack dress on her body to her name. She had no shoes. Her direction was not readily apparent. Village elders spoke of a village called Benguela by the Sea. She overheard their conversations by the communal fire, saying it was fingers-and-toes days' walk from B'Douro in the direction where the sun sleeps. They said that there one could be fed and given clothes from the spirit women, and they had many "children of war" living with them. The children of war were protected from the soldiers. She decided to follow the stream in the direction of the sleeping sun.

Frogs and grasshoppers were frequent fare and never cooked. She stripped off the frog skin with her teeth and snapped the grasshopper legs with her fingers. She missed her mother's meals in the evenings by the fire, eating monkey meat brought in by the village hunters and roasted on a spit stick, with fresh honey and bananas. No one ever went without food in the village. The hunter men always came home with meat or speared fish from the river.

She had nothing to build a fire with. One village elder was charged with fire building at B'Douro. The children helped bring in cooking wood. She always saw and enjoyed the fire, but could not make one with sticks the way the fire maker could. Sometimes after tearing the frog skin off with her teeth, she lay the frog on a rock in the sun for a while before eating it. The warm rock made them easier to eat, and their legs quit twitching after a while in the sun. Sometimes she could find no rocks, and speared them on a stick facing the sun. She found no banana trees, only a few gobo roots to go with her stream frogs and brush grasshoppers.

Slowly, Jackaleena made her way toward the sleeping sun, following the stream. Every night she would count her toes for the time she traveled. The village elders said it would take all fingers and toes to get to Benguela by the Sea. The stream became wider and much faster than when she started. She did not know where the stream started or where it ended. She only knew it was moving much faster, and frogs were getting harder to sneak up on in the water. They seemed to be able to jump faster than she could grab them. When she could not catch them, grasshoppers had to do. Her belly was never close to full, and the grasshoppers were like eating straw with juice coming out. They did nothing to help her hunger pains.

She lost track of the days she had been traveling. The nights were long and scary. She felt safer sleeping in a tree at night as high as she could climb, always breaking off a sharp branch for protection if an animal came up the tree.

It was never easy to sleep. Balancing herself with her legs and arms in the branches, she gathered as much sleep as possible, forever fearful of falling to the ground and being eaten by a leopard or lion. Each night, Jackaleena called out to Toto to watch after her, clapping her hands twice at the end of her petition. Mostly the petition was to not let her fall to the ground and be eaten by a lion or leopard, to help her find her way to the spirit women at the village Benguela by the Sea, and to not let the soldiers find her and do what they did to the two girls in her village. She supposed that he was watching after her, as she had not even heard the call of a leopard or lion since she left B'Douro.

Jackaleena began feeling pain right above her girl parts after several days of travel. When she relieved herself, she noticed bright red blood with her free water. She screamed and immediately called on Toto to save her from something eating her insides and spitting out the blood with her free water. The pain subsided, but the bleeding stayed for three sunrises and sleeping suns. Then it vanished. She washed herself on the edge of the fast-moving stream every morning and evening. Maybe some spirit had taken over her body. Maybe one of the dead girls had taken up her spirit in Jackaleena's body.

Her mind raced with this thought. If Toto demanded it, it would happen, and she could not stop it. She washed herself and her tunic, letting it dry on the rocks by the edge of the stream while she stuck her toes in the mud. She was careful to remove the remnants of the dried blood. If it ever returned, she knew she might be under a curse. It seemed like long ago when she was looking out her tree root hideaway by the stream and cooling her toes in the mud.

She heard a noise. She grabbed her tunic and put it on. Rushing behind a tree, she listened carefully to what appeared to be approaching footsteps. She peaked behind the tree and glimpsed a boy, not much older than she, trotting down the path in the direction she had been traveling. He did not look to be a soldier boy, but did not look like boys in her village. His hair was braided. He had on a pair of breeches and sandals, but no clothes above his waist. He carried a water sack on his shoulder that may have come from an animal's insides.

He stopped by the stream and knelt to drink. He splashed water on his face. Suddenly, he stopped. Sensing someone's presence, he slowly turned around. His piercing eyes were scanning the ground and the trees, trying to detect any sign of movement. Jackaleena froze in fear and tried to keep her breath from making noise. Her heart felt like it was bursting from her chest. She thought he might hear it. He slowly stood and pulled a small knife from his breeches. He walked toward her tree. She dared not peek around the edge, and crouched frozen at its base.

The boy appeared from around the tree. His knife was drawn and ready to strike. He froze in his tracks when he saw Jackaleena crouched on the ground. She dared not speak, and kept her eyes on the ground and the sandals that stood there.

"What is your name, please?" he said. Jackaleena said nothing. "I said, what is your name, please?" Still she crouched motionless. "Girl, I say, what is your name, please? I will not hurt you. I am traveling away. What are you doing here? Is your village a close walk? Stand up please. I will not hurt you. Do you speak Umbundu? Do you speak Portuguese? I Joao Cubala. I go to be a priest and help people. It is where was going when he caught me. If the soldiers catch me again, I have to fight again. I do not want to fight."

Jackaleena stood up, never taking her eyes from the ground. The boy's voice gave her hope that he was not a soldier boy. He did not have the soldier boy's cap on, either. Slowly she brought her chin up and looked him in the eyes before turning away. He was not mean in the eyes but she was still not sure.

"What is your name, please?" Joao asked again.

"My name is Jackaleena. I am protected by the witchy man Toto. He guards me night and day and is with me now."

"So you do speak Umbundu. Good, we will talk. I do not see your witchy man, is he like a frog and jumped into the water?" Joao said, laughing.

Jackaleena angered. "He is not a frog. He is the guard of all villages and people and can fly. He lives forever and knows where the village of Parrot People live."

Joao laughed. "Maybe he has gone to the village of the Parrot People because he is not here. Anyway, my Jesus Man will protect us."

"I know nothing of your Jesus Man," Jackaleena said. "Is he your village protector?"

Joao laughed heartily. "Jesus Man is the builder of the jungles and the whole world. He is the builder of the bright lights in the sky at night. He is the maker of the stream and the water and of the big water the stream flows into. He made the animals and he made you and me."

"My mother made me," Jackaleena said, "and you better be not speak again of such things or Toto may curse you. He may curse me for hearing your words. Where did you meet your Jesus Man?"

Joao studied the girl closely as he looked away for a moment. "I met him at the village of Benguela by the Sea. There was a woman. She was not our color. She is the color of that rock. The rock was the opposite of our color. There she takes care of us who do not have a village to go to. She fed me and let me stay at the Benguala by the Sea after I escaped from Mingas the killer man. There are many women at Benguela by the Sea. There are some good men, too, but they stay behind the walls. Mingas never attacks the village, but has his army guard it. It is sometimes hard to sneak in. He made me fight for him against village people who hurt no one. People that have done nothing to him."

Jackaleena began trembling and ran to the stream. She wept uncontrollably. Joao approached cautiously, taking off his water bag and laying his knife on the ground.

Jackaleena wept. She sat on the ground with her head buried in her arms, crossing her knees. "Did I say something bad?" Joao asked.

Her sobs were deep. She recalled the killing of her village and the man Mingas, the boy soldiers, and the two girls. Maybe this Joao was trying to trick her and take her to the soldier boys. She saw a sharp stick a short distance from where she sat. She grabbed it and was on her feet as fast as a leopard. She held it up to his throat.

Joao batted it away. "Jackaleena, please be calm, I will not hurt you."

"You were with Mingas, were you not? You probably killed people and cut off their heads. You probably did things to girls like the soldier boys did." There was venom in her eyes. Her mind was racing. She might try to run away from him. Maybe she was quicker. If she was not, he was much stronger than she. He could hold her until the soldier boys came. She had not heard them, but she imagined they could be close. Jackaleena froze, not wanting to say anything.

Joao quietly turned his back on her. "My father was captured and made to fight for Mingas. I do not know who he was made to fight against. Mingas just kills people with his soldier boys. He made me go with my father and his other soldiers. He beat me in front of our village. My father was not the same man he was before he was captured. His mind was not the same. He did not talk the same. Mingas would talk loud at the evening fire, when he allowed us to have one. He smoked the brown-brown and became crazy-eyed. He made all of the boy soldiers smoke it too, and the grown men. It made my father crazy. I acted like I was, but did not do it. He spoke about an army of fighters against a government while holding his rooster in the air. Their name was Unita. He would become angry and start shooting his gun into the sky. Everyone was very afraid of him. I do not know what the government is. I think it is like a king. Mingas did not like the king, and wanted to kill him and his people. I ran away, after many days in the jungle, which I did not count."

Jackaleena listened carefully. She could feel that Joao was probably telling the truth and came around to look at him. His eyes were furrowed and worried.

"I tell you the truth, Jackaleena. I am going back to the village of Benguela by the Sea. You can come with me."

"I still do not understand why you left the village of Benguela by the Sea," Jackaleena said.

"I left to return to my village. I had to see if my father had been allowed to return. Maybe he escaped. But he was not there."

"What about your mother?"

"My mother is dead. She died when I was born. My father took care of me every day until Mingas came. I am going back, to be a teacher and shepherd of the people. I will teach people about the Jesus Man. He has saved me. I now have a purpose."

Jackaleena scowled. "I do not know what is the priest or this Jesus Man. I have my Toto, the witchy man. He takes care of me. What did your Jesus Man tell you your purpose was?"

"The women at Benguela by the Sea taught me to pray to my Jesus Man. They showed me a book that he wrote through other people about his life. It says not to worry about what to eat or wear on your back; he will see that you get it. He wants us to tell other people about him, that he can save them too."

"Save them from what?"

"From the devil and going to hell."

Jackaleena stared in awkward disbelief. "What is hell?"

"It is a place of constant fire and pain where people go if they do not believe in Jesus Man."

Jackaleena said, "I have already gone there. My village was hell when the soldier boys and Mingas came. How can it be worse than that?"

Joao looked away for a moment. "I don't think Toto has taken very good care of you, or your village."

"Don't you say that. He is very busy and there are many important things."

Joao cut her off. "Jackaleena, the witchy man is not a true healer. He is full of tricks and useless powders. Jesus Man is the true healer. He is the keeper of people. Sister Francis taught me about him and what he has done. He saves the world, he saves people that believe in him. Everything he does is good. Everything he thinks is good."

"Have you seen him?"

"I have not seen him."

"Then how do you know he is there?"

"I can feel him at my side and in my mind," Joao said. "I pray to him and he gives me great comfort."

"Why did he let you not have your mother's milk? If he saves the world, why did he let Mingas and his soldiers kill everyone in my village? Why did he let the boy soldiers hurt and kill the two girls in my village?"

"I cannot know the answer to this," he said.

"Then I do not believe this about a Jesus Man."

Sensing that the conversation was going no further, Joao dropped the subject. "I think maybe my Jesus Man helped me find you to take you to Sister Francis. She told me nothing ever happens out of the sky that Jesus Man has not planned to happen. Also, my friend Margaret Mavungo lives there and helps with the children. She is a woman from Kabinda."

"I have never heard of Margaret Mavungo," said Jackaleena.

"That is because she is much older than you. You are going to Benguela by the Sea, yes?"

"That is right. I heard they will protect you from the soldiers, give you food and clothes."

"You are right about that," said Joao. "Why don't I lead you there?"

"You can lead me there if you will not speak about your Jesus Man," said Jackaleena.

"And you will not speak about your Toto witchy man," said Joao.

*   *   *

With a pact now in place, Joao proceeded to follow the stream to Benguela by the Sea. Jackaleena was but a few short steps away. They moved along the stream like wisps of smoke, easily hiding behind trees at the slightest sound in the forest. Several nights were spent in trees to stay off the forest floor. Joao knew many edible jungle plants. They were able to find a few banana trees, but mostly the bananas were green and bitter. Most of the plants he found were bulbs. He cracked those with his teeth. They had a soft white inner core without much taste. However, it left the stomach not craving food a few moments after it was eaten.

"How much longer to Benguela by the Sea?" asked Jackaleena.

Joao checked his surroundings, looked at the sun above the canopy top. "I guess about two more sunrises. When we get close, we have to be very careful of Captain Mingas and the boy soldiers. They are on patrol, looking for boys coming to Benguela by the Sea. They will try and capture them if they can, to fight for them in the war against the government. If they catch me, they might kill me, because I escaped. They try to catch girls if they can."

The very thought of the boy soldiers sent Jackaleena's heart racing. She clapped her hands to summon Toto, and asked him to put a curse on Mingas and to protect them in their travels.

Joao said, "Remember our pact, Jackaleena? You cannot speak of Toto and I cannot speak of my Jesus Man. Besides, I have already prayed that you get safely to Benguela by the Sea. Jesus Man has given me peace that you will get there safely. He already has a big plan for you in your life. Maybe to help someone as he will help you."

"Toto will protect us," Jackaleena said quietly to herself.

* * *

The sea was closer to the stream as they began to get close to Benguela. Joao's cheery mood did not belie the dangers of the area as he led them along. He sang and quietly hummed a song.

Halting behind a group of trees, Joao put his finger to his mouth, signaling complete silence. He held out his hands like he was holding a gun and pointed to the white campground in the distance.

Jackaleena could not hear any soldiers, but that did not mean they were not there. Slowly they crept toward the campground of Benguela. First four stone throws, now three, and then one.

There was a sound above from one of the trees. "Stop right there, skinny boy!" someone screamed.

There were several soldier boys perched in the trees with their guns aimed straight at Joao. "We know you, you piece of goat shit."

"Jackaleena, run now and run quickly. Go to the village."

Without thinking, Jackaleena ran hard as she could. The soldier boys started shooting their weapons. She ran side to side and was fast approaching the village encampment doors. She could feel the bullets zing past her. The massive doors swung open as she sprinted the last fifty meters. She ran in the gates, not knowing the outcome of Joao or what awaited her on the inside. She dared not turn around.

Outside, she heard many rifle shots as someone closed the big gates. She surmised that Joao was probably now with his Jesus Man, either by bullet or machete. She remembered what Joao said: "I prayed for Jesus Man to get you safely to Benguela by the Sea." She prayed for Toto to protect both of them. He did not. Did Jesus Man get her safely to Benguela? She saw Toto, she could not see this Jesus Man. Was he a ghost?

Jackaleena ran through the gates and ran to a stairwell. At the top of the stairwell stood two men with guns, guarding the gates. They must have seen her and Joao as they approached and arranged to have the gates swing open as she ran in. She hid under the stairs and crumpled close to the ground. Several girls and young boys ran up to her, pointing and laughing. She did not recognize their language, but knew they were laughing at her.

Two Milano women appeared in neat tunics that were clean and pretty. One approached her cautiously, and bent to touch her. Jackaleena pulled herself into a ball and kept her head tucked between her knees. The woman said something in a language she did not understand. She gently stroked Jackaleena's arm, speaking in a calm voice. She heard the woman say "Margaret Mavungo." She recognized this woman's name from what Joao had said about the village by the sea. He said she was from Kabinda.

A dark woman appeared. She was dressed in a neat tunic with a bright headwrap. She and the Milano spoke briefly, and then she sat on the ground in front of Jackaleena. She began to speak a language Jackaleena did not understand.

The woman tried one more, and still Jackaleena did not understand. Then she began to speak Umbundu. Jackaleena peeped up over her knees. "Oh, you must come from Kabinda." She turned and spoke to the Milano. "I think she is Ovimbundu from Kabinda Province." The woman then said something else in another language. All of the children and the Milano woman left. Only the dark woman with the bright headwrap and the guards above were left.

"My name is Margaret Mavungo. What is your name?"

Jackaleena had not been this close to a woman since she last saw her mother alive, the day all of her village were killed by the boy soldiers. "What is your name, child?" Margaret repeated.

"Jackaleena."

"Oh, that is a lovely name. Are there more words in your name?"

"Jackaleena Karino N'Denga."

"Hello and welcome, Jackaleena Karino N'Denga. This is the village of Benguela. We help children here. You are safe behind these walls. Have you had anything to eat?"

Jackaleena had not really thought of food, but her stomach was telling her she needed something in it. She had nothing to eat in the last two days but some bulbs that Joao had dug up.

"Where is Joao?"

"Who is Joao?" Margaret asked.

"Joao Cubala. He is the boy that helped me get here. There were soldier boys in the trees in front of your village. They shot guns at us. He told me to run and I ran to the gates. Have you seen Joao?"

Margaret clasped Jackaleena's hand warmly. Her eyes welled up, as they had many times before, as she began to speak. "I know Joao very well.

He was a young soldier boy we took in. He was going to be a priest, you know. He was a great helper inside these gates. He helped lead in at least five children past the soldier boys of Unita that I can think of. You make number six," holding up six fingers. She looked up at the two men guarding the gate. One made the sign of a machete cutting off a head.

Margaret held Jackaleena's hand tightly. "Joao has gone to see Jesus."

"What do you mean?" Jackaleena asked.

"The soldier boys killed him before he got to the gate."

Jackaleena began to sob quietly. Everyone she knew was dead. Joao, who helped her get here, was dead just outside the gates.

Margaret put her arms around her and held her for the longest while. The sobbing subsided after a while. Margaret then quietly said, "We will try to get to his body in the night, if we can, and bury his body under the earth. I believe they may have cut off his head. We will get it, too, if we can."

Jackaleena, now in somber awareness, did not cry further. "I will help you get him in the gates."

"No, Jackaleena. You must stay inside the gates until you are ready to leave for good. It is not safe for you outside. We have everything we need here. Food and water are brought in every few days. The soldiers do not attack the people that bring food. They are only after the young boys, to put them in the fight. If you go out, you can be caught, and then you will not wish to be alive.

"Right now, let's get you into a bath and out of your tunic. You have dried blood on your legs."

Jackaleena looked down and saw the blood. She looked up at Margaret. "I am making blood from my water maker. I think Toto has made me a witch."

Margaret stared in disbelief. "Come, Jackaleena, let us go get you a bath."

Margaret led her by the hand to a quiet room inside the walls. She could hear children and older people laughing in another room. There was water being heated in a great iron pot on an earthen fire in the center of the room.

Margaret began to pour water into a metal basin. The water steamed as she poured it in the basin. She told Jackaleena to take off her tunic. The tunic was made of burlap and had two arm holes and one head hole. It was barely holding together, and was all she had in the way of clothing.

Jackaleena shyly took it off and turned away from Margaret. "Jackaleena, we have the same parts. Do not be afraid. Turn around, I will not hurt you. Let's get you into the warm water."

Jackaleena had never had a warm bath. She had only soaked in the stream from time to time because her mother told her to do so. It was more fun in the cold stream because she got to put her toes into the mud.

She stepped into the basin carefully and quickly jerked her foot out. "You must go slow," said Margaret, "this water is not like a stream. It will make you feel very good."

Jackaleena stuck her toe in the basin slowly, then her foot. Then the other foot. She stood there in amazement at how good it felt on her feet. Margaret said, "You must sit in the water."

Slowly, Jackaleena sat all the way in the tub. She was able to stretch her legs. Then Margaret began to pour something into the basin that smelled very good, and began to make bubbles.

"What is that?"

"This, Jackaleena, is bubble bath. It is a soap that makes bubbles. They bring it to us."

Margaret picked up a cloth and handed it to Jackaleena. "Dip this into the water and wash yourself, all over. I will return in a little while. Wash on top of your head as well," pointing to Jackaleena's hair.

With that, she left the room. Jackaleena washed herself and it felt good. She had never used a cloth before, and certainly had not used bubbles before. It made her skin feel soft and smooth. The warm water made her relax. She leaned her head back on the back of the basin. She fell quickly asleep.

Suddenly, the door to the room cracked open. Margaret in the bright headwrap appeared. "Well, I see you have enjoyed your bath. You were sound asleep. You will sleep in a real bed tonight, after we have given you something to eat. First, let's rinse you off."

She picked up an urn from a table and filled it with warm water. She poured it over Jackaleena's head.

"Please stand up, Jackaleena."

Jackaleena, covering her water maker, stood up. Margaret said, "Young lady, we have the same parts. Do not be afraid." She handed Jackaleena a towel. "Dry yourself off from head to toe."

Jackaleena had never used or heard of a towel. She always dried off in the sun on a rock. She began to wipe the towel on her wet body until it was completely dry.

"Now, let's get you into some clothes," Margaret said.

Jackaleen stood amazed at the dresses as Margaret lay them on the bed. They were many different colors. Bright and beautiful. She looked at her old tunic that lay beside the water basin. It was dark and dirty, full of stench, with a little blood on it.

She said, "What will you do with my old tunic?"

"Well, dear, I believe we will not use it again." Jackaleena smiled and shook her head. "Well, you have a beautiful smile, Jackaleena. That is the first time you have let me see it. I hope to see it again soon. Which one of these tunics do you like?"

Jackaleena looked them all over carefully. She felt the fabric between her fingers. Some were softer than others. All were softer than her old tunic. After touching each for several minutes, she finally picked a bright red one.

"Oh, that one is lovely, Jackaleena," said Margaret. "First, you must put on something underneath it."

"Something on underneath it?" said Jackaleena.

"Yes, dear. They are called undergarments." She went to a wooden cabinet and brought out two Milano garments. "This one goes on bottom. See the holes for your legs? This one goes on the top. They will feel good when you put them on, and even better when you put your red tunic on. We call the tunic a *dress*. Here, put these on." Jackaleena fumbled with the bottom undergarment, as she had never seen one. "No, dear, that is backwards. They go on like this." She demonstrated. Jackaleena put them on. She slid the top undergarment over her head. Both were soft like baby leaves, but even softer. Margaret helped her put the bright red dress on. "Now, let's see what you look like."

She took her to a mirror on the wall and stood before it. Jackaleena had never seen a mirror. It looked like the stream she looked into and could see herself in, except it was very clear. She stood and gazed at herself in the bright red dress.

Margaret said, "You are a very *beautiful* young lady, once we got you cleaned up."

"What is '*beautiful*?'" asked Jackaleena.

"It means you are delightful to look at. *God* made you special."

Jackaleena pretended not to hear the words Margaret spoke. Who was this *God* she spoke of? Maybe he was like the Jesus Man that she and Joao had a pact never to talk about again. She looked at herself for a long time. Her head was on Margaret's shoulder. She felt she had found a friend, but still she must be careful. She did not know if there were enemies within these walls.

"Come, Jackaleena, let us get you some hot food. I bet it has been a while since you have had some."

She led Jackaleena out of the room through a main courtyard with flowers planted along a rock pathway. There were several chickens scratching around in the yard. Margaret paused to look at them for a moment. Like everything else, the chickens had been given to the orphanage by someone in the United States, and had arrived by ship along with enough feed for a year or so in burlap sacks. The idea of having fresh eggs daily for the staff and especially the children was well-received. Along with their canned goods and small garden, they barely got by, but were able to feed everyone every day. With the donations of flour, sugar, salt, and cured sardines, they would make it until the next shipment of donations, usually around four months. The shipments always included drums of diesel for the generators. Without the generators, they had no lights. Without lights, they were not as safe against the guerilla army at night. The diesel always seemed to last, but they were usually down to the last drum when the next shipment arrived. There were always sighs of relief when the ship arrived.

Of late, the numbers of chickens had decreased, as they had killed and eaten a few, and without the benefit of a rooster they never had baby chicks to replenish the small flock. Maybe the folks would send one or two by ship from the United States. The staff had sent requests back for a couple of roosters with the ship captain and his staff on the last two or three shipments.

Jackaleena paused to look at the chickens with her and perceived through Margaret's eyes that things could have been better in some way, concerning the chickens. Jackaleena thought perhaps the chickens did not have enough to eat, and it was bothering Margaret. Maybe she would bring them some of her food.

"Come along now. After we eat, we will visit a while." She handed Jackaleena a pair of slippers made of leather. "Put these on like mine," pointing to her feet. Jackaleena took the slippers and stared at them. "Here, dear, let me put them on for you." Margaret knelt, placed the slippers on her feet, and lashed the tongs in back to secure them. "Stand up, Jackaleena and see how they feel."

Jackaleena have never had shoes on in her life. The bottoms of her feet were heavily calloused. The slippers were very soft when she stood up. They felt good on her feet.

"Now walk a few steps and see how they feel."

Slowly Jackaleena walked around the room. The shoes mysteriously stayed on her feet, and she got the knack of it quickly. She smiled as she looked again into the mirror with her new tunic and her new slippers. Shipped over in sea containers on a cargo ship, the donations from folks in America were the only things that kept the orphanage going and the volunteer team that worked there. Margaret was the only person helping locally.

Jackaleena stared, mesmerized by the image in the mirror.

"Come, dear, let's go together to eat. I will be with you."

Margaret led her out of her room and into a courtyard area where there were many children playing, a few boys and many more girls. Some children stopped playing as she and Margaret walked by, on their way to the meal room. Jackaleena noticed some girls with tribal tattoos, others with teeth sharpened to a point, and others with pieces of wood in their earlobes. Some tried to speak as she came by, but she could not understand their language. Margaret kept Jackaleena close. Then a Milano woman began to speak, but she could not understand her. When the woman finished, she made a motion for all to begin eating.

Margaret leaned over and said, "That was our lunch prayer, thanking Jesus for the food that was brought and prepared for us to eat."

Jakaleena's questions began to pile up, but she remained silent. Food was brought in on trays. First came the bread, freshly baked and on a board. Next came the freshly heated sardine fish with rice. Then fresh bananas and pineapple.

Jackaleena had never seen food like this. Her father had trapped fish in a stream that was cooked on a stick over the communal fire in their village. This food smelled very good. The children were all eating with utensils, some more clumsily than others. If they tried to pick up the fish and rice with their fingers, one of the women would gently remind them to use their utensils.

Margaret picked up her fork and instructed Jackaleena to do the same. The cold fork felt unfamiliar in her hand and awkward to hold onto. She noticed that some children held the eating part of the fork upside down, scraping the food on the fork while others held it the other way and scooped the food. She looked at Margaret quizzically.

"There is not a right or a wrong way, dear. Whichever way is easier for you."

Jackaleena tried the scooping way and it seemed to feel better. The food was met by her stomach with great desire. She had not eaten in a while, and certainly not food that was prepared like this. She ate silently while observing the other children in stolen glances from time to time.

Margaret cautioned her to not eat fast, as her stomach might get upset. Cautious as the leopard eating its prey in a tree—her father always said she was smart as a leopard.

After everyone had finished their banana or pineapple, the Milano woman stood up with her little bell and stick. She struck the bell two times and waved her hand toward the door they had entered. Margaret leaned over and said, "It is time to go. Would you like to go back to your room for now?"

Jackaleena nodded. Slowly they made their way across the courtyard, while the other children began to play. Some chased each other, some swung from a tire hanging from a tree. Others sat by trees.

Margaret and Jackaleena entered her room. Jackaleena immediately took off her slippers, looking to Margaret for approval. "That is perfectly fine, dear. Now, what would you like to do?"

Jackaleena looked toward the gates. "What about Joao?"

"We will try and get his body tonight when the sun is black. If we can get it when the soldier boys are not watching, we will place him in a hole dug in the earth. We will read from God's holy word."

Sensing the moment, Jackaleena asked her, "What is this God's holy word? Is he part of the Jesus Man tribe?"

Martha slowly opened a drawer in a wooden dresser in Jackaleena's room. Some family in America had likely sent it over with the furniture shipment. From inside the drawer, Margaret pulled out a black Bible.

"This is God's holy word. From it, God tells us all about him and all about us. Is there something you would like to know?"

"Yes," Jackaleena said. "You said God made me special. How do you know this?"

Margaret smiled warmly. "Well, let's go into God's word and see what he has to say about it." She opened the Bible and turned to Jeremiah 1:4

through 1:5 and read: "(4) The word of the Lord came to me, saying: (5) Before I formed you in the womb, I knew you. Before you were born, I sanctified you: I ordained you to be a prophet of the nations."

Jackaleena looked puzzled. "What are the signs on the book? How do you know what they say?"

"Well, they are words, much like the tracks of an animal. You look at them and they say and mean something. I will teach you if you will let me. Any more questions?"

"What do the words mean that you just said?"

"Well, it means that God (our creator) knew each of us and created each of us in our mother's *womb*."

"What is a *womb*?"

"It is the place where babies are made and carried inside of their mothers. Just like you were. One day, you will probably be married and have a baby created inside of your womb as well," said Margaret.

"No, not me," said Jackaleena, "I am thinking that Toto has cursed me and I am a witch. Witches in our tribes are cursed and do not have children. I have blood coming out of my water maker. Not always, but this many times over this many suns-go-to-earth and held up three fingers. I put a pebble on a flat rock to see when there is more blood from my water maker and maybe I am a witch. It was this many pebbles and my water maker bleed more." She began to touch each one of her fingers as she remembered the pebbles.

Margaret counted thirty. She realized that this child appeared to be intellectually above her peers at the orphanage. She had learned to count by the sun going down and coming up and tracked it with pebbles.

Margaret smiled. "Let's see what God's word says about it." Slowly she turned through the pages, looking for the answer she knew was there. She finally found the passage. She read from Luke chapter 8, verses 43–48:

"(43) And a woman was there who had been subject to bleeding for twelve years, but no one could heal her. (44) She came up behind him and touched the edge of his cloak, and immediately her bleeding stopped. (45) 'Who touched me?' Jesus asked. When they all denied it, Peter said,

'Master, the people are crowding and pressing against you.' (46) But Jesus said, 'Someone touched me: I know that the power has gone out from me.' (47) The woman, seeing that she could not go unnoticed, came trembling and fell at his feet. It the presence of all the people, she told why she had touched him and how she had been instantly healed. (48) 'Daughter, your faith has healed you. Go in peace.'"

Jackaleena took in the words, staring at Margaret. "What have you told me?" she said.

Margaret thought for a few moments about her question. "First, God knew you when he formed you in your mother's womb and made you special, as he does all of his creations. Second, you are not a witch. All girls reach an age where they begin to bleed for a few days out of every set of sun-to-earth cycles. It is part of being a girl and a woman. I bleed at the same time on a cycle, just like you for this many moons, sometimes this many moons, but, every this many moons," counting all of her fingers and toes and her fingers again. "I am not a witch. The woman in God's word that was bleeding was doing so all the time. She had faith that Jesus would heal her and touched his cloak. Of course he did."

"I do not understand why you call him God. Joao called him Jesus Man, and you say God's holy word but talk about Jesus."

"Jackaleena, I think that is enough for one day. You have seen much change in the few hours you have been here at Benguela. Let's visit again tomorrow. We may be putting Joao in the earth. You will need your rest."

Margaret touched her warmly on her shoulder and exited the room. Jackaleena looked at the mirror for a long while in her bright red tunic. Tears welled in her eyes, which she could not control. She did not know why she was weeping, but she began to feel better as she cried.

Finally, she lay on the stick bed with blankets on it. It was soft and warm. When she awoke, the sun was above the earth by one finger.

Margaret tapped lightly on her door. Jackaleena brushed aside her sleepiness and approached it shyly. She had never had someone tap on a door. Martha tapped again and said, "Jackaleena, it is Margaret. Please open the door."

Jackaleena turned the knob and pulled the door open.

"It looks like you have rested well, Jackaleena. We found Joao's body and brought it here. We are preparing it for burial below the earth."

"Did you find his head?" Jackaleena inquired. "Yes, but it probably does not look like what you remembered. Come, let us go."

Slowly they made their way to the back of the walled compound. All of the Milano women were there. Margaret held Jackaleena's hand as they approached. There were at least one hundred crosses in rows, each painted white with word tracks on them. Jackaleena somehow knew this was the land of the dead and tried to turn away.

"No, Jackaleena, it is all right," said Margaret. "We come today to honor Joao, not to run away."

Slowly they walked to the small hole in the earth with a wooden box beside it. There was blood draining between the boards in a couple of spots. When they stopped close to the Milano women, one of them began to speak.

"Dear God. As with all of the children we have buried here, we commit Joao's body to you. He believed in You and was firmly committed to You. He brought in at least six children here without fear of death, so they would have a better life, and have a chance to come to know You. In fulfilling his purpose in life, he lost his life. In doing so, he gained his life."

As each sentence was spoken, Margaret bent down and said the words spoken to Jackaleena. Jackaleena's eyes were wide open with wonder as her mind raced to determine what the words meant. How could Joao have lost his life fulfilling his purpose in life?

The Milano woman said, "Earth to earth, dust to dust." She reached and grabbed a handful of dirt. She sprinkled it on the wooden box.

Each of the Milano women did the same. Margaret held onto Jackaleena's hand and walked toward the wooden box. She picked up a handful of dirt, sprinkled it on the wooden box, and walked away. When they were away from the Milano women, Jackaleena asked Margaret, "Why did you and the other woman put dirt on the wooden box with Joao inside?"

They walked a short way to a wooden bench. Margaret sat and motioned Jackaleena to sit beside her.

"When the body is dead, it will eventually turn back to dirt. So, we place the body in a wooden box, if we have wood to make it and put it below the earth. We use the wood pallets off of the shipments to make the box. It is all we have. If we do not have a wooden box, we put the body in the earth because in time, it will turn back to dirt."

"How do you know this?" said Jackaleena.

Margaret held her hand and said, "Because it is in the Bible. God's holy word says it, my dear."

"What did the Milano woman mean when she said in fulfilling his purpose, he lost his life? Why did the soldier boys kill Joao and when are we going to kill them for killing Joao?"

Margaret peered off into the distance, looking at the children play. She turned her gaze back to Jackaleena. Her questions were provocative. She had never seen a child ask questions like this girl. None of the other children who came before her had ever asked questions with such intensity or insight. She silently asked God to help her with the answers.

"Let's go see what God's word has to say about your questions."

They got up, Margaret holding onto Jackaleena's hand, and made their way back to her room. She asked Jackaleena to bring her the black Bible from the drawer. Jackaleena pulled the drawer open and saw it there. Carefully, she picked it up and handed it to Margaret.

Margaret thumbed through the tracks and finally stopped. "To your first question, I read in Luke 9, verses 23 and 24. Jesus is speaking: '(23) Then he said to them all: If anyone would come after me, he must deny himself and take up his cross daily and follow me. (24) For whoever wants to save his life will lose it, but whoever loses his life for me, will save it.'

"Now, let's move on to your next question. I have to say, dear, your mind is like a *sponge*."

Jackaleena looked at her with great interest. "What is a *sponge*?"

"It is a creature that comes from the sea where the ships and boats are. Sometimes men in my village went to get them at the bottom of the sea. You can squeeze them in your hand," closing her fingers together. "This squeezes all of the water out. When you put them back in the water, the sponge pulls the water into itself. You pull it back out of the water, squeeze it, and it will release its water. If you keep doing it, it will empty out a tub, just like you took your first bath in, one moon ago. So, you are like a sponge when it comes to learning about things. You ask me questions, you drop yourself in me, and get the answers to the questions, just like dropping a sponge in water. Understand?"

Jackaleena smiled as she thought what a leopard sponge would look like.

"Now, you asked me how did I know that once someone is dead, they turn back to dust or dirt. Let's see what the Bible says about that." She thumbed her way through the tracks for a while. Finally, she found what she was looking for.

As Margaret pondered what she was preparing to read to Jackaleena, she paused and looked at this very bright child, full of wonder, full of questions. She was preparing to tell her that God created man from dust, and so when he died he would return to dust. *How can a child absorb such information?* she wondered. *It is difficult for anyone, regardless of age.*

Like Margaret's great faith, she reasoned that, like her, Jackaleena was free to hear and absorb, retain and possibly reject what she was preparing to read. But she also reasoned that it was all in God's hands, as she had no specific power, just faith in God that a seed would be planted in this fertile mind.

"Jackaleena, I am reading from the Bible in the book of Genesis, which is when God created this world we live in. He created man, or should I say, the first man and the first woman. They were called Adam and Eve. Genesis 2:7 reads: 'And the Lord God formed man of the *dust* of the ground, and *breathed* into his nostrils'"—at this, Margaret pointed to her own nose—"'and man became a living being.'

"Then in Genesis 3:19, God is speaking to Adam and Eve, and says: 'In the sweat of your face you shall eat bread. Till you return to the ground. For out of it you were taken: For dust you are, And to dust you shall return.'"

Jackaleena sat speechless, absorbing what she had just heard. After a few moments of thinking, she said, "I want to know why they kill Joao? When are we going to kill them for what they did?"

Margaret knew the question would come again and began looking for the scripture. She said, "Let's see what God has to say about your questions. Just give me a minute. Your questions are good but require me to really look into the Bible for the answers."

Margaret's hands were trembling as she fumbled through the scriptures. She said a silent prayer that God would settle her down and help her find the scripture she had in her mind.

After a while, Margaret cleared her throat and began: "I know what I am going to read to you will be very hard to understand, but here it is. I am reading from Matthew 5:43–45. Jesus is speaking. '(43) You have heard that it was said, "You shall love your neighbor and hate your enemy." (44) But I say to you, love your enemies, bless those who curse you. Do good to those who hate you and pray for those who spitefully use you and persecute you. (45) That you may be sons of your Father in Heaven: for He makes his sun rise on the evil and on the good, and sends rain on the just and the unjust.'

"That means that there are good and evil people in this world. God lets the sun come up each morning on them as well as letting it rain where they reside.

"As for killing the boys that killed Joao, I read in Romans 12:19: 'Beloved, do not avenge yourselves, but rather give place to wrath: for it is written, Vengeance is mine, I will repay,' says the Lord.

"I do not know how you say what you say," said Jackaleena.

Margaret said, "I know, my dear. But maybe in time it will be easier to understand." *Heaven help her*, Margaret thought, as she often did not completely understand the true nature of God.

"I need to leave, dear, and take care of some other things. I will see you tomorrow when the sun comes up. We shall go eat together. Will that be good?"

Jackaleena nodded. "What things do you take care of?" she asked.

"Well, I am trying to figure out how we can help our chicken situation, nothing you should worry about. We need more of them. I am sure God will provide somehow, I just don't know what that is right now."

Margaret was ashamed of herself for talking about the chickens in front of Jackaleena, or any other child for that matter. She and the others were their guardians for the time being, and passing on her worry was not appropriate.

"Jackaleena, I am very sorry for talking about the chickens, they are not a worry. Please do not worry about what I said. I will come by in the morning for you. Sleep well, dear. I am going to the *chapel* to pray."

After she closed the door, Jackaleena stood and went to the window. She watched Margaret walk away, to what Margaret had called the *chapel*. It was a small Milano building in the courtyard. *Maybe Toto can bring her more chickens*, she reasoned.

She looked out the window at the courtyard and watched Margaret disappear inside. Margaret had instructed her not to leave her room for any reason when the sun turned black. All she wanted to see was what Margaret was doing in the chapel.

Quietly, she slipped on her dress and opened the door. She looked around everywhere for a moment, especially at the guards on the wall. They were at each corner of the compound, high on the walls. She made her way around the edge of the courtyard trees, stopping behind each one for a moment. Finally she made her way to the steps of the chapel. Making her way across the porch, careful not to make a noise, she peeked around the doorway and did not see Margaret. She could hear her speaking.

Finally, she saw Margaret kneeling at the front of the chapel at a step. She had her hands clasped together and her head on the step.

Margaret's words were spoken quietly, but with her excellent hearing she was able to make them out.

"God, I know I am just someone that you have allowed to live and teach at the orphanage. I believe my purpose is to help these children be safe, eat, have clothing, and most of all to come to know you. I am not sure I am very good at this. I am asking you again to help me, if this is my purpose, so I do it well. The only thing I have to offer is myself. I give you what the Bible tells me I should give, as far as money that I earn here. It is not much. You have blessed me with a place to live, with walls, food, and Milanos that taught me about you. I am also praying for more chickens, not just for the eggs but for the meat. The children love to eat the eggs, and every now and then a chicken. I know that is a lot to ask, but it is on my heart and mind.

"I thank you for all you have given to me. I thank you for Jackaleena coming to us. She is a very smart young girl who lost her entire village when the soldier boys killed them. I am not judging, but she is probably one of the smartest girls I have ever come to know. She has many questions, many of them hard for me to answer. Please help me to explain when she asks me questions, because I do not think I have done well so far. Forgive me where I fail you, amen."

Jackaleena had listened carefully to Margaret's requests. She thought of the many requests she had made of Toto. None of these had been answered.

As she watched Margaret stand, she saw her reach into her dress and remove a small pouch with a string on it. She untied the string and removed something from the pouch, and put it into a small metal box on the step. Margaret said, "God, please use this *money* to your benefit. I wish I had more to give."

With that, she started out of the chapel.

Jackaleena bolted across the steps and hid behind a tree. She held her breath while Margaret made her way down the steps and started toward her living quarters. Jackaleena watched her all the way before turning to go back to her room.

Not knowing exactly what she had just seen, she could not go to sleep thinking about the words Margaret had said to Jesus Man. What is *money*, and why did she put it into the box? She also heard her ask for more chickens. Would Jesus Man give her the things she asked for? Why was she asking Jesus Man about answering the questions she was asking Margaret?

It was deep into the night before she drifted off to sleep.

* * *

Several days passed with the same daily routine for Margaret and Jackaleena. Margaret would tap on her door every morning when the sun was one finger high. They would hold hands and walk to the place where all the children ate.

The same boys and girls would watch her every day. She did not understand their words.

After they ate their food, Margaret would take her hand and they would walk around the compound. Margaret would describe trees, flowers, birds, plants, and would say the word in what she called English. She said, "If I teach you English, you will be able to read the Bible tracks that are in English. You need to know how to say it and then how to write the tracks like the animals make in the ground. Is that something you want to do?"

Jackaleena nodded. It was scary to try and learn what Margaret was speaking about. The Bible was heavy, with many tracks in it, and it would not be easy to learn the words and make the tracks. She saw nothing in the Bible that looked like a track on the ground like the chickens or a grasshopper. The tracks in the Bible looked different, and some looked alike but in different spots when she looked up and down a page. So, it began.

"Jackaleena, this is going to be your first set of words in English. Are you ready? *Let us walk.*"

The words rolled off Margaret's tongue so easily. Jackaleena listened attentively.

"I will say them once again in your language, and then in English."

Jackaleena laughed at the English and tried to say what she had heard: "*Leet oos ewak.*"

"That is very close," said Margaret. "*Let us walk.* Try it again."

This time Jackaleena listened intently and tried again. "*Let os walk.*"

"You are very close, dear. One more time. *Let us walk.*"

Jackaleena listed carefully to the slight difference in how Margaret said the words. "*Let us walk.*"

"That is very good, Jackaleena. You have just spoken your first words in English. They mean, me and you taking a walk through the compound," pointing to Jackaleena and herself. Then she held her fingers up, imitating legs walking. "*Let us walk.*"

Jackaleena beamed with pride.

"You really have a beautiful smile, Jackaleena. I know you went through a lot before you came to us. Smile your smile every time you think about it. Now, would you like to see how to make the tracks of the words I just taught you?"

They knelt in the dirt, and Margaret took a twig and began writing the tracks in the dirt.

"See the first tracks? Each one is called a *letter*, from now on. When letters are put together, they make what we call a *word*. When you say, 'Let us walk,' you have spoken a *sentence*." She showed here the letters in "let," "us," and "walk." "Now, why don't you try and make the letters just like mine?"

She handed Jackaleena the broken twig. Jackaleena carefully made the letters to look like the letters Margaret had put on the ground.

"Very good. Now please read them to me, starting on this side," pointing to the left side. Jackaleena pointed to the first letter on the left. Margaret said, "That is called the letter *L*," and breathed the word out of her mouth making the *luh* sound. Jackaleena repeated the sound. "The next letter is *E*, and in this sentence is said like this: *eh*," Margaret said, putting Jakaleena's hand to her mouth, to feel her breath when she spoke. "The last letter in this word is *T*. It is said like this." She put her tongue to the top of her mouth and made the *tuh* sound.

Jackaleena said, "*Luh eh tuh.*"

"Very close," said Margaret. "This time, say them faster, and just say '*let.*'"

Jackaleena shortened the word to "leht." "Very good, Jackaleena." She went through the same sequence on the next two words until Jackaleena understood how to say "let us walk" and was able to look at the letters and identify them.

The daily walks and learning started to move at a faster rate than Margaret had ever experienced. She brought Jackaleena a tablet and pencil, so she could write the English words as they walked and looked. She wanted to know how to say everything in English. Margaret would draw a picture in her tablet and spell the word. Jackaleena quickly learned the letters of the English alphabet, and her vocabulary grew rapidly. Her questions were rapid-fire and to the point. She missed no opportunity to expand her vocabulary. "Look, Margaret, there is a blue bird flying in the sky. I am going to write that down." "Margaret, I like my red dress. I am going to write that down."

One morning, when Margaret tapped on her door, Jackaleena opened it.

"I do not see your beautiful smile, Jackaleena. Please tell me who robbed you of it."

Jackaleena looked up with tears in her eyes. She held out her tablet and pencil. "My tablet can take no more words. My pencil is nearly gone."

Margaret wrapped her arms around her and held her tight. "Dear, we have many more tablets and pencils. You will never be without a tablet or a pencil to write words with. Now, put that smile on your beautiful face and let us walk."

Jackaleena hugged her. "Thank you, Margaret. You are my friend." She grabbed her hand and they began to walk. Margaret could not help but wipe away tears of joy and gratitude to God. She quietly thanked God for putting a child such as this in her life.

Jackaleena stopped and turned to face Margaret. Her eyes were welled up with tears.

"What is wrong, Jackaleena? Why the tears?"

Jackaleena was trying to gather the courage to tell Margaret about seeing her in the chapel. She knew what she did was wrong. "I left my room the other night and followed you." The tears came in waves. Maybe she needed to cry as she had held her feelings in since Mingas and his soldiers had killed her village. She could not seem to stop crying.

Margaret gathered her in her arms and held her tight against her chest until the sobs subsided. "Dear, why did you follow me after dark? I know there had to be a good reason. Also, you know I told you it is not safe after dark for you to be out. Tell me about it." She held Jackaleena's hand. "I am not displeased with you, I just want to understand why."

Jackaleena stared down at the ground looking at her toes. "I always watch you leave, and you did not go to your room. You went to the little Milano chapel. I wanted to see what you were doing, so I went out of my door and went there. You were kneeling at the front, talking to Jesus Man. I saw you take out a bag and put something in a box from your bag. I heard all that you said while I was there. I do not know what I am thinking. Your words to your Jesus Man made me glad and then sad. You talked to him about me and then you asked for more chickens. Will your Jesus Man come see you when you ask him these things?"

Margaret prayed a silent prayer: "You see, Jesus, this is what I was talking about in my prayer. She asks me very hard questions. Please help me with the answers." She opened her eyes and noticed that Jackaleena was still holding onto her hands and looking deeply into her eyes when she opened them.

"Jackaleena," she said and paused, "I am not happy that you left your room. I am happy that you heard me talk to Jesus Man. You see, I go to the white or Milano chapel to talk to him. It is called a prayer. When you pray to Jesus Man, you pray from your heart and tell him what is on your mind. You ask him for these things. You also ask him to forgive you for all of your wrongdoings when you pray. The Bible says he will forgive each of us. So you saw me put something in the box, and you heard me ask for more chickens. When I work here, they give me what is called money for working here. With the money, I can trade for clothes like you wear and food to eat. No one gives these to me. I would do it for free because I love children like you. I believe that my purpose in life is to take care of children, whoever Jesus Man brings through those gates. When he does, I take care of them, feed them, put clothes on them, and tell them about Jesus Man. Each one of those children also has a purpose in life. Also, if there is interest, I teach them how to count and how to read and write. Not all of them want to do that. You are the first one, in fact. Jesus Man answered a prayer when he sent you through these gates, you see. As far as the money, Jesus Man tells us in the Bible to give back part of it to him every time we are given money or anything of value."

Jackaleena stopped her: "Does Jesus Man take the money out of the box?"

"No, dear, he knows when you put it there, even though I do it in secret. The Bible tells us to pray in secret and to give our money as well."

Jackaleena was bewildered by that statement. "What does Jesus Man do with the money?"

Margaret was doing her best to keep up with these questions, as they had never been posed to her before. "Help me, Jesus, she is too smart for me."

A calm came over Margaret, like a dove descending on a branch. Her thoughts, as if delivered by Jesus Man, became lucid and clear.

"Jackaleena, the Bible (Jesus Man's word tracks) tells us that every person has a purpose in life, and Jesus Man will help guide you to what it is if you trust in him to do so. In one book of the Bible, the one call Acts, there was a man called Saul. He was a known persecutor of Jesus Man's people, the Jews—much like the man that struck your village. He was traveling down a path when Jesus Man struck him blind. As he lay on the ground blinded, Jesus Man told him to go to a village. In the village was a path called 'Straight.' Jesus Man told him to go to that path and wait. The people that were with Saul led him there.

"Then Jesus Man sent a vision to another man that lived on that path called Straight in a village called Damascus. There was a man there named Ananias. Jesus Man told him in a dream that he was sending Saul to him. Ananias said to Jesus Man, 'This man hurts your people.' Jesus Man said, 'I have chosen him to be a chosen vessel for me. He will take my name before all people including kings.' Saul's sight was given back by Jesus Man. He became a teacher to people about Jesus Man's love for them. Those people could be counted as sands of the sea. The ones he spoke to, the ones those people spoke to, and the ones they spoke to. The circle keeps going, today and forever."

Jackaleena studied in her mind what she had heard. Toto the witchy man was surely watching from somewhere. He probably knew Margaret was telling her about this Jesus Man. She wondered if he would be angry with her for thinking about this Jesus Man.

Out of the clear blue sky she asked, "If Jesus Man has a purpose for everyone, what is mine? Why do you think I am here? Why am I the only one that is alive from my village?"

Margaret looked into her eyes. This wonderful child, so full of questions, so full of mystery, she could hardly contain her emotions. *Jesus*, she thought. *You really overdid it this time by sending me more than I ever asked for in this young lady.*

"Jackaleena, you are what I will call very special. You are like the ocean sponge we talked about." Jackaleena smiled at this comparison. "You want to know everything about everything. Most people are not like that. When you eat, you are hungry. Your mind is hungry for knowledge and information at every turn. It makes me tired but happy that Jesus Man made you that way. It simply means he has something very large in mind for you. Your purpose will be big, I am afraid, but you have to trust Jesus Man to help you see what that is. I will teach you how to read and write, how to count with numbers. Some of the Milano women here can help you with other things they teach in their country called America. I do not know of all of these things, but I believe you will learn them all because Jesus Man gave you a mind that questions everything. You want to know how everything works. This is good, but when he gives you that kind of mind, much will be required of you, I am afraid."

Jackaleena took in all that Margaret said and still studied the ground while she talked, looking up occasionally to gaze across the compound or look at her toes. "I still do not understand what you say about the money Jesus Man says to give back to him," Jackaleena said.

"Dear, Jesus Man tells us in his Bible that we are to give him a certain amount of our money. Here is what he says. Hold out your hands." Margaret counted each finger. "If your money was one piece of bread, like we eat every morning with our breakfast, and if Jesus Man gave you ten pieces of bread, just like you have ten fingers, you would give one piece of bread back to him for him to do with as he wishes, since he gave you the bread to start with. Understand? I earn money from the orphanage to buy clothes and food, and it helps me have a place to live. Out of the money I earn, I put one finger's worth in the metal box for Jesus Man to use. One of the men that is in charge of all of us takes the money from the box every day. He takes this money and uses it to help pay for things for the children.

"Jesus Man tells us in his Bible to test him with this. Most people would not think of putting money in a box to Jesus Man, who they have never seen, who will use the money through a man that they work for. I know it sounds like something that is not true, but Jesus Man says it is in his Bible. He has helped me because of trusting him with one finger's worth of my money."

"How would Jesus Man use a piece of bread?" asked Jackaleena. "I do not have money. I only have my clothes you gave me and food you feed me with."

"Well, you have to figure out how to give one finger's worth of what you are given back to Jesus Man. He will decide how it is to be used. Jesus Man created all of us, and every living thing that you see. He created the dirt, the sun, the night sun, the bright lights in the sky when the sun sleeps, birds, frogs. He created all of it. It is written in his Bible. He says in his Bible, that whoever believes in him, will live forever with him. I plan on doing that."

The words that flowed out of Margaret's mouth astounded her and surely did not seem like her own. She felt she had spoken too many words that may surely have overwhelmed Jackaleena in just one conversation. However, this child called for drastic action, as she would not be restrained for long and probably would not tolerate anything short of the truth.

And she had spoken the truth. Actually, she felt Jesus Man speaking through her with great peace. It was nothing short of magical as it unfolded. She did not know what she was going to say next, but Jesus Man seemed to put the words on her lips. She had never had this exact thing happen before, and it was quite scary yet exhilarating to experience. Truly a heaven-come-down moment she would cherish as a Jesus blessing. She could never give enough back to Jesus to be the recipient of what he gave her. Just like he said in his Bible about giving money.

She thanked him silently. Her faith in Jesus was multiplied at that moment.

Jackaleena sat silently before her. Margaret wondered what thoughts were pouring through her mind at the moment—mostly they must have been like the thoughts she had when she first came to Benguela by the Sea for work. One of the Milano women from America told her about Jesus Man, just like she was telling Jackaleena. She was quite bewildered at the time, but over time she accepted him. She hoped Jackaleena would do the same.

But as with all people, Jesus Man does not make you accept him or believe in him. Only you can do that on your own, out of faith.

"So you are saying that if I take my bread and break it into ten pieces, I can eat nine and give the other to Jesus Man? Jesus Man will take that one piece and do something with it? If something does not eat it, it will be wasted, or a grasshopper will eat it."

"That is what I am saying, dear," said Margaret. "Jesus Man will take what you return to him and make it useful to him. I can only tell you that."

Jackaleena, deep in thought, grabbed her hand and said, "Let us walk."

No more words were said as she and Margaret strolled through the compound. They went by the crosses of the children. Margaret stopped and checked on the chickens to make sure they had water. They sat under the large tree for a while.

Jackaleena lay in her bed most of the night thinking about all that Margaret had told her. Everyone has a purpose, and hers would be a big purpose, giving Jesus Man back one finger's worth of everything that was given to her. And he would bless her for it.

She knew she wanted to believe that he existed. Toto existed, but he had never helped her. Where was he now? She did not know.

Margaret came by the next morning, as she normally did, and hand in hand they walked to breakfast with the other children. After the food was served and the prayer of thanks was said, Jackaleena looked briefly at her piece of bread. She was very hungry. Quietly she broke off a piece of her bread and placed it in her dress pocket while no one was looking.

She continued to eat her breakfast as if nothing had happened. Later that morning, Margaret told her she should stay outside with the other children for a while. She had to take care of some things that the Milano women asked her to help with. Jackaleena had become used to her being with her most of the day, and had come to not want to let her out of her sight for long.

Margaret sensed anxiety in her eyes. "Jackaleena, I will be right over there in that room. If you need me, come over there. You will be fine, dear."

Jackaleena watched her walk away and sat on a rock under the large tree. She saw the slight bulge in her dress pocket. She stood and started walking to the chicken pens in the compound. Holding onto the screen wire, she smiled as she watched the clucking chickens scratching for bugs in the dirt. They gave her peace just watching them. She took the piece of bread from her pocket.

"Jesus Man, this is Jackaleena. Margaret told me that I should give one finger's worth of what I am given back to you, and you will decide how to use it. If I leave it at the box, someone may eat it or maybe a grasshopper. I do not know how you will use this. Margaret asked you for more chickens when I heard her pray. I have decided to give this finger's worth of my bread to these chickens. I do not have any money, and have never had any. I only have food and some clothes she gave me. Margaret tells me that your Bible says you made all of us and even these chickens. Maybe they will have more chickens if I give them some more to eat. She says it is up to you to decide how to use this finger's worth."

Once she finished talking, she flipped the small piece of bread into the chicken pen. Two hens made a run for it, and it was quickly gobbled up as they fought for it. It was gone so fast she could not believe it. How could Jesus Man use what she had just thrown in the pen? As she watched the hens gobble up the small piece of bread she sighed deeply.

"Jesus Man, this is Jackaleena again. I do not know if you can hear me. If you can hear me, why am I here? Margaret told me that I have a big purpose. I do not know what it is. Since you cannot talk to me, how do I know what it is? Maybe it is to feed the chickens every day with my piece of bread. What happens if I do not have enough bread to feed them?"

This became her daily custom, as she waited to see what Jesus Man would do with her offering. Maybe he would not notice, she thought. She began to spend a little time away from Margaret with the Milano women on a daily basis. Margaret encouraged her to do so. Each of them brought something new and exciting to her mind, which was full of wonder. She began to learn and excel at reading and writing English, math, and science, as well as how to be a young lady of social graces. Now instead of fearing the flow of blood from her water maker, she embraced the time monthly as she now knew she was not a witch, but just like the other girls her age.

She learned to engage them as she encountered them daily. Her laughter and wit became contagious, and she was viewed as a leader among the other girls and even some of the boys. Some could not understand her language, but they understood that she cared for them, and that was all that mattered. It was not long before several of the children were breaking off and putting a piece of bread in for the chickens.

CHAPTER EIGHT

As usual, when I got back from the hills, I felt nearly human again. Bea gave me an unusually big hug and kiss at the door when I arrived. Her eyes were puffy and red. She seemed genuinely glad to see me.

My red flags went up. Did something happen to somebody or to the livestock?

"No, Alfie, I am just glad to see you. I was really lonely while you were gone. Not much happened around here or at work. Did you have a good time?"

She always asked me that question when I returned. It always seemed curt and pissy, but maybe I was reading too much into it.

"It was okay, I guess. Covered a lot of miles, saw a lot of country. Enjoyed the stars at night. That is about all," I said.

She just smiled and said, "That's nice. I'm really glad you enjoyed your trip."

Maybe she was trying to imply that we had not taken a vacation together for many years. In fact, she just always stayed home. Of course there is absolutely 100 percent no chance I would take her with me to the mountains. She would turn that into some kind of train wreck before the week was out. No way was I going to let that happen.

"If you're hungry, I'll fix you some bacon and eggs," she said.

That really sounded good. "That will be just fine. I hope we still have some hot sauce left to go with it."

I sat in my easy chair, smelling the bacon as she fried it. I watched her in the kitchen. She was a damned attractive woman, to this day. It was that snippy attitude I could not stand.

She stood there in her red apron, picking the bacon up with rubber-tipped tongs, and flipping it over. Her auburn hair was pulled into a pony tail. Her glasses fell slightly to the edge of her nose. I felt the need to ease up behind her and give her a hug, but did not. She finished cooking the meal and brought it to me on a tray with a fresh cup of coffee and her homemade hot sauce. Two pieces of toast cooked in the frying pan, just like I liked.

"Thanks, Bea, I really appreciate it."

I ate in silence. She watched me for a little while. "Maybe if you are not too busy, we can go see a movie or maybe go take a walk," she said. "I don't mean tonight, just sometime. We never do anything together anymore."

I nodded while I sipped coffee.

I checked in the next morning with Captain Burris before I headed to the Couch place. I was careful to put the picture of Jenna Couch in my shirt pocket, knowing I had to return it to Pap's trailer. Maybe this time someone would be there.

I made my way out of town to their place. When I approached the driveway, there were no vehicles in the yard. I turned off the ignition to take in the surroundings. I caught movement coming out of the chicken coop. Out stepped an old man in his white underwear. He had on leather sheepskin-lined house shoes and no shirt. The cowboy hat atop his head appeared to be the one I saw hung on the wall in the picture. He was smoking a cigar and had on an old pair of steel-rimmed sunglasses. He was carrying a shotgun.

I unsnapped the strap on my service revolver as I exited my vehicle. "Howdy," I said.

"These damn grackles are killing my sparrows that stay out at the chicken pen. I ain't having it."

He was quite a sight, with his bowlegged, bony legs. Not a hair in sight. By the looks of all of the scars on his legs, he had seen some misery.

He noticed me looking at his legs. "Barbed wire. Horse rubbed me up against a fence. Couldn't get away from it for a while."

He laughed. He swung around wildly and fired his gun at a black bird flying toward the chicken pen. My right hand was already on my revolver handle, but I kept it in the holster. He missed the bird. Breaking the barrel over, he ejected the shell of the .410 shotgun. "I ain't got no more shells with me. What you want out here? By the way, they call me Pap," as he stuck out his hand.

"Alfie, Pap. I am a detective for the police department."

"Well, I kind of figured you was something, with that pistol and all. You got a badge?"

I pulled out my billfold and opened it, revealing my service badge.

"Well, I guess you are the real McCoy. What do you want?"

"Well, I was hoping to visit with someone about Jenna Couch, your granddaughter, I believe."

"Yeah, she was my granddaughter. My only one."

He began making his way to the trailer, mumbling to himself and puffing on what remained of his White Owl. He opened the old screen door, leaving it wide open as I followed him in.

"Sit down, sir. Alfred, you said?"

"No, sir, it's Alfie. Alfie Carter."

"How in the hell did you get a name like that? Was your mama mad at you?"

"I guess so," I said.

"I can make you a cup of coffee," said Pap.

By the looks of the cups in the sink, I thought it better to decline.

"Thanks, Pap, I have had my fill for the day."

I took a seat in the area around his eating table. He pulled up a canvas folding chair.

"You don't mind if I smoke, do you?"

Of course I minded, but shook my head no. He pulled a White Owl out of the package and was eyeballing me while he lit the thing. Even though he appeared to be in his eighties, his eyes were still bright but appeared weather-beaten and saddened around the corners.

"I need to go take a leak," he said. "Seems like I need to pee every thirty minutes. Damn prostate stays swolled up. Takes me a while to get it out."

He shuffled out of the chair to the toilet I had seen on my first trip. He did not bother to shut the door when he went in.

Seizing the moment, I pulled the picture of Jenna out of my pocket and lay it back where I found it. He trickled pee for two minutes before sighing deeply. He flushed the toilet. It seemed like it did not flush quickly.

"I am tied into my boy's sewer system. It takes that damn thing about a minute to get to the sewer tank."

He sat in his canvas chair with his underwear pulled up to his navel. I tried not to look.

His dark skin was shriveled. His hair was mostly white with areas of yellow. I saw many years of labor in the sun. He was marooned in a small travel trailer, to live out his days; maybe it was by choice that he did not live with his son in his house, but it was not my concern.

Pap looked out the screen door south towards town. His eyes watered. "You know, I knew something was up when those girls came by the house."

"What girls are you referring to, Pap?"

"Well, the girls in the Bronco. The day they found Jenna hanged, they came by here the evening before."

"Did they come to see Jenna?" I asked.

"Well, they went into the house and then left a little while later. Jenna did not leave with them. I saw her leave the house right after dark out her window. I could not see very well, but she left walking down the driveway and took a left on the road. Then next thing we knowed, she hanged herself. Or at least that is what they told us. I do not know if that is true. She never talked about ending her life. She spent a lot of time visiting with me, sitting right where you are sitting. She liked to ask me about my cowboying days and how I trained my horse to rear up while I swung my hat off and things like that."

"Mr. Pap, can you tell me more about the girls you saw, maybe how many, hair color, height, or maybe clothing they had on? That may help me find the answers on what happened to Jenna."

Pap sighed deeply and pulled a long drag off of his cigar, slowly exhaling the smoke through his nose and his mouth at the same time, coughing all the while with phlegm rattling his throat. When he finally cleared his throat, he was in need of air.

"Take your time, Mr. Pap, I have all day."

"Stop calling me Mr. Pap. Just Pap will do. I ain't never been a Mr.

"There was four of them. They was all dressed alike. Real short bottoms on. Nearly like shorts. Them and the tops was yellow and black."

"Yellow and black?"

"Yes, yellow and black, nearly like a uniform. They all had on yellow and black tennis shoes with little socks on. The socks like them golfing folks wear that just come to their ankle bones. You know what I'm talking about?"

I nodded. "How long do you think these four girls were here that evening, Pap?"

"Well I didn't keep no track of no time, but maybe about twenty minutes. Could a been thirty. It was before sundown, though."

"Can you tell me what color the Bronco was, and maybe the model?" I asked.

"Well, it was dark blue with some chrome around the middle, like they do them things. One of them big Broncos, not one of them little ones, you know. It was a pretty vehicle. I don't know how old it was. It wasn't new and it wasn't old. Maybe three years old?"

"Was it solid blue, Pap?"

"No, it seems like it was two-tone blue. Dark blue on top, light blue on bottom maybe?"

"Did you notice anything particular about the tires?"

"Not really," Pap said. "Seems like they had them big letters on the sidewall, like they do, you know. I only saw that when they backed out, but wasn't paying no attention to any details. My damn eyesight ain't near to as good as it used to be. If it was, there would be a damn sight less grackles around here, pestering my sparrows."

"Well, you certainly have helped in your recollection so far on details, Pap. Most folks would not remember half of what you told me so far."

"I always had a detail area in my brain when it came to horses and the like. I still remember a lot of the horses that I rode and the other cowboys rode. Remember their riggings, too. Some liked a bear-trap hackamore, some liked the leather-wrapped bosal. But me, I always was a bit man. Better head control, you know. And a steel curb chain. Never liked the leather ones. Seen a horse run away with a feller with a leather one. That big roan gelding chomped down on that bit and took off. He could not pull him up. Ran all the way to the ranch barn. Lucky he did not get hurt. Never would have happened with steel curb chain. Pull that sucker down and put the whoa on his ass quick."

"I bet so, Pap. I have a few more questions for you, if that is okay."

"Sure it's okay, Alfie Carter. All I got is time."

Did you notice the color of the girls' hair, any of them at all?"

"Well, just when I was bragging on what type of riggings the boys had, I cannot remember exactly about the girls' hair. I think two of them was blonde-headed. The other two was probably darker-headed. I don't recall it being black or brown. They was wearing something black on their lips. All of them had it on them. I looked at them with my little pair of binoculars over there," he said, pointing his bony finger toward the cabinet. "They parked that Bronco right over there by that piss elm tree. That is a good thirty yards from here. Don't ever park by one of them things, they piss tree juice on your car. You ever seen that?" he asked.

"I have heard that," I replied.

"Well, it's true. It will squirt all over your vehicle, then the flies will swarm all over it the next day, trying to get at the juice."

"I will remember that," as I looked out to see exactly how close my vehicle was to the tree.

"You're safe where you are parked, but you got close. I don't know what they had pasted on their lips, looked like painted-on clown lips but not as big. That is about all I could see. And I'll tell you another thing, if you find that Bronco it will have piss elm juice on the roof, I will bet you."

"So Jenna did not leave with them, but you saw her sneak out of her window after dark and head down the road."

"I did indeed see that. That vapor light comes on at dark on the edge of the house there. He pays $3.50 a month for it. Good for seeing snakes at night, but it also calls up every moth and flying bug in the county. We got a bat around here that takes care of the bugs by golly when the night comes. I reckon she snuck out her window about one hour after the light came on. She pulled some leaves off of that tree and wadded them up. I saw her wedge them between the screen and the frame. I don't know right particular why she did that. I thought she did not want the screen flapping and would come back in the same way when she got back. Only thing is, she never came back. How do you figure she got all the way to the lake? That is quite a few miles out there. Long way to walk in the dark."

"Well, Pap, I do not know the answer to that question. None of it makes any sense. But I can't say for sure at this point what happened. We may never know exactly, but I am looking."

"You can't say for sure, or you won't say for sure?" he asked.

"Pap, you can rest assured, if I knew, I would tell you. I simply do not know. Can you tell me where your son and his wife were that night?"

"They was in the house. She brought me supper before the girls stopped by in the Bronco. I sat right here and ate it. They were for sure in the house."

"Where are they now, Pap?"

"I do not know for sure. They used to play a lot of tennis at the city park, because it was free. They don't do much of anything now that Jenna's gone. I don't know for sure where they are at right now."

"That's fine, Pap. I will come by again. Here is my phone number, if anything comes up down at the station."

"I don't have no phone. Just leave it there on the table. The boy has a phone at their house. I never had much use for one. Never had one back in the day, and got by pretty damn fine."

"Yes, sir, pretty damn fine. Well, thanks for your time. I need to head out."

"Where you heading next, Alfie?"

"Oh, just around. Got a lot of ground to cover." I shook his bony hand. He was still fairly stout in his grip. I did not squeeze hard, as his knuckles looked arthritic.

He smiled broadly as he squeezed my hand. "Pretty good for an old man, huh? There was a time I could take a man to his knees."

"I am sure that is right, Pap. See you later."

He stood to bid me out the door, with underwear sagging. I backed out of the driveway and pulled over about a mile down the road to compile all of the notes I had taken mentally in our conversation. His recollections were better than most, and who knew where they would lead. I needed to get a cup of coffee before I headed to Rose's Feed Store.

I stopped at Merle's Café on 34th Street in Spring. The coffee there was always hot and fresh. Merle as always had on his white café hat and his white, grease-stained apron.

"What you having, Alfie? Breakfast, early lunch?"

"Just coffee," I said. "No creamer."

"Coming up."

I sipped on the cup, taking in all that Pap had relayed to me. For a man who appeared to be in his eighties, his faculties were better than most, setting aside the underwear of course and maybe shooting grackles with his house shoes on and no shirt.

Maybe we should all be so lucky in our elder years. At least he could still carry on a fluid conversation of sorts, even if it was in his underwear.

My first thought on the girls was their uniforms. Maybe they were part of a club, maybe cheerleaders, maybe pep squad members at the high school. Only time would tell.

CHAPTER NINE

Rose McDonald owned the local feed store in Spring on Lockhart Street. She bought out Old Man Weatherford when he was well into his eighties. He was the crankiest of sorts, who loved a lively conversation on politics, mainly. He hated "Jake-Legged Democrats." Every last one of them. It was always hard to buy horse feed without him going into the political scandal of the day. It never mattered if a Republican was involved in some type of provocation. Those damn Jake-Legged Democrats were behind it. Socialists everyone of 'em. "They would rather take your money and blow it on their stupid social programs than take care of the country," he would bark. "I bet half of them are red-communist, they just won't own up to it in public."

He always ended with, "I need to run for mayor of this place and start cleaning out the local red-communist Democrats in the town. They have run up my property taxes nearly 15 percent since I bought this place. And for what? That stupid statue down at the courthouse? Or that new turning circle downtown? I nearly got killed trying to navigate that thing. Why can't they use our city money better than that? They are just like those Jake-Legs in DC."

The feed store pretty much looks the same as when Old Man Weatherford owned it. The same six leather chairs and woodburning stove remained when Rose bought it. Of course Merle always had a means to which Rose came up with the down payment for her loan at the Better Citizens Bank. "I bet she was passing out favors to the rodeo cowboys for money back when she was barrel racing," he would say. "How do you figure I asked after hearing that story for the fiftieth time? Well, I have just heard she liked the boys back in the day and still does today some say. Some say, huh? Damn skippy, aye. I've even heard she will take you for a ride today for a twenty."

"Who tells you these things, Merle?" I asked. "That is pretty rich storytelling."

"Well, I just know her husband ain't done too well in his hardware business, and she is probably supplementing the kitty with herself. You know he likes to get to Vegas now and again, to play the blackjack. I hear he never makes no money at it, and it has caused some hard financial times on them. And another thing, I hear tell her old man is good with it."

"Good with what?" I asked.

"Can you imagine that? His old lady is turning tricks in the back room of a feed store and that fool thinks that is okay."

"Merle, I think I would be very careful taking that kind of hearsay public. Rose seems like a very nice lady. Even if any piece of that is true, that is her business, not yours."

"Well, turning tricks is against the law, Alfie," he would say.

"Indeed it is, if it can be proven."

I always watched Merle tilt his head toward any conversation going on with the barstool patrons up front. With the never-ending supply of naysayers, hearsayers, and make-it-uppers, he never ran out of sordid stories to rehash. His little white cap looked like an upside-down boat, listing slightly with red pinstripes down each side, when he was in one of his most active listening modes, taking in every word while drying coffee cups and placing them on the dry mat. When he used to smoke, he always had a cigarette tucked above his ear. He would turn over the front to his oldest waitress Gracie McCowan for a few minutes, and go out back by the dumpster and smoke.

Merle opened at 5:00 every morning, and I have seen his '69 Chevrolet truck there at 4:30 a.m. many times. His coffee was fresh, eggs cooked over easy to perfection, and his thick-cut bacon was cut from pigs he purchased at the local 4-H livestock auctions. His biscuit recipe was "my mama's from scratch," he would say, "and she taught me how to make them." He always had several pies made up in a pie rotator. He could make lemon and chocolate meringue pies better that Bea. His apple pie with ice cream on top was as good as they come.

It seemed that the gossip just came with the café, with an endless supply of roughnecks on shift change, retirees, and cowboys coming in from early morning gatherings at the Moorehouse 66 Ranch, or the tennis club brunch gathering twice a month from the country club. Then, of course, there were the boys from the refinery. There were never-ending stories, unedited gossip, salacious hearsay, lies, and probably some bit of truth in the nonstop chatter. It was and is an epicenter of people talking about people, people looking at people, and quite frankly a place to eat and listen for clues on past and present cases. Most of it can be thrown out with the trash. But every now and then some tidbit will come out of someone's mouth that is worth looking into.

I had Rose on my mind, as she was my next stop after coffee at Merle's. All of his past commentary was flashing back in my mind as I drove slowly down Lockhart to the feed store turnoff. Not being but two miles from Merle's, I tried to drive slowly while my mind was moving faster than my vehicle. My investigation into Jenna Couch's death was in full swing, with no stopping until I got it completed. As Bea always says, the bulldog has bitten and won't let go until he is finished. She was probably right.

I parked my service vehicle beside the feed store. The sign always made me smile, with its single rose and "Rose's Feed Store" beneath it in bright red letters. The city sign ordinance limited her to a 36 x 36 for some reason. Of course some of the larger approved signs in the city were business interests of some past and sitting city council members.

There were several old cars parked in front of Rose's—probably the same group of old retired men that gathered there six days a week after they left Merle's Café.

I opened the ancient wooden door and walked in. I wore my usual uniform. Creased jeans, cowboy boots, brown issue shirt, straw cowboy hat, and service revolver. My eyes required constant sunglasses outside. There were five old men sitting around the unlit woodburning stove in the old leather chairs. "Howdy, boys," I said as I walked in.

"Howdy," one said, polite waves from the other. I could feel them looking me over, head to toe. They really did not know if I was here on a case or personal business, but probably assumed business, as I did not have on my civilian skivvies. I spotted Rose behind the counter in the back room. She had a little bell that would tinkle every time someone opened the front or side door to the feed store. She hollered out that she would be there in just a minute.

Rose was tallying up receipts and entering them into a ledger in the book room behind the counter. I walked up to the counter, taking note of her from behind. She was in her late forties, I guessed. Her blonde hair probably came from a bottle, as there were dark roots showing. She had on her usual poured-on blue jeans and white shirt with a little, artificial red rose in her hair on the left side clipped with a bobby pin.

When she entered the last ticket, she stood and turned around. "Well hello, officer. I did not know it was you," as she adjusted her hair. "To what do I owe this pleasure? You buying horse feed?"

"No, ma'am. Just here to visit, if we can find a place to talk in private."

Old man antennas were up at half-staff as I gingerly turned my head toward the old men, pretending to look at the merchandise. Rose looked into my eyes and quietly said, "Why don't you come back around 12:30 today?" She cocked her head toward the old men. "They will be gone home by then. I am going to run home and have a sandwich with my husband and will be back then."

I agreed. I walked over to the water trough floats and picked up one to inspect. Hopefully the old men thought I was asking about a float. Of course, the next thing out of their mouths would be, "He is handling personal business on the city's time."

I held it up and asked Rose: "Do you have only brass or something in galvanized? Big difference in price, I would guess."

"I have both but will have to order the galvanized. Will be about half of the price for that brass one you are holding."

"Thanks. The Mounted Sheriff's Posse water trough at the stables is cracked. They asked me to pick one up for them next time I was close to the feed store." Even though this was somewhat of a stretch of the truth, the old men seemed to be satisfied as they resumed their visit.

When I arrived at 12:30 p.m., there were no other cars at the feed store, with the exception of Rose's Jeep truck. I parked my service vehicle around back by the hay loading area to not draw too much attention. Our conversation would have to be quick.

When I walked in, Rose was wearing a skirt and different top. The top buttons remained unbuttoned. I could smell perfume I did not smell earlier. "Howdy, Rose," I said as I walked in the front door.

"Howdy, officer. As I said, they are all gone."

"Yes, I can see that. Good call. Can we sit?"

"Why, certainly, officer."

"Why don't you call me Alfie?"

"Okay, Alfie, do I need to lock the doors for privacy during our conversation?"

"No, ma'am, let's leave them open."

"How about you call me Rose instead of ma'am?"

"Okay, Rose, I will do that. If you see someone drive up, I will simply get up and go to the water trough area and you to the front desk. Good enough?"

"Yes, sir, Mr. Alfie," she said as she smiled and saluted me. She had on bright red lipstick. I did not recall her having that on earlier. "Now, to what do I owe this pleasure?"

"Well, I am sure you read the papers, Rose."

"Why, yes I do," she said. "Am I supposed to have read something? Are you going to write me a ticket or something?"

"No, no ticket. Just a few questions."

I got up and walked over to the horse tack. She carried everything: snaffle bits, curry combs, lead ropes, saddle conchos, latigo, and girth straps. She got up and followed me to the area.

"What are you looking for, Mr. Alfie?"

I took one of the red-and-black pleated lead ropes off the hook. They were all marked twelve feet and had two-inch, spring-loaded, easy-latch brass clips woven into one end. The other end was a single knot.

"You sell many of these?" I asked.

"Well, we sell them on occasion. Probably a few more around rodeo time. I would say about ten a year, something like that. Are you needing one, Mr. Alfie?"

"No, nothing like that. I will have to ask you to keep our conversation quiet, even from your husband."

She smiled wryly. "I sure will, officer," as she readjusted the rose in her hair. "Whatever you say."

"Well, Rose, you may or may not be called as a witness or possibly for a deposition in a pending investigation."

Rose sat up with eyebrows raised. "What do you mean, an investigation? I've done nothing wrong. Did someone tell you something? Is my husband in trouble?"

"Rose, just calm down," I said. "This has nothing to do with you or your husband."

"But you just said I might have to sit for a deposition or be called as a witness. Sounds like I am involved in something."

"Well, a lead rope, just like this one, was used by a young high school girl to hang herself a short time ago at the lake in a cabin."

"Oh no," she said as she covered her mouth. "I read about the girl in the paper. I had no idea."

"Well, I am investigating the case. Do you have any idea who may have purchased one of these ropes in the last, say, twenty-four months or so? The rope we have in evidence has been used little but that does not tell us how old it is. The brass clip is shiny, the rope is not well worn from use. It could have come from anyone's tack room."

"Well, I order these from one specific place that custom braids them. No other company makes one just like it," she said as she took it from my hand. "Each brass clip has the company's logo engraved in the underside and a stock number. In other words, each one they have ever built has a number. They started with one." She looked under the brass clip. She took her cheater glasses out of her blouse and put them on the end of her nose. "I can't see like I used to. Of course there are some things I can't do as good as I used to. But," she said, "there are some things I am still doing good, Mr. Alfie," with a smile as she inspected the buckle. "See," Rose pointed, "this one is marked number 4605. That means it was the 4,605 lead rope they produced."

"So what does that do for my question? How do we know who owned the one used in the hanging?"

"Mr. Alfie, just get me the number on the brass clip and I will see what I can do. Those numbers come with the shipment from the company in South Texas that makes them. We should be able to tell what month and year it arrived here. I track those numbers in my daily ledger for inventory purposes. I should be able to see who it was sold to and when. Of course, it could have been given to anybody."

"I know," I said. "But like any investigation, it is a starting point. I will get you that number as soon as I get back to the station and stop back by or call you."

"I will enjoy seeing you," she said, "why don't you just stop back by?"

"Well, I may," I said, "but it will be whatever is in the best interest of time."

"I hope stopping by to see me is in your best interest of time," she said.

"Thanks, Rose. I will be in touch," I said as I turned and walked away.

"Yes, sir, Mr. Alfie," she said as she saluted me again.

"I really wish you would not do that, ma'am."

"Yes, sir, Captain," she said, she saluted me again. "Anything you say, Captain, sir."

I started my service vehicle and turned on the air conditioner. For some reason, Rose embarrassed me with her flirtations. Or maybe she wasn't flirting at all. Maybe I just listened to too much of Merle's salacious gossip on Rose.

No, she was flirting. And the perfume, the wardrobe change. She was flirting.

I did nothing to encourage her, I reasoned, as I retraced our conversations. I absolutely gave her no reason to flirt with me. She saw my wedding band. Come to think of it, I did not see her wedding band on her hand. I knew she was still married to the hardware man.

Maybe Merle was partly right. Maybe I am reading more into the thing than there is. I have done that plenty of times before. Pre-drawn conclusions always reap a bad result. I recognize that perfume, it was the same kind Bea wore.

Maybe I would put cotton up my nose the next time I saw her. If I went in again. Maybe it would be best to do it by phone.

I was still debating Rose's intentions when I pulled into the station. I nearly ran a red light by not paying attention about two blocks from the station. That would make headlines if someone saw it. Luckily, there was no one coming or behind me. I went straight to the locked evidence room without stopping to talk to anyone. I waved as folks said hi when I passed through.

"How was your vacation, Mr. Alfie?" the new receptionist asked. I just shook my head to affirm it was okay. "Good," she said, "glad you are back." She did not even know me.

When I arrived at the evidence room, Mr. Orville Black stared at me with his thick horn rim black glasses. Straight out of the Marine Corps, a twenty-year man, and into the police department. He still wore a high and tight crew cut. All business and no smiling, ever. I do not believe he had any personal friends, in or out of work. All business, all of the time. Completely structured to the ninth degree, and uncompromising. You did not get anything from him without the proper clearance and credentials.

"What can I do for you?" as he unlocked the slide up see through metal window.

"Hello, Orville."

He did not acknowledge my hello.

"What do you need? Also, you can refer to me as Mr. Black? I do not go by Orville."

"Why, yes, sir, Mr. Black. I need to see a piece of evidence, please."

"Name and badge number, please," he said.

"Mr. Black, it's me, Detective Alfie Carter. You know me."

"I said name and badge number, please," he said, holding out his hand under the slide door.

I pulled out my service badge in my wallet with my driver's license opposite the badge. "Will this do? I asked.

Mr. Black recorded my name and badge number, driver's license number, date of expiration, and time and date in his log. He looked carefully at my driver's license, noting that I should be wearing prescription lenses to drive. "I see you are not wearing glasses, sir, your driver's license requires prescription lenses."

I yanked my billfold from him and leaned toward the cage. "My vision is none of your business. I happen to have had eye surgery."

He did not draw back but only stared at me blankly. "Sir, what piece of evidence do you require to see? You realize you are not allowed to leave my sight while the evidence is in your possession, you will be on camera. Do you understand?"

"Certainly I understand," I said, "I am a detective."

"Please sign and date the log-in and initial the section pertaining to handling the evidence and the camera," he said, pointing to the square box on the form. "Also, you will be issued a prepackaged set of neoprene gloves, to not contaminate any evidence you may touch. You will need to check off and initial that box as well."

I suppose I should appreciate his matter-of-fact approach, as it would stand up in court. It was his lack of facial expression and general attitude or lack thereof that got under my skin. After I had signed my life away, he opened an electric-operated door and asked me to come in through the door. "Please have a seat in that chair." He pointed to a metal frame chair at a small, round evidence desk. Same procedure every time. He turned on the light above the chair and the recording camera. "The light is set proportionate to the camera angle," he said. "Now, case number and the piece of evidence you require?"

"Well, it is the Jenna Couch case, and I require a red-and-black pleated lead rope with a two-inch brass snap on the bottom."

Mr. Black strode away like he was in military formation, turning down an aisle on his heel. He looked to be marching. A moment later, he returned with the lead rope in a plastic bag.

"Please be careful to wear your gloves at all times, careful to remove the object from the bag. Do not let the object touch any part of your body hair or the floor. Understand?"

"Perfectly," I said.

"I will also be in here with you at all times. Also, be reminded that the camera is rolling, with audio. You may now proceed."

I split the wrapper the gloves came in and carefully put each one on.

"Careful not to tear the gloves, please," he said. "The forensic team looks at each piece of evidence under a microscope."

"I will try my best," I said.

After I carefully removed the lead rope out of the bag, I stood to hold it up in a loop. Picking up the brass clip, I looked carefully underneath. The ring was stamped with the company logo and number 3404.

Mr. Black watched every move carefully. The thick glasses made him look like an insect eyeing its prey. I put the lead rope back in the bag and sealed it together, handing it back to him.

"That's all I needed, sir."

"Please remain in the chair until I return," he said. He spun on his heel and marched to the aisle of retrieval. In a moment he returned with a new plastic bag. "Please remove your plastic gloves, sir, and carefully place them in the bag I have here. They will be labeled with today's date, time, and person, and entered into the evidence file. Do you understand?"

"I am certainly doing my best, Mr. Black," as I stripped the gloves off my hands, dropping each into the bag.

"If there is nothing further that you require, I will escort you to the door and open it for you, to formally leave the evidence room on camera."

Mr. Black pushed the button for the electric door to open and I made my exit, glad to be out of there.

"Thank you, Mr. Black," I said in parting.

He just stared at me with those praying mantis eyes through his black-framed glasses, a steady sentry at the guarded gate. Devoid of human emotion but essential to the task.

"Goodbye, Orville," I waved as I walked out the door.

I went straight to my office and closed the door. A refreshing moment from the day's events. I looked at my watch, it was now 4:00 p.m. I had not sat in my chair for five minutes when there was a three-tap knock on my door. Captain Burris's calling card.

"How do, Alfie? How was your trip?"

"Good, Captain. Could not have been better."

"How is Bea? She doing okay?"

"Fine, I guess. No complaints, as far as I know."

"She still down at that place that, what, houses kids or something?"

"Yes, sir, she's still down there."

"Well, I guess that is a Good Samaritan thing to do," he said. "Kids always need a mama. Especially someone like Mrs. Bea."

"Yes, I guess so," I replied.

"How is the Couch girl case coming?"

"Well, I am just getting into it good. Interviewed her grandfather but not her parents yet. Working on gathering evidence now."

"Damn tragedy, that girl's death," Captain said. "Why would she hang herself like that?"

"I don't know, Captain Maybe I can find out."

"I am sure you will, Bulldog. I am sure you will." He walked out and closed the door behind him.

I had one more item for the day, and that was to call Rose at the feed store. I looked up the number in the phone book and dialed it slowly, hanging the phone up before allowing it to ring. *Do I really want to call her, rather than go to the feed store?* For some reason, her charming presence was pulling me in. Maybe it was that "yes, sir, Captain" and saluting stuff.

No, I would call. I redialed the number. The phone rang two times before Rose picked up.

"Rose's Feed Store."

"Rose, this is Detective Carter."

"Well, hello, Captain, you coming down soon?"

"Well, it has been a long day and probably not."

"I can stay past quitting time if you need me to, Captain."

"Well, I have a number for you on the lead rope we were talking about. Can I give it to you over the phone?"

"Well, it would be better in person, Captain, but if you must, I will take it over the phone," she replied. "Let me get my pen and my cheaters out of my shirt."

My face blushed at her inferences and tone. What could interest her in me, a married detective?

"Okay, Captain, I am ready," she laughed, "sometimes those glasses just get stuck in there. What is that number?"

"Well, it is 3404," I said.

"3404," she repeated. "Okay, Captain, I have it written down. I will go to work on it. Give me at least a day before you come by. You will be coming by, won't you, sir?"

"Rose, please do not call me sir. I guess I could come by day after tomorrow for a few minutes. How about 3:00 in the afternoon, does that work for you?"

"You bet, Captain, sir. I will be here with bells on. Do you drink coffee in the afternoon, Captain? I can have a pot on when you get here and we can sit and drink a cup while we visit."

"I appreciate it, Rose, but probably not. I am not an afternoon coffee drinker."

"No problem, Captain, I will just have some fresh tea."

"See you then, bye-bye."

I was going to have to pay particular attention to all of my dealings with Mrs. Rose. It seemed that with the least bit of encouragement things might go off the rails quickly for both of us. Maybe Merle was warmer to the truth than I thought.

I made my way home with Mrs. Rose and her comments on my mind. Bea had long been home from work at the orphanage. I walked in the door and found her in the den facing the backyard on her reading bench. Her beautiful hair, usually tucked neatly in a bun, was flowing freely on her shoulders. The west sun sent rays through the tilted blinds that reflected off her. Her hair and skin glowed in the rays of sunlight.

I stood at the entrance of the den for a few moments undetected. Maybe both of our lives could have been different, but I don't know how, with our circumstances. She did her thing and I did mine. Never the twain will intercept. We don't seem to communicate much, other that the morning peck on the cheek, courtesy talk, and the occasional sexual encounter. It was always short and probably unfulfilling for both of us. Still, she was beautiful in the sunlight.

"Hey Bea," I said. "How was your day?"

"Alfie, I did not hear you come in."

"What are you reading?"

"Oh, just a book. Kind of a love story, I guess. How was your day?"

"Same old, same old."

"Are you working on the girl's case that hung herself?"

"Yes," I said, and left it at that.

"I really don't feel like cooking. How about we go get a hamburger?"

"I was just thinking about a bowl of soup, grilled cheese sandwich, and a beer."

"Let me fix you just that," she said, laying down the book.

She stopped when she reached me and gave me a tremendous bear hug and kissed me on the lips. "I thought about you today," she said and headed off to the kitchen.

"If you were thinking about me, you must have been bored."

She laughed out loud when I said this as always. "And why would I not be thinking about you?" she asked with her hands on her hips, feigning incredulity that I would say that.

"Well, I am just saying that you probably have better things to think about than me, that's all."

"Well, I will determine what I choose to think about, thank you. That is something you do not do, understand?"

"Yes, ma'am, understood. I will go wash up."

She brought me my supper on a tray while I watched the evening news. Our conversation dried up pretty quickly after that. I watched the news and a Western then turned in at my normal 9:30 time. As usual, she washed the dishes and then returned to her reading.

It was 2:50 p.m. on Friday when I pulled up to the Feed Store. Be it by chance or by her own doing, there were no other vehicles in the parking lot but Rose's white Jeep truck. Our appointment was for 3:00 p.m. When I got to the door I understood why. There was a "closed for inventory" sign on the door.

Rose opened the door as I was reaching for the handle. Her perfume carried out the doorway. "Come in, Captain," she said, waving her hand. "You look hot in your uniform. I'm closed for inventory. Didn't wear my normal clothes, it is so hot."

Rose had on a pair of very red and very tight shorts, tennis shoes with little matching ankle socks, and a white t-shirt. Everything she had on accentuated her shape. I tried not to look.

"Let's go sit down, Captain, and have a glass of tea. Sound good to you?"

I sat in one of her leather chairs while she poured two glasses of tea. She sat them both on the little, round table and pulled her chair directly in front of me.

"I appreciate you seeing me today, Rose. I have a pretty tight schedule. Did you come up with anything on the lead rope?"

"Captain, you can't be in that big of a hurry. Let's enjoy our tea and visit a little."

"Ma'am, I really have to move on pretty quick, it would be nice to see what you have on the lead rope if you have anything."

"You are such a killjoy, Captain. I do have a name that matches up to the tag number you gave me, it was 3404, right?"

"That is correct."

"I kept it on me all day in my shorts pocket." She stood and made quite a show trying to get it out of her pocket. "It is real tight in these shorts," she said, finally fumbling the receipt. She handed it to me.

"What is the signature on the receipt?" I asked.

"Well, Captain, it is Turtle Vines."

"Do you know him?"

"Why, yes, Captain, he is the Ag teacher at the high school. He's been there many years and a steady customer of mine. Looks like he purchased this about six months ago." Rose was sitting directly across from me, sipping on her glass of tea. "What else can I get for you, Captain?"

Her forward behavior made me blush. "I think that will do. You have been very helpful," I said.

"I like a man in uniform. My husband is a nail salesman. His uniform is a nasty apron in a hardware store."

Donning my hat, I stood and thanked her for the tea. "Remember, Rose, this information is extremely confidential."

"Don't worry, Captain, sir," as she saluted. "Everything between you and me is safe. I mean everything."

"Very well," I said. "That is good. Can you let me out the door?"

She was still standing in front of the front door when I started my vehicle. Hands on hips. I could not get out of there quick enough.

CHAPTER TEN

Turtle Vines had been employed by Spring High School for nineteen years, and was into his twentieth when we met. I arranged to meet him on a Monday afternoon during his conference period at 2:00 p.m. He was a short, stocky man with blue eyes. He had on what I would expect from an Ag teacher: boots, jeans, and a western yoke shirt with pearl snap buttons and a genuine smile. His cap came from the ag co-op. His belt buckle was large with a man on a horse roping a steer.

"Are you a steer roper, Mr. Vines?" I asked, looking down at his buckle.

"Hell, this?" he laughed. "I used to be, back in the day. I used to do a lot of things back in the day. Yes, you could say I was a steer roper," he laughed. "It helped me pay my way through college. Made enough money to pay for my riggings, gasoline, and pony. Maybe a few dollars thereafter. But never was good enough to go professional. Maybe that was a good thing. Well, my conference period is only thirty minutes, detective. Let's get on with it. Am I in some kind of trouble?"

"No, I wouldn't say that, Mr. Vines."

"Please, call me Turtle."

"Okay, Turtle, I wouldn't say that. I am investigating the death of a child from this high school. The Couch girl."

Turtle teared up immediately and began wiping his eyes.

"I will tell you, detective, I love all of these high school kids. Spend a lot of time with the Ag girls and boys in FFA. And I don't care where they come from, I love all of them. That broke my heart. Such a young girl. Me and Mama never had kids. I treat all of them like my own. Exactly what happened out there? Rumors in the teacher's lounge are running rampant. I try to stay away from that gossip crap and just keep my mouth shut."

"Well, Turtle, I am working on the case now and I cannot tell you exactly, that is why I am paying you a visit." His eyes narrowed. I pulled out the receipt Rose had given me. "What can you tell me about this receipt?"

Turtle looked it over carefully and handed it back to me. "Detective, that is for a lead rope I bought from Rose McDonald down at the feed store. I buy all of our Ag lead ropes from her. For consistency, when we show. Want them all to look alike. Besides, no one else in town sells them."

"Yes, sir. That is what I understand," I said.

"Well, what is the deal, detective? What does this have to do with the Couch girl?"

"Turtle, all of these ropes have a specific number on the inside clasp. This particular rope was the one that was around Jenna Couch's neck when we found her hanged at the lake house."

Turtle's eyes widened. "Why, how in thunder did she get it? She is not in Ag." His mind was running ninety miles a second as he pondered. "Let me see that receipt again," he said. He studied it carefully.

"Where do you keep all of the lead ropes, Turtle?" I asked.

"Why, down at the Ag barn, where they belong," he said. "Only the Ag kids have access to them."

"This particular rope looked new. Are they kept locked up, can anyone access them?"

"They are hanging on a wall on little individual hangers. I guess anyone could grab one if they wanted. They would have to have a key like the Ag kids do to get into the barn to check their animals." Turtle stood and looked out the conference room window with his arms crossed and one hand on his chin. "How in thunder? How in the thunder? You know, detective, there are a lot of kids with a lot of projects, and I'm not just talking about Ag projects. I give them what I can if they ask me."

"Exactly what are you trying to say, Mr. Vines?"

"Well, it is coming into a little better focus now, but there was this girl."

"What girl?"

"She was one of the senior cheerleaders at the school. I think her name is Brittany, or something like that. She came to see me about a month ago. Maybe a month and a half."

"Go on, Turtle."

"Well, detective, she asked me if she could borrow a rope. I swear, I forgot all about it. Kids are asking for stuff all the time. Do you have a horseshoe, can you spare a bale of hay for our project, or some damn hay-ride? But she sure did ask for a rope. I guess it was this rope."

"Do you think she gave it to the Couch girl?"

"Hard to say, Mr. Vines. But it got to her somehow, someway, I guess. I would have never loaned it to her if I would have known it had come to this."

"Mr. Vines, that is the way the world is tilted, I am afraid. There is really nothing in our control, is there? How would you have known about where and what this rope would be used for?"

"Well, I guess I wouldn't," he said. "I damn sure would not have loaned it."

"I understand. Also, Mr. Vines, this investigation is confidential. You may be called to testify. I would ask you to keep our conversation private and under no conditions share it with anyone, agreed?"

"Absolutely, detective. I understand completely. It is still a sad day when it comes to this. I am available anytime, day or night, if you need me. You might want to visit with the school superintendent. Not telling you how to run your business. Thomas Orlager is a good man. Of course, he is the only one I ever worked for, but he is honest. I'll tell you that. Never lied to me in all of these years. When he says it's red, it is red."

For some reason, I thought of the tight shorts Rose had on at the feed store on "inventory day," as she said. She had a way of embarrassing you when she was not around.

"You look flushed, detective, need a glass of water?"

"Yes, that would be good."

I thanked him as I walked out of the conference room. Turtle Vines appeared to be an honest man with a big heart for kids. He had gained my respect and admiration. Anyone that wants to work with high school kids is fairly tough and must like the job. I still did not understand the attraction for Bea, working down at the orphanage with those kids. They did not seem to have much hope for a real life, it seemed to me. All of their clothes were donated by the local good folks, wanting to feel better about themselves. I thought about the pair of boots the neighbor gave me when I was young.

As usual, I tried to move as quickly as possible on this case. It was always a puzzle, with one piece connecting to the other until a complete picture came into view. This one was no different. "Loose lips sink ships" was my motto. You never knew for sure who would keep their word and keep their mouth shut. I have been on multiple cases where they knew I was coming before I got there. I just wanted to find out exactly what had happened to Jenna Couch. It was starting to sound like there was more to the case than just a girl taking her own life. I was confident Turtle would keep his word. Rose? I was not so sure.

I could not go higher than Tom Orlager in the Spring school system. His secretary confirmed he was not available for a few days, due to meetings. She put me down for the following Tuesday at 9:00 a.m. She said he was meeting with the president of the PTA at 8:00 that same morning. She also said he may be in a foul mood after that meeting, so be prepared. I could only imagine a meeting with the PTA president. Like any organization in the school system, when there were parents involved, it generally centered around their kid or kids and the promotion thereof.

The parents seemed to live vicariously through their kids' lives, pushing and promoting their kids to make themselves look good.

Bea and I quit making the football games a long while back, due to the behavior of the parents. We sat in the stands for years, dutifully cheering on the team. After several near-fistfights, cuss fights, and family against family, we quit.

In any event, I would give Mr. Orlager the high side of the road after the meeting with the PTA president. Of course I could not repeat what his secretary had said in private. Maybe the visit with Mr. Orlager would prove to be pivotal in the search for answers. Maybe it would not. Sometimes in protecting an institution, which may or may not bear any responsibility, answers get lost in whirlwinds of minutiae. Giving an answer that is not an answer. Lawyer-speak. Evasiveness and twisting of words. Based on what Turtle Vines told me, though, I should expect that of this individual.

I sat quietly in the waiting area in the superintendent's spacious lobby. The local tax revenues from the oil companies in the county had been good for the school. They had put the money to good use in building a new junior high school. They were able to put a new football stadium in, with a little bond money. Every time there was a bond election issue with more tax revenue needed to pay for a dream, there was conflict. The new football stadium did not seem to cause the normal stir, as all they had to raise was about five million dollars, with the oil revenues providing the rest.

The lobby was adorned with new dark cherrywood furniture and Western artwork. Nine a.m. came and went with no Mr. Orlager. His secretary stepped out and approached me. "I am sorry, Mr. Orlager will be about thirty minutes late. His first meeting is taking longer than expected."

I assured her that would be no problem. It must be quite a meeting. Finally, around 9:40 a.m., the door swung open and out marched a woman in a tennis outfit. She appeared fit to be tied.

"I have a doubles match at the Country Club in twenty minutes. Because of you, I will be late."

An exasperated Tom Orlager offered a feeble, "I'm sorry it took so long."

"Well, Tom, you just remember what I said. The PTA will not tolerate it, and you better not either."

"We will stay in touch," he said. "I promise."

She turned smartly and strode out the door and into the hallway. He looked at me with his spectacles on the end of his nose.

"Are you Detective Carter?"

"Yes, sir. Perhaps a better time, Mr. Orlager?"

"No, there is not a better time. I am sorry you had to witness that spectacle. Let's go to my office."

Mr. Orlager quietly shut the door behind him and seated me.

"No one can hear us in here. I am sorry you had to witness that ogre of a woman," he said, his face reddening, "and I should not be calling her names. She is one of the reasons I may retire early. Always threatening. I cannot imagine how she was elected to head the organization. She is so overbearing, I think no one will ever challenge her. Our only hope is when her daughter is out of school. Seems like the apple did not fall far from the tree. Don't mind me, I am just venting and should not be. Especially to you. I don't even know you."

"That is okay, Mr. Orlager, it is safe with me. Vent all you want. What is she threatening you about, if I may ask?"

"You may ask and I will tell you. She wants a separate van to haul all of the cheerleaders on all out-of-town games. Can you imagine such a waste of dollars? Everyone else rides on the school buses, for gosh sake, including the teams. The sanctimoniousness is nearly unbelievable."

"Well, I guess so," I said. "What are you going to do about her request?"

"I'll be damned if we are ever going to let her get by with it. She claims that the cheerleaders represent everything good about the school and should be treated as such. Again, I am sorry. Every time I deal with her it is like a preparing for and having a colonoscopy. You ever had one,

Detective? Well, there is nothing fun about it. Drinking the juice, crapping all night, and then getting a rotor rooter shoved up your rear. She leaves my butt irritated every time. It takes me days to get over it. Want a cup of coffee? Let me get us one and I can settle down a little and visit when I get a little caffeine in my system. I did not have time to drink my morning cup of coffee before she burst in my door."

Mr. Orlager disappeared for a few minutes. I could smell the coffee being brewed. He brought in two steaming cups on a tray with milk creamer on the side.

"You take cream, Detective?"

"No, straight will do."

When he finished doctoring his coffee, he took a sip and let out a long sigh. "Now, that is better. What can I do for you?"

"Well, in light of the morning's events, I am afraid to tell you."

"Go ahead. Go ahead," he said. "If I can handle her, I can handle anything you have to tell me. Someone in trouble at the school?"

"Well, I cannot say at this time. But based on my current investigation, someone maybe needs to be talked to."

"Go on, detective. What does it concern?"

"It concerns the death of Jenna Couch, sir."

"You know, detective, I don't consider myself an overly perceptive man, but somehow in the back of my mind I thought that might be why you are here. I gave my condolences to her parents by phone the day after it happened. That girl was a lovely girl. She was not in the top-tier group, we shall say. She was a very good athlete. I did not know her personally. There have been all kind of rumors floating around. I simply disregard them. I cannot imagine why she took her own life. What do you need from me?"

"Mr. Orlager, again, after what transpired this morning, I am nearly afraid to tell you, but here goes. I went to the lake house and met the JP right after her death was reported. I personally gathered evidence at the scene and was there when they took her down and to the funeral home. It seems that the rope used in the event was somehow borrowed from the Ag teacher, Turtle Vines. He indicated that kids borrow things all of the time from the Ag department for use in projects. He thought nothing about loaning out this rope. However, this rope is a lead rope for use on animals, leading them by halter in livestock shows and training them to lead. Mr. Vines uses only one type of lead rope with a certain type of swivel."

Mr. Orlager leaned over his desk with deep interest. "Go on, detective."

"Each swivel is stamped with a number. He buys all of them from the only place in town that sells them, Rose's Feed Store." I paused for a moment.

"Yes, Mrs. Rose. We have met on occasion when I was buying flower seeds for our flower garden. She is quite a, shall I say, an interesting lady."

"I could not agree more, sir. Rose keeps very good records, it appears, and records each sale in a handwritten ledger. She keeps the signed receipt of each purchase categorically. In this case, the rope that was used in the hanging death of Jenna Couch was purchased by none other than Turtle Vines. He in turn loaned it out to one of the students of the high school."

"Was it Jenna Couch, Detective?"

"No, I am afraid not. Turtle indicated it was one of the cheerleaders at the school. I believe he thought her name was Brittany, something like that."

Mr. Orlager stood slowly, rubbing his head. His slightly balding head creased at the forehead. "Detective, this is beyond something I could ever dream up. That is beyond coincidental. That girl's name is Britanee Phelps. She is captain of the cheerleading squad. That was her mother you saw coming out of my office. No worse chain of events could unfold, if she is tied up in this somehow. What are you saying happened?"

"Well, sir, I don't know. I only know that the current set of facts as stated. Somehow this lead rope was used in the hanging death of Jenna Couch. I cannot say how it got to her. How many girls make up the cheerleading squad, Mr. Orlager?"

"Six on the main squad, and twenty-six on the pep squad."

"Can you give me the names of all of the cheerleaders on the main squad and the pep squad?"

"Yes, sir, I can. I will type them up if that will do, so they are legible. That good with you?"

"Yes, sir, as long as I leave with them today, if possible."

"That will not be a problem. I will start now."

Carefully he inserted a blank sheet into his electric typewriter. Pausing before he started, he turned to me.

"You do realize, Detective, that once this can is opened, it can never be shut."

"Yes, sir. That is what an investigation is about. All I want is to get to the truth of what happened on that night or evening and work accordingly from that. A young girl is dead. No one knows why or how it happened exactly. If it was by her own actions or others. But she is dead. There is an answer, and that is what I will find. Whoever lies in the wake of that boat will be called upon to tell what they know, understand?"

"Oh, I understand, Detective, I just know when a stink bomb goes off, you can smell it in every nook and cranny. I have a feeling this is going to be a bigger stink bomb than we both know. I know this woman. Her mama. Good grief, her mama. When you go to questioning her child, it is going to break loose. Be prepared."

"I can handle her mother. Is she married?"

"Well, she is married, but the father is an absolute go-along-to-get-along kind of guy, as far as I can tell. He will not buck her. She is the king of their household. Maybe I should say queen. In any event, she absolutely rules the roost around that place. I attend all sports events surrounding the school. Every time I have seen them together, she is in the lead and he is two paces behind her. He never says much to anyone."

"As I said, Mr. Orlager, I will be fine. If you will just give me the names, please, I will be on my way.

"One more thing, sir, is there someone in charge of the cheerleader squad, like an adult teacher or something?"

"Well that would be Ms. Samantha Divine, Detective. She teaches senior government classes. She is in charge of the troupe. Goes with them everywhere. I am not sure she is the one that came up with the need for a van to haul them separately from the rest of the girls. My bet it is that's Britanee's mama. Maybe both of them conjured it up.

"She has a conference period at 2:30 today. You want me to set it up to visit with her?"

"That will be fine, Mr. Orlager."

"Please, Detective, call me Tom."

"Okay, Tom, please set it up. Looks like we are at least moving in the right direction."

Tom carefully typed the names of the cheerleading squad and members of the pep squad below them. He eyed the document and pulled it from the typewriter and handed it to me.

I studied the names of the cheerleaders first: Britanee Phelps, Wiley Arrott, Tempest Livingston, Olivia Rodriquez, Shiloh P. Jones, and Amber Plessington.

"If the cheerleaders cheer, what does the pep squad do, if I may ask?"

"You may ask. They cheer, just not on the field. The cheerleaders are the only ones allowed on the field. This subject has been brought up multiple times at the PTA meetings. The cheerleader moms obviously want the limelight for their girls, claiming that allowing both groups on the field would demean the meaning of being a quote 'cheerleader' in comparison to just being a pep squad person, if you will. I know that does not make much sense, and I wish we only had one big group that took the field with a rotating leader each week, or something like that. Would be a much fairer way to operate, and it would take the good looks and popularity out of the equation.

"I could never say that kind of thing publicly, you understand. I just cannot stand their social cliques and how they treat the other girls. Some of those pretty faces have a terrible heart and a less than high intellect. Crap, I should not have said that. I have just seen a lot, you understand. Their mamas are just as bad, if their girl is one of the six. Bad deal all the way around, and been that way for a long time. As I said, Britanee's mama is a bully and won't be shoved around by anyone. That is why I said earlier, this is going to be a stink bomb, I am afraid."

"I thank you, Tom. You have been very helpful. It will go where it will go, stink bomb or no. Thanks for being candid. I am going to grab a bite to eat at Merle's and then tag up with Mrs. Divine at 2:30. I am assuming at the teacher's lounge area?"

"Yes, Detective. She will be there. She will be the one with red hair, usually in a ponytail, chewing gum. Won't be hard to miss."

"Tom, please remember this case is highly confidential, and the information we have discussed is not to be shared. Please inform you secretary. I know folks saw me come in, with my badge and gun. Please ease her fears and let her know she is not at liberty to share with anyone. You may be called to testify."

"I got it, Detective. This ain't my first rodeo. However, when the dust settles on this thing, it may well prove to be my last one." He laughed.

"Maybe so, Tom, but I bet not."

I made my way to the parking lot and got into my service vehicle. My mind was not in full pursuit mode, knowing the next bit of trail was going to be a little bumpy. But, I always rode in a good saddle. I might have to tie my rope tiedowns to my belt loops before it was over.

Merle was his usual gossipy self. I ordered a cheeseburger loaded with onion rings and a glass of tea.

"What you been up to, Alfie?" he asked. "Any big cases going on?"

"It's pretty boring out there, Merle."

"Crap, that is what you always say. I bet you have a big one going on. Any politicians in trouble? Arrest anyone for DUI or something?"

"Like I said, Merle, it is pretty boring out there."

"Yeah, I know," he said.

He went back to the bar, head tilted toward the conversations going on. I finished my meal, trying to burn time. The hamburger was delicious and the onion rings were just the way I liked them. If he did not serve good food, it would not be worth putting up with him.

Merle came by to fill my tea glass. "How about some chocolate pie, Alfie? Made it last night."

"Yeah, go ahead and bring me a piece. That sounds good."

His chocolate pies were to die for, as they say, the pecan pies even better. He always had just the right thickness of chocolate to meringue on top, ratioed just right. His pie crusts tasted a little bit like the few my mama made from time to time.

Merle brought me my pie and a cup of coffee I did not ask for. But it smelled downright heavenly. "Coffee is on the house, Detective. That will help your mind on any big cases you are working on and won't tell me about," he said, smiling as he set it down.

"Why, thank you, Merle. Like I said, it is just plain boring around here."

I ate the pie slowly and sipped my coffee. It was always fun to observe the people in the café and Merle. If the military could have captured his ears, we would never have to worry about the incoming enemy, as he would hear them well before they reached our shores.

I arrived at the high school at 2:15 p.m. on the money and went to the teacher's conference rooms. I sat in the small lobby outside the three conference rooms. I felt like the investigation was fixing to take a turn with Samantha Divine. It would lead to direct interviews with the rest of the cheerleading squad.

This would have to be handled especially carefully. Teenagers are a precariously tough group to interview. Testosterone, hormones, and sometimes less than steady brainwaves may have led to a few disturbing outcomes in past interviews. Even under the most basic questioning some would cower, become extremely defensive, cry, or bust out in uncontrollable giggles. I had become much better at interviewing them, the older I'd gotten, but it was still not one of my favorite things to do.

At precisely 2:30 p.m., Samantha Divine burst through the door. Exuberant is a good word for her. She had on casual blue jeans, a gold shirt, and, true to Mr. Orlager's description, a bona fide footlong red ponytail. I think her hair may have been dyed that dark of a red. In any event, it was a striking visual when she burst through the door with her ponytail bouncing.

"Detective Carter, it is a pleasure," she said as she grabbed my hand with both of hers. She did look me straight in the eye. "Tom told me you wanted to sit down in conference with me. You don't have a child in school I am aware of, do you? Maybe from another marriage, with a different name? I know all of my government students like the back of my hand."

"Ms. Divine," I started.

"Please, Detective, call me Samantha."

"Okay, Samantha. No, ma'am, I do not have any children at your school."

"Well, then, Detective, what may I ask do we have to discuss?"

"Well, Samantha, you do remember Jenna Couch that was on the pep squad?"

"Why, yes, sir, I do. What a tragic suicide. It really shook up the whole squad. We have done our best in the leadership group to assist with any questions the girls might have."

"Did any of the girls have questions?"

"A few of the girls on the pep squad did ask why she would take her life like that. You know, all of the basic questions a teenager would ask during a time of tragedy like that. I think most of them have just moved on in their circles."

"What about the cheerleading squad?"

"The cheerleading squad?" she asked. "Why, they are not part of the pep squad, like Jenna Couch was. They are a completely different group. In fact, it may not be long that they will be traveling by van to all games, kind of goodwill ambassadors of the school, you know."

"Well, Samantha, I guess that would be okay if that occurs, being ambassadors and all. However, with that being said, this complete interview is confidential. I am letting you know right now that you may or may not be called upon in a hearing or trial, do you understand?"

She stopped chewing her gum and stared dumbfounded at me. "A trial? What on earth are you talking about? I have done nothing wrong."

"I did not say or imply you did anything wrong. I am just saying that things have occurred that lead me to have to interview all of the cheerleaders."

She gasped with her hands over her mouth. "For what, for crying out loud? These are just girls. They are my girls. You better have a very good reason, Detective.

"Please forgive me, I did not mean to say that, I mean, this is just so much to take in. What happened?"

"First of all, Samantha, I will ask you to lock entrance and exit doors in this conference room and draw the shades. I would like to conduct our interview in normal tones, as walls can be thin, you understand?"

She got up and locked both doors, pausing at each in deep thought. She looked at me as she closed the shades on the outside wall. Composing herself, she sat down.

"Okay Detective, I'm ready. Or at least I think I am."

"Samantha, as you may have heard, Jenna Couch was found at a lake house a short time ago. She was found hanging from a rope with a stool under her. I will not tell you all of the evidence I have gathered thus far, but there are a few things you need to know."

Samantha looked straight into my eyes with deep concern. "Was any of my girls involved, detective? I mean, that would be really bad for the school."

"Samantha, we have a dead teenager, and I am trying to get to the bottom of it. The reputation of the school is not my priority.

"On the night before Jenna Couch was found, it has been reported that four girls came to her house in the county for about twenty minutes."

"So how does that pertain to any of my girls?"

"Well, two of them were blonde, they were all dressed alike in short bottoms and matching tops. Each girl was reported to have on black and yellow shoes and socks. It was hard to see clearly at that time of day."

"It could have been any girls dressed up like that," she said.

"The girl driving was in a two-toned blue Ford Bronco with raised white letters on the tires. Chrome strip in the middle."

Samantha gasped.

"Ms. Divine, do any of your pep squad or cheerleaders drive something that meets that description? It was reported to be maybe three or four years old."

Samantha bent over and put her head in her hands.

"Are you okay, ma'am?" I asked.

"Britanee Phelps has a vehicle like that," she said.

"Can you tell me a little more about her?"

"Detective, she is the head cheerleader and her mom is head of the PTA. It cannot be her. Maybe she loaned it out or something."

"Samantha, it has also been reported that she may have borrowed the rope from the Ag dept in your school, the rope that Jenna Couch was found hanging with."

"Are you saying that Britanee hanged her?"

"No, ma'am, I am saying that the lead rope used in the hanging was purchased locally and has a definitive stamp on the shank clasp. It was traced to purchase, date and time, to the head of the Ag department at your school."

"Are you saying that Turtle Vines was involved with this?" Samantha said.

"I interviewed Mr. Vines, and he indicated that one of the cheerleaders, Britanee, as he recalled, asked to borrow a lead rope. He loaned it to her, believing it was for some type of high school project."

Samantha sat and looked blankly at the ceiling. "I just cannot believe that she would have anything to do with Jenna's death. It just does not make sense."

"Do you know if there was any animosity between the two, or with anybody on the squad for that matter?"

Samantha's eyes began to tear up. "You know, Detective, now that I think about it they may have dated the same boy. Do you know of ET Junior? You know, Efron Tillman's son. Do you know Efron Tillman?"

My heart skipped a beat. *Damn, this is Effie Tillman's son*, I thought, not letting on to Ms. Divine.

"Why yes, I know Mr. Tillman. We went to high school together and ran track together, as a matter of fact. I read that his boy is a candidate to go to a division-one school on a football scholarship."

"Why, yes indeed, Detective. The team is doing great because of his leadership on the field. Our girls are there to boost him on."

"So you believe Jenna Couch and Britanee Phelps were dating ET Junior?"

"Yes, sir, at some point. I know I saw Jenna and ET Junior walking down the hall together. I think she had on his class ring. Are you saying Britanee had something to do with this hanging, and Jenna did not kill herself?"

"No, ma'am, do not jump to conclusions. The investigation will take us where it goes. The county coroner called me this morning with the autopsy report on Jenna. It seems she was pregnant. Very early in the pregnancy, but pregnant nonetheless."

Samantha burst into tears. "Do you think it was ET's baby?"

"Well, we certainly do not know that at this point, but blood tests will probably be in order shortly, if needed."

"Why, this whole thing is so bizarre. So surreal. It does not seem like it can be happening to my girls."

"Samantha, like I said, I will follow where it takes me, and we do not know the answers to most of the equation as of yet. Like I said earlier, there are other pieces of evidence that I cannot speak about. You know I must interview the cheerleader squad, as a group first, and then individually. They will all hear the same thing from me as a group before I take each one in a closed interview session. This will be done at the police station, so as not to attract attention, do you understand?"

"I understand, Detective. When do you want to see them?"

"At this point, I will contact each of the parents and set the time for next week. The parents have the right to show up, but cannot intervene in

the questioning. You are not to say anything to anyone about our conversation, do you understand?"

"Yes, Detective, I completely understand."

With that said, I stood and put on my hat. I offered my hand, but she
did not accept it. She stood and walked to the door, to let me out without
saying a word.

"Remember, Samantha, not a word."

She never looked up as she nodded.

"One more thing, Samantha. This is a very serious case with potentially serious consequences for anyone involved. I will be in touch."

CHAPTER ELEVEN

Mingas sat quietly, away from his small band of guerilla fighters, looking through his ever-present spyglass. They were mostly captured and indoctrinated young boys and two steadfast lieutenants. The two older men's intelligence might have been in question, but their loyalty to the leader was not. Eduardo, the one with the machete wound close to his eye, was a fierce and deadly killer. He wore only boots and pants, with a cotton vest wrapped with the ever-present leather bullet strap. His bloodlust was paramount. He was known for his extreme cruelty to the boys in the band. Mingas let him have at it with little interference. Fits of rage, threatening to kill and behead each of the boys was a daily performance. But when Mingas completed his plans for the next attack or raid, it was he alone who was in complete control. Eduardo feared him above all other things. Mingas, void of any type of feelings for human life, was first and foremost a self-preservationist. Mariel, the second lieutenant, was of no sound mind. Years of smoking brown-brown had left his brain void of continuous thought. He was fraught with fits of laughter and loved to crow like Mingas's prize lookout roosters, firmly tethered around Mingas in a large circle.

All of the group knew and were warned routinely by Mingas: Anyone caught inside the circle guarded by his roosters would be killed. No exceptions. If they needed to talk to him, they were to give the clucking hen sound, day or night.

Mingas deemed Mariel a fool but kept him around because he would always relentlessly kill anyone Mingas pointed in his direction, including the young boys in the band. Mariel loved to run into a fight, crowing loudly as he unloaded his gun on the villagers. Then he would climb on the tallest rock or structure and crow loudly while flapping his arms like rooster wings. Sometimes this made the boys laugh. Mingas simply told him to not crow out loud until the attack was finished. The terrified young boys were forced to stay in line. Adequate food and water were acquired only through attacks on small villages in their path.

Mingas had been studying the orphanage compound for some time with his spyglass. He was somewhat certain they had a small number of guns, if they had any at all in the compound. He could see two men on the compound wall at all times, but they never had a shouldered weapon. Every now and then he could see something reflecting the sun, possibly a mirror. He never saw it for long, and it did not appear they were trying to signal someone. Maybe their firearm was leaning against the wall.

The orphanage had long been off-limits to any type of military attack. He was well aware of the fact that the compound not only had food supplies and water but possibly young boys hidden behind those walls.

The band had not eaten well in several weeks. Eduardo had killed two monkeys with his gun a few days hence. By the time the three adults had their fill, there was precious little left for the boys, mostly the meat off the tail. Eduardo and Mariel made it a point to throw any bones for the boys to chew on. They dared not approach the fire, where the adults were eating. The bones were quickly grabbed and devoured by the hungry boys. At least they were getting a little subsistence from the marrow inside the skinny bones.

Mingas calculated that if the compound was taken over, his band would have immediate food and water, and possibly a stronghold where they could bring other fighters. Others might be eager to help him join the fight against the government, if they knew he had a compound with sleeping quarters. He would take the biggest room.

It would also give the government a place to kill his entire group in one setting, if they found out they were holed up inside. Maybe they would attack and overcome the compound, take all that they needed or wanted, kill all of the men and rape the women and girls.

That would make his entire band happy for a while. He might even let Mariel crow from on top of the wall after they were finished. He could see the men and boys raping the women, and then Mariel climbing to the top of the compound to begin flapping his arms and crowing.

He laughed quietly to himself. This would surely put everyone in good spirits. Timing of the attack would be critical. Mingas was good at planning attacks on innocent villages with little or no defense. Surprise, kill, and leave. Often the villagers were frozen in fear and the men unable or unwilling to fight off the intrusion. The attack on the orphanage would have to be shortly after daylight. He knew the men changed shift shortly after daylight, and were absent from the wall for five minutes. They would use their machetes to build enough ladders to put in place a short distance from the compound walls.

Maybe six ladders would do. They would dry camp a short distance from the ladders in the jungle, out of sight of the wall. They would have to ensure complete quiet. The tree monkeys were quick to detect an intruder, and would begin barking at the least sound in the night. This in turn would alert the guardsmen on the wall. Better that they be in place well before sundown the evening before.

He would tie each of the roosters' beaks together with twine during the night, to avoid the morning crowing at sunrise. He would keep his main rooster with him as usual through the night. Even if he could not crow, he would gurgle cluck when someone or something approached.

Lions would have to be killed if they approached the group. If that happened, the whole attack would be off. When the men were changing guard the next morning, the band would quietly rush to the ladders and get them to the wall. He figured they could get the ladders set up at each corner, and get over the walls before the guards got back. He anticipated that Eduardo and Mariel, along with the two oldest boy fighters, would need to be first over the wall. They would have their guns ready and machetes strapped to their backs. The element of surprise was crucial, as the compound occupants believed they were safe from attack within the walls. His men would have to kill all men they encountered without reservation. Once those threats were eliminated, the women and children would be rounded up and assessed. At that point, the fight would be over and they could slow down and enjoy the fruits of their labor.

Per his normal regimen, Mingas went over the fine details and timing of the planned attack. He knew of no other villages in the immediate area that would detect gunfire and come running. Through his area surveillance, he knew of no government troops within miles of the area. The only boat he could see from the shoreline was the big white Mercy Ship, which was normal for this time of year. The ship normally stayed offshore about two kilometers for the first day or so after its arrival from the United States. He figured that even if anyone on the large ship heard the gunfire, they were in no position to make an immediate response, and would not know where to respond. He figured that even if they lowered a boat, put personnel in it, and headed to shore, it would be at least one hour before they got there. Then they would have to approach the compound carefully, if they did at all. No, he figured they were safe enough with his plan. If someone did come their way, they would have to come over the wall with the ladders to get in. He would have to ensure that the last person up the ladder pulled it over the wall, if there was time. They could kill anyone below the wall if they approached.

Mingas really did not like to travel in the jungle at night, unless it was an absolute must. Full-moon nights were desired, if they must travel. When they camped, he liked to have a fairly good fire next to him and his rooster's sleeping spot. He would sleep on his bedroll, gun and machete by his side, rooster secured by foot tether within a few feet of his bedroll. The slightest alert from the rooster had him up, gun in hand.

He would continue to flesh out any weak spots in his plan overnight and tell the troops in the morning. The moon would be full in two days.

Mingas slept lightly. The animal night sounds always made him feel uncomfortable. He never showed any fear of any kind to his fighters. To do so would be death. His total grip of fear on the men and boys was his control. Without that he would lose control quickly. He had watched the younger lions drive out and many times kill the pride leader when he demonstrated the least ability to keep them at bay. Although wary of night sounds, he was fearless. The group knew he had killed countless men, women, and children. He loved to utilize the machete and work on the head, often slicing off ears before whirling like a samurai warrior with a sword and taking off the entire head at the neck. He was deadly accurate at hitting the victim's neck just about midway. The aftereffect was extremely disconcerting to the viewers of the kill: the chickenlike neck spurting blood as the heart continued to pump, the head falling to the ground, and then the body crumpling to the ground following the head. The band had seen him kill many in this fashion after the main attack was over, and the men and women were all huddled in fear in a group. With no means to protect themselves, nor the will to fight, they were easy targets for his cruelty. He kept a whetstone in his side pocket on his pants. He continuously kept the machete razor sharp under the attentive eyes of the men and boys. Just sharpening the blade kept them wary and careful of not being his next victim.

Eduardo had started a morning fire when Mingas arrived in the main camp. He carefully set his rooster down and tethered him to a tree. The boys had already gone out with Mariel in search of food to bring back to the camp for some type of breakfast. Mingas stood by the fire. The flames reflecting off his dark eyes gave away nothing of his intent. Eduardo knew it was useless to try to question him when he was in this mindset. Better to wait and see what he had to say.

He was always quiet and moody like this when an attack on a village was imminent. Then, when he was ready, he would lay out his precise plan and timing. After that was done, there was no turning back or questioning. He could not and would not be reasoned with. He was the absolute leader and authority.

Eduardo knew if he wanted to challenge him, he would have to kill him. He knew he did not have the nerve and possibly the skills to kill him. He also knew that Mariel was too stupid to attempt to kill him, and the boys were scared of looking him in the eye. He would wait and see what the boys brought to eat, and see what Mingas had to say.

Shortly after midmorning, Eduardo could hear the boys making their way back to the camp. They were carrying bananas in each hand. He had hoped for some type of meat. Their bodies were in need of protein.

The bananas would do for now. Mariel came behind the boys carrying two large frogs. He probably hit them with their machete as they stared back at him at the edge of a stream. He had killed many in this way. The legs would be tasty, cooked over the fire, but there was not enough to feed but one person. That person would be Mingas. As the leader, he always got first choice of any food and particularly meat. Mariel or Eduardo was always close to the boys when they were sent out for food. They normally stayed a short distance away, in case the boys were detected by army troops and captured. Then they would be able to report back to Mingas and escape.

The boys sat the bananas by the fire. There was enough for everyone in the group of ten boys and three adults to have a banana each. Mariel cut off the frogs' legs and placed them on a pointed stick above the coals. He did the same with the body of the frogs, though they would be last to be eaten if at all.

Mingas did not acknowledge that they had arrived. He did not look in their direction, only in the direction of the Benguela by the Sea compound. They all knew something was up.

After the legs had cooked a while, Mingas turned around and went to the fire. He picked up the stick and blew on the legs before, pulling one off, and began eating. He motioned with his head and the boys each took a banana. He motioned to Eduardo and Mariel in the direction of the frog bodies on the sticks. "Those are yours," he snarled. They took a frog body apiece and began eating the portions he allowed them to eat. Mingas finished his legs and grabbed a banana. He washed down the meal with stream water from his canteen. "Hurry up and finish your meal. I have something to say."

The group knew it was no-nonsense time and sat around the fire. Each boy threw his banana peel into the fire, as they had been taught. Eduardo and Mariel threw the remainder of their frog bones into the fire and stood. All eyes on Mingas, he began to lay out his plan.

"It has been a while since we ate good meat and slept off of the jungle floor and not on the ground or in trees."

While speaking, he surveyed the face and emotion of each person in the band. He was looking for any potential noncompliance or disobedience.

"I have found a place where we can have good food for a while, good water for a while, and women for a while." Eduardo and Mariel smiled at this announcement, their unbrushed teeth gleaming. Never mind the sweat and grime on their bodies, women sounded good. They knew from the past that Mingas would order them killed when they were done. He would only keep them alive for the men, and possibly some of the older boys, and to cook for them.

When the boys saw that Eduardo and Mariel were allowed to smile, they began to smile as well. They remembered the attack on the village where the village men's heads were placed on sticks around the fire. They remembered the two young girls and the killings. They would have to be careful not to get the girls' brains on Mingas's boots, if he told them to shoot them. He would probably kill them this time if it happened again.

"I have decided we will overtake the compound where the children are. Benguela by the Sea." The boys tried to look straight ahead without emotion. They all remembered the young girl who had escaped into the compound and the boy who led her there. They remembered dropping out of the trees and cutting off his head and hanging him upside down from the big tree.

"The moon will be full in two days. We will attack when the sun is one finger from the ground."

He described the attack plan in vivid detail, covering the preassembly and placement of the ladders, their height, and pulling them over the wall. After he completed the lists of duties and timelines, he turned away.

As usual, he asked if everyone understood their task and if there were any questions. As usual, everyone nodded. He carefully opened his cigarette pouch and doled out brown-brown cigarettes to each person. He also gave each person a wax-covered match to go with the cigarette.

"Do not smoke these until before we attack. I will tell you. Get the ladders prepared. I will be back."

With that, he gathered his rooster and headed back to his camp spot. It was time for him to sleep. He tethered his rooster and lay on his blanket, safe from the challenges of a rival.

CHAPTER TWELVE

Jackaleena was en route to give the chickens her one finger's worth of bread when she noticed the girl with the long stick. She was holding it where the top of it cleared the top of the compound wall.

Jackaleena observed cautiously for a while, sneaking a peek every so often, so as to not draw the girl's attention. The young girl, about Jackaleena's age, would look toward the top of the stick and then lower it down. She did so multiple times before laying the stick down parallel with the wall, so as to not be seen easily by anyone passing by.

Quietly she slipped away. When she had been gone for a little while, Jackaleena carefully walked along the wall without moving her head as she walked by the long stick. She shifted her eyes downward and walked slowly past the stick. She stopped to pull off one of her sandals. While she appeared to look at her sandal, she shifted her eyes to the stick. The end of the stick was split and a small mirror was stuck in the split.

Jackaleena determined the girl was attempting to look over the wall. She had heard the large boats steam past on the seaward side of Benguela. She remembered that the jungle was on the other side. Maybe the girl was looking at the sea.

Jackaleena carefully looked around in all directions, to ensure there was absolutely no one watching her, including the men on guard duty. She picked up the stick and stuck it up over the top of the wall. The mirror was not easy to see, but her eyes were sharp. She moved the stick around a little and only saw ocean and waves. She could make out birds flying above the water. It was then she spotted the large white ship with a red mark on it. It was sitting in the ocean a distance away. It did not appear to be moving.

She lowered the stick and lay it down as she had found it. If there were people on the ship, maybe they were going to attack the compound.

She ran to her room. She must tell Margaret so she could warn the others before it was too late.

Margaret was in the lunch room, helping the other women prepare the noon meal, when Jackaleena walked through the door. She was worried. Standing quietly at the door, she said nothing. All of the women turned and looked at her, as no children were allowed into the lunch room until someone hit the bell. Margaret saw her and knew there was something terribly wrong. She wiped her hands on her apron and ran to the door.

"Jackaleena, you look terrified. Did you have a bad dream last night? Did something happen?" Jackaleena motioned her to come outside. "What is it, dear?"

"I saw a girl holding a stick over the top of the wall by the sea. She had a looking glass on the stick where she could look at the ocean. Just like the one I have in my room."

"You mean a *mirror*, dear?"

"Yes, a *mirror*," she replied.

"Okay, so what happened exactly?"

"She laid the stick by the wall and left. When I was sure no one was looking, I picked it up and looked over the wall to the sea. I saw a big white boat with a red mark on its side. Do you think they are going to attack us?" Jackaleena's eyes were wide with fear. "Maybe they had machetes. Maybe they would cut our heads off." She began to cry.

Margaret held her tightly and caressed her hair and cheeks.

"Jackaleena," she said quietly. "Jackaleena, it is okay. They are not going to attack us. What you saw is called a Mercy Ship. And the big red mark is a cross. That means they are a boat with *doctors* and *nurses.*"

Jackaleena pulled away and looked into Margaret's eyes. She dabbed away her tears. "What is *dockters* and *nusses?*"

"Well, the ship comes one time a year. That means one time every time the sun has come up and gone down many times."

"What do they do?"

"They send a small boat to our compound with supplies for people that may be sick or that may get sick. A small group of people are on the small boat that can help sick people. If they are very sick, they will take them back to the ship where they can help them more."

"Where does the ship come from?"

"It comes from the United States of America. Very far away, I am told. That is where most of the people in the compound came from. They came a long way to help children just like you."

"Why would they want to come a long way to help children?" Jackaleena asked. "This is not their village."

"I would say because they care and they feel that Jesus Man has given them a purpose in life. Do you remember I told you many times that everyone has a purpose, they just have to find out what it is?"

Jackaleena considered what Margaret had just told her. "Do they have compounds like this one in the place where the big boat came from?" Jackaleena asked.

Margaret marveled at this question. "Why, I do not really know. I have heard that it is a very big place and that all of the people live very good lives. I think this means they always have food to eat and clothing to wear, but I do not know much more about it, only what the women that work at the compound have said when they are talking to each other. Why would you ask that question?"

Jackaleena looked away and thought for a moment. "If they have a compound like ours with children, maybe I could go there when I get older and help them. Just like you are helping me. I can teach the other girls about their water makers and making blood and that they are not witches. I can teach them how to take a bath and to read like you are doing me."

Margaret's eyes began welling up with tears. She gathered up Jackaleena in her arms and hugged her. "That is a very nice thought, Jackaleena, but I don't know how easy that would be for you. It is a long way to America. How would you get there, and how would you find a compound like ours?"

"You told me Jesus Man had Joao lead me to this compound. You told me that Jesus Man gave Jaoa this purpose. I think Jesus Man would lead me to a compound in Amerika. He would make me my purpose. Do you think Jesus Man will make my purpose? There is no one left at my village. I have no people left. Maybe my purpose is not here."

Margaret was taken aback by Jackaleena's thought process. How could she argue against what she had been telling Jackaleena nearly on a daily basis? How could she turn loose such a gifted wonder that God had sent her way? If she did somehow get to go, how would she get there, where would she go in that faraway land? Who would take care of her? How would she survive in a world of Milanos? She was beginning to speak good English and was smarter than any child she had ever come across. While she was thinking about it, what did the future hold for her here? Would she stay in the compound forever? Where would she go when the warring ended?

She had no one. No one but Margaret.

"Jackaleena, I think we need to pray to Jesus Man for answers to your question. It is very troubling for me to think about right now."

"I have been praying for your chickens to Jesus Man," Jackaleena said. "I have been giving one finger's worth of my morning bread to the chickens. Maybe Jesus Man does not hear me. Toto never heard me when I called on him."

Margaret's intuition was to remain strong and to offer comfort. Her insides were screaming for relief. To burst into tears would upset

Jackaleena. Just thinking about a child giving a portion of their food to chickens made her eyes tear up and filled her with overwhelming emotion. To remain stolid would not do.

"I am sure Jesus Man has listened to your prayers, dear. Just because he has not done something does not mean he has not heard you." With no more available energy, Margaret said, "Let us walk, dear."

They took each other's hands and walked in silence, Margaret fearful of any and all implications of Jackaleena's questions and consequences, and Jackaleena's mind full of wonder at this place called Amerika. If the ship came from Amerika, maybe the ship could take her to this place. Jesus Man would have to help her, if he was who Margaret said he was. He had not made any chickens come to the compound. Maybe they had some on the ship, she thought.

Margaret walked Jackaleena to her room, giving her one last hug before she turned and left. "I will see you in the lunch room when the bell rings." She turned and left.

The women working in the lunch room all turned as she walked through the door. Margaret slowly approached the women. "Jackaleena saw the Mercy Ship with a mirror on a stick," she said. "I told her the ship was from America. She asked me if maybe her purpose is to go there and work in a compound like ours." She burst into tears as the women gathered around her. "I can't bear to think of her leaving. I have grown to love this child. I know it sounds bad, but she is the smartest child I have ever seen. She has a mind like a sponge. I know that God sent her to me."

Beth Goodchild, the oldest of the Milano women, put her arms around Margaret. "I love you for who you are and what you do, Miss Margaret. But I am afraid that Jackaleena is not in your hands. You see, none of these children are really in our hands, are they? We will do the best we can for her and all of the children God sends our way in this wretched hell on earth. No child deserves to live like this or grow up in this kind of environment. I know my children could not have survived it. These kids have nothing except us, as long as the war is raging. I say us, I mean those of us in this compound. I don't see the world knocking down our doors to rescue these orphans of war, do you? There is not an end in sight. Their only safety net is our compound, which the warring factions will not touch. After this war ends, I am sure there will be something else that follows. With that said, we can change none of that, only do our best with what we are given and who we are sent. If one of these children wants to go to America, maybe we should help them. Or help them all. The question is, how would they get there, and then what would happen to them when they get there? America is a land of people that have come from all over the world for a better life, a better opportunity to do something with their life. I think Jackaleena is in God's very capable hands."

As always, Beth Goodchild's pearls of wisdom were right on the money. Margaret held her hand as a comforting anchor as she dabbed her eyes with her apron.

"I know you are right. I just cannot stand the thought of losing her somehow. She is like my little girl."

Beth squeezed her hand. "Margaret, whatever she does or wherever she goes, she will be an extension of you and whatever you and the others here have taught her. Remember, she had never heard of God until you told her about Him. She has yet to believe that He exists and has not turned loose of her witch doctor completely. She has no family remaining in this world that we are aware of, no home, and you are the only one she has learned to trust. There are no other adults in her life but us. Why don't we just pray that she put her faith in God and us as well? Maybe that is best for her and better yet, for all of the children. It is not like they will all grow up and live in the lap of luxury. For whatever time God allows us to have each of them, let us do our best to prepare them for whatever path that they will take, if and when they leave."

Margaret wiped away tears and hugged Beth Goodchild. The embrace seemed to last forever with both women and those around them weeping.

Finally, they separated. Holding each other's hands and looking deep into each other's eyes, Margaret insisted that she be allowed to leave before the meals were prepared. "I will be back. I simply need to be alone. I need to talk to God about this situation. I need to—" She let go of

Beth's hands and slowly turned around, gathered her skirt, and walked out the door.

Margaret sat alone in her room, thinking about all that had occurred. She knelt beside her bed and the tears began to flow like a mighty river. She could not begin to pray until she had no tears left to cry. "God, You know all about me and where I came from. You know that I believe in You and that You have put me here, this is my purpose in life. I love helping these children that have no other place to go. At least the ones that make it here. I often wonder how many are killed that don't know about our compound, or are killed trying to get here. It seems we always have just enough to get by, and I guess we cannot ask for more. I forget that You are the mighty commander of our world and beyond. You made it and everything and everyone in it. I am a weak vessel, but I am asking You to make me strong. Help me with Jackaleena. I love this little girl like no other that has come to us. You sent her here. I pray that she will believe in You and You will be her God like You are my God. Please forgive my insecurity and fear. I do not mean to be a bad person. I only want to help with what You have instilled in me. I love You for giving me a purpose, a place to live, food to eat, clothes to wear, and most of all the children. I do not know what will happen to Jackaleena. I trust You to take care of her wherever she may go, once the war is over." She smiled as she slyly hinted, "Perhaps she can stay here and help us? I know that probably will not happen, but it does not hurt to ask."

CHAPTER THIRTEEN

Mingas sat in silence as he watched the men and boys finalize the ladders. Eduardo and Mariel smelled horrible, never ones to bathe in a stream. Mingas could smell their stench from thirty feet away. He hated both of them, but they served his purpose. Neither would ever challenge him. He worried more about Eduardo than the shit-for-brains rooster-crowing Mariel. He still thought it would be a good morale-builder for the boys to allow Mariel to crow from the compound wall when the men were killed.

They would place the ladders close as the sun was going down, and make their attack when the guards were changing in the morning. All of the boys clung to their brown-brown cigarettes, but dared not light them until Mingas gave the okay. He always gave them a brown-brown cigarette before an attack. He called them his boy-courage builders.

The sun was nearly down as the band approached the compound. Mingas could see the guards on the wall corners with his spyglass. He motioned the boys to carry the ladders just to the edge of the forest tree line, a short distance from the walls. Quietly they spaced the ladders out down the tree line fifty yards apart. When they were placed on the ground and covered with leaves, Mingas motioned them to recede into the forest and back to camp. This night would be a cold camp, with no fires and only bananas to eat. But tomorrow, they would quench their hunger after the attack. He could not wait to get his hands on the girl that escaped and maybe one or two of the Milano women. Once the men were all killed, he would let Mariel climb up to the guard post and crow with all of his might and stupidity.

Mingas ordered all of the outer-ring roosters tethered and their beaks tied shut. He did the same with his inner circle. "I want no noise at all tonight. We will put the ladders on the walls in the morning when I tell you. You will all eat and sleep well tomorrow night, and we will have a fire and women bringing us food." Mingas rarely smiled, but let go of a tooth-gleaming smile as he spoke of the women and food.

Eduardo and Mariel were quick to follow up and turn their heads to the boys. "Also, Mariel, when we are in the compound and all resistance is taken care of, I want you to get up on the wall and crow like a rooster. Will that make you happy?"

Mariel jumped up and, much to the satisfaction of the boys, began to flap his arms and throw his head back, but not crowing. The boys laughed quietly to themselves.

"Me rooster," Mariel said and continued to flutter about.

"Okay, Mariel, that will do," said Mingas. "Don't exhaust yourself. I need you in the morning. I know that Eduardo told each of you how the ladders will be carried and how to set them on the wall at the exact time, yes?"

All of the boys nodded in unison.

"Good, then there will be no mistakes, yes?"

Eduardo said, "There will be no mistakes, capitão."

Mingas eyed him warily and with contempt. "Good, let there be no mistakes." He pulled out his machete and whetstone and began sharpening an already razor-sharp edge. He smiled wryly, "I do not like the mistakes, no?"

Everyone got the message as always. Completely driven by fear, all of them capitulated to his madness.

"Now, I am getting ready to sleep for a little while. If my rooster interrupts my sleep, let there be a great reason, yes?"

He carefully sheathed his machete after first picking a piece of grass off of the ground. He dragged the grass across the blade and it parted.

"My machete is very sharp, yes? It makes the ears and head come off easily." Each of the boys sat in fear as they watched his psychological parody play out in front of their eyes. He always gave them the impression he was actually talking about cutting off their ears and heads if they made a mistake. The brown-brown made them fearless for a while, after they had smoked. When the effects finally wore off, the reality of their killing came at them full-bore. Killing families in huts at night gave them nightmares. They could never let on that they were scared to carry out whatever Mingas told them to do. After all, each of them had been captured to serve him in his fight.

They never knew what killing innocent villagers had to do with a fight with the government. Cutting off men's heads with machetes and putting them on sticks around fires made no sense to them. Mingas's bloodlust did not run in their veins, but if they were to survive, it had to appear they enjoyed the killing and the raping. They were afraid of the ever-watchful Eduardo. Mariel was more of a clown, but seemed to go back and forth between sanity and insanity. They were afraid he would kill them when he went to either extreme. They had heard Eduardo and Mariel talking quietly in the bush on food runs. Eduardo said he would kill Mingas if he ever had the chance. He also said, "I will kill you, Mariel, if you ever betray me. I will kill you that very minute, do you understand? Before I kill you I will cut off your rooster arms, then pull out your tongue and cut it off. Then I will cut off your penis and testicles."

Mariel was fully wide-eyed, mouth open and quivering.

"Then I am going to cut your stomach open and pull out your insides and string them out on the ground." Mariel grabbed his stomach. "Yes, and then I will shoot you on each side of your heart with my gun. And then, Mariel, I will kill you. Never betray me, do you understand?"

Mariel said, "I will never betray you, Eduardo. You know I am just a rooster. I am just a little rooster," as he flapped his arms and began crying.

"Good, good, Mariel. You be my little rooster and you will stay alive."

The boys listened closely nearby and stared at each other at the exchange. Mingas kept Eduardo and Mariel in check, Eduardo kept Mariel in check, and all three of them kept the boys in check. They each missed their families or what may be left of their families.

Dawn brought the usual forest sounds. The barking monkeys in the distance. There was nothing that gave away the band's presence to the compound. Mingas approached the others from his sleeping spot in the center ring. His rooster sat menacingly on his shoulder with his tether leg and beak tethers secured. The others had long been up from a mostly sleepless night.

"Get out your brown-browns," he ordered. "Let us smoke them now."

The boys pulled the cigarettes out of their pockets and their wax matches.

"Light them," he said, "and pull the smoke deep into your chest. It will make you fearless. We do not have long to wait, so get busy."

Eduardo and Mariel had grown used to the prebattle routine over time and were drawing deeply on their cigarettes. The effect was nearly immediate. A calm enveloped each of them with each drag on the cigarette. The drugs in the cigarette seemed to take each of them into another realm of the world. It made them not care and most of all not fear.

When they finished, Mingas ordered Eduardo and Mariel to lead the way. The boys followed, with Mingas taking up the rear. Some of the boys carried the outer-circle roosters cradled in one arm, careful to ensure their beaks were secure. If one of them crowed, Mingas was sure to kill that person immediately.

They approached the ladders at the edge of the compound. Two boys each grabbed the ends of four ladders. The sun was making its way up to one finger above the earth. Mingas was watching the guard towers intently. Any moment now, the guards would be changing. They would have a brief time to run with the ladders, set them on the wall, and get over. He instructed Eduardo and Mariel to be the first ones over the compound wall when the ladders were set.

Anxiously, the men and boys watched Mingas for the signal to go. "Make sure your weapons are ready," he said under his breath. "You each know what your job is, yes? I do not like mistakes. My machete does not like mistakes. Now go, the guards are going down. Go now. Go now."

The boys ran quietly the short distance to the compound corners, standing the ladders up on the wall. Eduardo and Mariel had just began to climb two of the ladders when they heard the gunshot from the forest.

They could hear Mingas screaming. "Quick, everyone, back to Mingas," Eduardo ordered. The boys had stayed a short distance from each corner to signal when time to go over the wall. They made the throat cut signal, which meant the mission was being aborted. They too had heard the screams of Mingas and the gunshot. It would only be a minute before the guards swarmed the walls.

There was no time to remove the ladders as the boys ran to the edge the forest. When they got to Mingas, Eduardo and Mariel were already standing above him. The black mamba was still attached to his neck and writhing to remove his fangs. The position of the snake's fangs would be fatal. Mingas's eyes were fixated and his breathing labored. He was making gurgling sounds, foam coming out of his mouth. The snake's fangs were pumping deadly venom into an artery.

The boys, mesmerized, looked on in horror. Eduardo quickly took command. He took out his machete and cut the snake right at the head. The snake's head continued to bite, even with its body detached. "Pump him full before I kill him." Then he proceeded to cut Mingas's rooster loose from its tether. "You won't be warning this shithead again. Now go, before I eat you," he laughed. He grabbed Mingas's gun and removed his machete from its sheath. He looked into Mingas's hollow eyes with no recognition. "You treated me like shit. I am going to enjoy killing you, even though this snake has really already killed you. You will never treat me like shit again," he said, kicking Mingas in the head. Taking Mingas's machete, he cut off each of his ears and stuck them in his open mouth. "Better than brown-brown, capitão, yes?"

He turned to the boys and proclaimed, "And now I am going to cut off this shit-for-brain's head." He turned around and brought the machete up slowly and deliberately.

The bullets' impact at close range killed Eduardo and Mariel instantly. Eduardo collapsed on top of Mingas and Mariel fell to the side. The younger boys stood in complete astonishment as the two older boys pulled their pistols and killed the two tormentors.

And it was over. One of the older boys took the machete and whacked the snake's head away from Mingas's neck. "I will let the poison kill you. You are not worth a bullet, capitão." He cut the cord holding the spyglass and pulled it away.

"Put your guns on top of him," the older boy demanded. "We are through killing. Now, I said."

Everyone pulled out their guns and put them on top of Mingas.

"Now, all of your bullets, too. I want you to cut the roosters loose and their beaks and then go home to wherever you live." With that, he turned and walked into the jungle. "Do not follow me. You do not live where I live."

The shift change guards ran back to their stations on the wall when the first shot rang out. They spotted the boys running back to the forest. They knew something did not go as planned when they saw the ladders. Taking out their binoculars, they saw the small group of boys standing at the edge of the clearing when they heard the two shots ring out nearly at the same time. One guard with the good binoculars saw two men fall.

"I think the boys just killed the two men with them. I think they were going to attack the compound and something went wrong. They are throwing something on top of those men and now they are leaving. They look like little boys," he said. "They all have on some type of little uniform."

Mingas's rooster flew straight to the wall and over. He was followed by the other roosters the boys had released. The boys had removed their beak ties, but Mingas's rooster remained tied shut.

The hens began to cackle and cluck wildly at the sight of the crowd of roosters. The roosters began to flap their wings and crow loudly as they descended into the pen. Mingas's rooster was quickly overwhelmed by the other roosters and dispatched with their talons, with relentless flogging. They pecked his eyes out and began pecking his body for a long while, seemingly in a fit of revenge. When they were satisfied, after careful looks that his body contained no life, they walked away and to the hens.

The men of the compound carefully opened the two big doors and peeked outside in the direction of the gunfire, leaving one guard with binoculars on top of the wall to warn them if he saw anything. Carefully they made their way to the edge of the forest. They could see the crumpled bodies of the three men, pistols and bullets lain on top of them. Mingas stared with dead eyes and his ears sticking out of his mouth. They could smell the stench of Eduardo. They stared in amazement at the blown-out heads of Eduardo and Mariel.

"What do you think happened here?" Gustoph Abernathy said. "It looks like this is a guerilla group and they had them boys working for them or something like that. Looks to me like the boys turned on them and killed them all. I don't understand the first gunshot we heard and then the boys and two men running over here. Maybe the feller with the ears in his mouth saw some trouble and was signaling the others."

The others shrugged their shoulders and shook their heads in agreement.

"Well, whatever happened, they are dead. Let's get ready to bury these bodies. A couple of you need to go back to the compound and bring us six shovels. Even killers like these need to be buried."

When the two men arrived back at the compound, the women and children were all gathered in the lunchroom. Beth Goodchild saw them coming and raced out the door.

"My gosh, what has happened? Is everyone all right?"

Jackaleena was clutching Margaret's hand and listening to Beth and the men talk as they described what had taken place and the ladders.

"We need to get shovels," one man said, "and get back. We got some burying to do. I think they are all gone for good. Looks like those boys left their guns and walked away. Got to go."

Beth stood watching them as Jackaleena appeared at the door. "Jackaleena, you must stay inside. It is not safe out here." Jackaleena walked out the door with Margaret close behind. "Jackaleena, come back. Come back inside."

Jackaleena walked to the gates. She peered out and saw the men gathered at the edge of the forest in the clearing. Slowly she began to make her way the short distance. All of the Milano men watched her approach unafraid. When she was close enough to look at the dead men she stopped. She saw Mingas with his ears in his mouth and the two other dead men. She saw the pistols on top of the bodies.

Jackaleena began to speak in a quiet voice, in English: "The man with his ears in his mouth is Mingas, their leader. The other two men are his followers. They guns belong to the boys. I have seen them before. They killed everyone in my village." She saw the fang marks on Mingas's neck. She knelt down to look closely before seeing the serpent head a few feet away. She slowly stood. "Mingas was bite there on his neck by this snake," she said, pointing at the head. "The snake that moves faster than a man. When he bites, man does not have long to live. He got bite on neck. He shot his gun but it was too late. The others," she said, pointing at the two men on top, and motioning to the forest for the boys, "must have ran back to see what why he shot his gun. He was not to live long. Then they killed him and the two men on top. I think they hurt all of the boys and they did not want to be with them anymore. They killed Joao, too. The boy that led me here. They had to do what Mingas and the other two men told them to do. But now they are all gone."

With that, she turned and walked to the compound. She passed the two men returning with the shovels as she remembered the dead men in her village with their heads stuck on sticks. The men stood in amazement, watching her walk back. They had never heard her speak.

Gus watched her go. "She is probably right, you know," he said, shaking his head. "That girl knew just by looking at what took place. I've never seen anything like that. Let's start digging before they start swelling and stinking."

* * *

All of the women were standing at the doors of the compound, not knowing what had taken place exactly. They watched Jackaleena make her way back to the compound.

Margaret ran to her and scooped her up. "You scared me to death, dear. We were afraid for you. Were you not afraid?"

Jackaleena looked back at the spot where the men lay. "Those are the men that helped the boys kill everyone in my village. One of the men there was their leader, Mingas. The boys that were with them are now gone and have left their guns. They are the ones that killed Joao when he led me here. The leader was bite by snake and shot his gun to try and kill the snake that chases men. All of the others ran away from the compound and ran to him. They cut off Mingas's ears and put them in his mouth. I think the other two men killed Mingas before he died from the bite of the snake. Then the boys killed the other two men that that acted bad to them."

Margaret held her close, still trembling. Jackaleena remained calm.

"Let us walk to the compound," she said, grabbing Margaret's hand.

When they entered the gate, Beth hugged her. "Well, I do not know how it happened, but during all of this ruckus we have some new birds in our chicken flock. They are roosters. I think there are six of them. They flew over the wall. One is dead but the rest are alive and crowing. Hear them?"

Jackaleena and Margaret ran to the chicken pen and spotted the roosters mingling with the chickens. Jackaleena looked at Margaret, not quite knowing what to say.

"What does this mean, Margaret? You wanted chickens. Not roosters."

Margaret had to turn her head away to hide the tears. She finally turned back and looked at Jackaleena. She knelt down and held both of her hands and stared lovingly into her eyes.

"Jackaleena, I believe that Jesus Man has answered your prayers."

"I do not understand," Jackaleena said.

"Well, you see, chickens lay eggs. They must have a boy chicken, which is a rooster, for the eggs to produce baby chickens. If no boy chickens, just the egg we eat. With boy chickens, we will have all of the chickens we can handle. I do not know where the roosters came from. I just know they came over the wall. Jesus Man has answered your prayer, dear. You just cannot see him. He works in different ways we do not always understand," and she began laughing. "Did you think he would send roosters to help make more chickens? Six of them? I did not."

"I did not either," said Jackaleena. "I have been praying to Jesus Man and giving the chickens one finger's worth of my bread every morning. I never believe this to happen. I cannot believe what he did for me."

"Well, dear, he did. He definitely did."

"I believe in him," Jackaleena said. "He did what Toto never would. I think he likes me."

Margaret smiled and hugged her. "No dear, he loves you."

"Maybe he will tell me what my purpose is," Jackaleena said. "This makes me know he is watching me and will give me a purpose. Do you think he will give me my purpose, Margaret?"

"I am sure he will, dear. I really am sure he will. Remember, the Mercy Ship doctors are supposed to pay us a visit tomorrow, for a little while, we have been told. I want you to meet one of them."

CHAPTER FOURTEEN

For the rest of the day, Jackaleena stayed close to Margaret. She looked to the gates and thought about all that had occurred. Even though she could not see Jesus Man, she could feel his presence. She knew that she was at a turning point in her young life. She was beginning to feel the weight of the world lifted off of her shoulders. If Jesus Man could do this after she prayed to him, he was the one who made the world and all things in it. Just like Margaret said to her and showed her in the Jesus Man Bible. She marveled at giving one finger's worth of her daily biscuit to the chickens and her prayer that Jesus Man would bring more of the chickens she heard Margaret praying for. She began to feel that Jesus Man heard her own prayer and answered it. Even though it was answered in a way she did not expect, he answered it in a much bigger way. While the women were busy in the kitchen, she slipped to her room in the late evening.

Jackaleena took off her shoes and knelt beside her bed. Her heart was light. Her feelings of joy and gratitude were immense. She felt like Jesus Man was the only one who had ever helped her, and besides Margaret she had no one in the world. She clasped her hands together and began to pray: "Jesus Man, this is Jackaleena. I know you know me, and I know you answered my prayers when I prayed for chickens. I think you helped with the men that were going to attack our compound. You are very powerful. I thank you for answering my prayers.

"I now have another prayer. Margaret tells me that everyone has a purpose and we have to pray to ask you what that purpose will be. I think you have a purpose for me. Maybe it is in Amerika. Maybe the big white boat with the red mark on it is for me to go to Amerika for my purpose. If you did not want me to see it, I would not have been able to see it. So I will go to Amerika on the boat when the doctors come tomorrow. I am not afraid. You will take care of me. I am pray that Margaret will not be angry with me. She will not know I am leave. When I get to Amerika, I am pray that you will give me my purpose and I will go do my purpose. I learn many things while I am here that will help me in America."

Jackaleena finished her prayer and stood. She went to the porch and looked up into the sky at the big night moon. She could see all of the stars beyond stars. "Jesus Man, you are very powerful because you made all that I see. I cannot hardly believe what all you have made. It is so very pretty and makes me smile. I am so little and you are so big. When I think Amerika, my heart is happy." She turned around and went back to her bed, unsure of what would happen the next day. She went to sleep thinking about the big white boat.

Margaret noticed that Jackaleena was gone from the dining room. She, like the other women, were deep in discussions over what had taken place at the compound. Simply trying to take it all in, they were a beehive of vocal activity.

It appeared God had spared them from a sure disaster, if the men and boys had actually gotten over the walls with all of their firearms. One thing all of the women were sure of, the men's intentions were not good. They gave great sighs of relief each time one of them spoke about the possibilities that did not happen.

Before the group broke up for the night, they joined hands, and Beth Goodchild led them in a prayer of thanks and deliverance. Had God not intervened, they might have all been killed. And the children! She thanked God for protecting the children they were entrusted to take care of, who had no one but them.

When the prayer was over, all of the women hugged each other. They wiped their tear-filled eyes with their aprons.

Margaret left the group and walked to Jackaleena's room. She peered through the screen, and because of the bright moon she could make out the form of Jackaleena, fast asleep on her bed. She watched her for a few minutes before walking out onto the wooden porch. She stood in amazement at the full moon and the stars. Her heart was full.

"God, you have blessed me greatly with this child. She is going to be something great one day. She is making me a better person. Thank you for putting her in my life. She is like a daughter to me. Her young life has seen many hardships. She is very smart and very strong minded and makes me smile. I will do my best to watch after her."

Margaret made her way from the porch to the chicken pen. Careful not to rouse them, she quietly listened to the clucks of the hens and roosters. What a pleasing thing to hear. It was nearly as if the hens were happy to have protectors. She walked slowly to her room, thinking how lucky she was to be here.

The next morning, everyone in the compound heard the horn of the Mercy Ship. Three loud blasts in succession signaled the imminent arrival of the doctors and nurses on a smaller boat. One of the guards had his binoculars focused on the ship. *Yep, they are lowering the shore boat down now. I can't see how many people are in it.* All of the adults were abuzz, waiting to hear news from the ship from America. The short time they were at the compound, the doctors would deliver ample supplies of bandages, antibiotics, and pain medicines. They would inspect all of the children and most of the adults. If someone was in need of x-rays, they would be shuttled back to the main ship. The ship even had a dentistry, for cavities or teeth-pulling if necessary. The women at the compound always gave each child a toothbrush and taught them how to brush their teeth twice a day.

Due to their schedule, they did not dally when they arrived. They would cast off to the bigger ship at sundown. Benguela by the Sea was usually their last stop before their return voyage to America. The crew generally made thirty or so stops on their month-long tour of the African coastline and saw as many villages as possible. Most of the staff volunteered their services free of charge, and had regular jobs and practices to get back to.

Questions were asked and answered while they went about their tasks. Jackaleena stood in line with the others with wide eyes. She watched as the children received vaccinations, teeth inspections, and inspections for lice and ticks. They rarely ever saw any lice or ticks. They knew that the women of the compound took exceptional care of these orphans, and made sure they bathed daily. The children were all taught personal hygiene. Most had never seen a toothbrush nor a nail clipper before they came into the compound. Some of their fingernails and toenails looked much like claws on an animal when they arrived.

Jackaleena did not flinch when she received her vaccinations and inspection. She looked at each of the four doctors that had arrived and the four nurses that helped them. She counted each on her fingers. With the one man that was the small boat captain, that meant there were nine people on the small boat. She would have to be quiet and careful not to be seen. It was a long day, with only a short stop for lunch that the ladies at the compound provided for the doctors and their staff. It only lasted about thirty minutes.

Jackaleena watched carefully from the courtyard as the doctors completed the last of their tasks. Everyone's attention was on them as they prepared to leave.

Jackaleena stopped briefly by the kitchen and poked her head in. Margaret was washing dishes when she approached.

"Everything okay, dear? You did very well today."

Jackaleena hoped Jesus Man would not be mad at her for what she was about to say.

"I am going to my room to sleep. The shots make me feel a little bad, I think."

Margaret felt her head. "You do not have fever. Sometimes they do that to people. You go ahead and go to bed. I will check on you in the morning. If you need me, come to my room." She held Jackaleena in a warm hug and kissed her on the forehead. "I love you, Jackaleena."

"I love you, too, Margaret."

"Maybe you will feel better in the morning."

Jackaleena paused at the door and looked back at Margaret, who had resumed her dishwashing. She looked at her for a while. The woman had become her mother and father and taught her so much. She taught her about Jesus Man, which was the most important thing. She did not know if she would ever see her again, but she knew that Margaret was the one who told her about praying and said she would have a big purpose. Surely she would not be angry at her for going to find her purpose.

Jackaleena quietly left the entranceway and made her way across the squeaky porch boards, across the pathway, and to her room. Pausing at her doorway, she glanced across the way with her hand shielding the sun. Slowing, she canvassed the enclosure that had become home. A source for food, shelter, clothing, and most of all companionship with Margaret. And that food was not frogs or grasshoppers like she had on her journey. It was real food.

She smiled as she recalled her biscuit, and how she gave her daily portion to the chickens. She could feel her heart picking up speed. Her eyes started to well up with tears. After a few moments, she wiped away her tears and turned away.

She planned to be over the wall and to the small boat at the guard change. She quickly pulled the pillowcase off of her pillow and packed two dresses and the extra pair of sandals she had been given. She packed nearly everything she had and tied the end in a knot.

She went to the door of her room, pausing, and turned around one last time. How far she had come up in the world, from sleeping in a thatch hut to a warm room on a nice bed. The warm baths and the mirror in her room where she could look at herself dressed in her pretty dress. Even though she had no idea of what lay ahead on her journey, she was not afraid. "Jesus Man gave me a place to sleep and eat, and he gave me Margaret while I was here. He will give me what I need," she said to herself. If it was frogs, she hoped they were good ones.

The dusk of the evening was casting shadows in the compound. It was always Jackaleena's favorite time of the day. But this day was like no other. The only way she knew she might get to Amerika was on the big white boat offshore. The only way to get to the big white boat was in the smaller boat that carried the doctors. She hoped there was a place to hide in the small boat.

She crept in the shadows of the trees, careful not to be seen. She could see the doctors and nurses getting all of their bags in one group and shaking hands with all of the adults in the compound. Time was short.

As soon as the guards came off of the wall, she knew she had a very short time to get up the ladder and over the wall. She thought she could throw her bag down first and jump down carefully. The large tree on the southwest corner of the compound hid her well in its shadow. She could see the man coming down the ladder and his replacement talking with the doctors. He made his way down and headed toward the group. She was lucky his replacement was not waiting at the end of the stairs.

She looked at the other guard posts, and they were empty as well. Quickly she climbed up the ladder and to the guard perch. She peered over the edge to the ground. It looked much higher looking down than it did looking up.

She dropped her bag over the edge. It landed with a soft thump. She crawled over the edge and hung by her hands for a short time before dropping to the ground, bending her knees on impact. She did not feel anything break and gathered the bag over her shoulder and made her way to the boat anchored at the beach. She could hear the front gates opening and fear overtook her. *They are coming now.*

She ran to the boat as fast as she could. It was out in the water. She splashed through the water until she reached the side of the boat. She threw her bag over the side and began to pull herself up and into the boat. It was bigger than she thought. Even though she was strong, it was hard to pull her body up and over the sides of the vessel. Her legs kept going under the boat. With all of her strength, she finally pulled herself up and rested on her elbows to catch her breath. With one final effort, she threw one knee up and pulled herself in.

She was breathing heavily, lying on the deck of the boat. She could hear the group coming from the compound, talking among themselves as they headed towards the boat.

She surveyed the inside of the boat. Each side had a latched compartment eight feet long. She pushed the button on the latch and pulled the door upward. Inside were lifejackets. She shut the door quietly and then opened the one on the other side. It had a small inflatable raft folded neatly in one end. There was room for her.

She stuffed her bag into the front of the compartment and crawled in, closing the door as quietly as possible. She could hear the group as they neared the shore, and could hear the captain talking to them.

"Okay, folks, I will load your bags and instruments first, and then we will board the nurses. When we get them on board, all of the doctors will go last. Please hold onto the stepladder handrail when I get it into the water. Also, please do not dally. There are sharks in the area. No splashing if possible."

Jackaleena barely breathed as she lay inside the compartment. She hoped they would not use the compartment. If they opened it, they would surely see her. She got as close to the wall of the boat as she could and away from the compartment door. They would have to lift it up if they opened it and might not see her.

She listened as the captain lowered a ladder. He picked it up off of the floor, pivoted it over the side of the boat, and lowered it gently into the water. He climbed down and proceeded to retrieve the bags. She heard him place six bags in the boat before calling for the nurses to come aboard.

Jackaleena heard him sit the bags three on each side. It sounded like he placed them in front of each of the storage compartments, or close to them. She breathed a sigh of relief, that he might not open the compartment in which she was hiding. Maybe the bags would hide the unlatched latch.

The captain helped each of the four nurses as they ascended the ladder. "That's good, ladies. Very well done. Please take a seat, two on each side. We have to make sure our weight is evenly distributed. Okay, doctors, please proceed to the ladder. I know you do not want me holding your hands, but you do not get the opportunity to say no," he laughed. "Now, give me your sweet little delicate paws and I will help you aboard."

When everyone was seated, the captain pulled the ladder back into the boat and proceeded to pull up the small anchor. She could hear him as he began to back-row the paddles a short distance.

"Okay, ladies and gentlemen, remember what I say each time we do this, the lifejackets are in that compartment there. If I tell you to put them on, you will grab them quickly and don them, and you will do it quickly, understand? I don't mean a few minutes, I mean now. If I tell you we need to activate the life raft, you will pull it out from that compartment and place it over the side, and then we will activate the cartridge that inflates it. Everyone understand? I know it is a short distance to the ship, but safety is first, ladies and gentlemen. If I don't keep you safe, you may not be able to return home, for which I would be to blame."

With his captain's hat and his burly white beard and mustache, surely he had sailed the mighty seas and was still alive to tell about it. Maybe he could get them back to the boat, as he had done getting them to shore and back every leg of their trip.

As always, his bravado turned to a smile, and with his familiar reproach he said, "Aye, me lads and lasses, let us go to yonder ship and sleep under the stars without fear of pillage and plunder. Aye?"

And their usual response: "Aye-aye, Captain!"

Everyone smiled and nodded in agreement.

"Aye-aye," he said.

After he oared them a ways, he turned around to address the engine. Choking the engine, he fired it up, gray gasoline-filled smoke filling the air. Slowly pushing the choke in, the engine leaned out nicely. Kicking in gear, they began to make their way to the mothership, on still but deep waters.

The spotlight on the Mercy Ship had been activated and was sweeping the shoreline until they picked up the boat.

"Folks, we have good water tonight. Pretty flat and maybe no one will get their stomachs upset. Here we go."

The short trip to the boat took ten or fifteen minutes as the captain slowly moved the boat along with the powerful spotlight leading them in. When they came alongside the anchored vessel, the captain kicked the engine into neutral. The ship crane operator had already begun to lower the boat rigging in front of them. Careful on the descending speed, he timed it where it was nearly to its destination before the boat came alongside. "Okay, Captain, pull your boat up even with the rigging," he said through his bullhorn.

"Heads up, everyone, please. Heads up." The captain pulled under the four-point rigging with a clevis dangling off each end of each cable.

"Okay, Captain, latch the clevises to each corner of your boat when you are ready. Make sure everyone holds onto the edge of the boat and stays seated exactly where they are. Even load distribution is a must."

The crane operator surveyed the position of each passenger and bag as the spotlight held steady on the craft. The captain proceeded to latch each clevis and secured them with their bolts. After he tightened each one of the bolts with a small wrench, he motioned the crane operator to put tension on the loading cable. As he took the slack out of the cable, the boat moved a little in the water.

"Easy, folks, this is a piece of cake," said the captain. "Sit tight and they will lift us up and over. Everyone ready, here we go."

He motioned the crane operator to bring the boat up. Slowly and steadily the boat cleared water and ever so slowly began to move upward.

In five minutes, it was over. The boom on top of the deck was pivoted ever so slowly until the boat was clearly inside the rails and lowered into its cradle. Once the clevises were removed by the crane operator and a deckhand, the passengers were allowed to step out of the boat. "Good job, boys and girls," said the captain. "Aye? How about we head to America?"

The passengers gave a hearty "Hear, hear." The night and day voyage would entail about twenty days to port in normal seas. They were all bone tired after thirty days of shore calls and countless shots and body checks. It was extremely rewarding, with mostly gladness but some sadness involved. Some they could not help or simply refused to be helped. They saw the hurt, the utter helplessness in the eyes of some children and certainly the adults that could not do for the children.

How bright the land of America is. Most of them said, "I will kiss the ground when we get there."

Jackaleena lay quietly in the compartment.

CHAPTER FIFTEEN

Jackaleena's legs began to cramp after lying motionless on the trip from shore. She dared not move as she heard someone approaching the boat. She could not tell how dark it was outside, only that it was very dark in her hiding place. Her wet legs had dried somewhat, but her sandals were still wet from the ocean water.

Someone threw something over the boat. She could hear them pulling it on top of the boat, possibly positioning it in place.

She heard the sound of a cord or rope being lashed to the boat. She lay breathless as each sash was pulled tight and secured. Finally secure, the worker made his way away from the boat.

After his footsteps faded, Jackaleena began to breathe normally. Slowly and gently she pushed against the door of the compartment. Surprisingly, it opened without much noise. She could see nothing when she peeked outside the cracked door. Her water maker was starting to really hurt, as she had not relieved herself since the early part of the day. She certainly could do so in the boat, but chose to hold on for now. Slowly she made her way out of the compartment after propping her sack under the door. Once she was outside of the compartment, she left her bag in place, holding the door in the event she needed to get inside again quickly. She reached up and felt the canvas boat cover and its rough texture. She pushed up on it, quietly testing its strength. It would be easy to poke a hole in and tear if she could feel around for something in the bottom of the boat. However, if she tore the top of the cover, surely she would be noticed.

Lying there, looking up into the darkness, she remembered that the man tying the lashings had tied only four, two on each side. She slowly made her way up the side of the boat to the edge. Pushing the canvas upward, she moved her fingers up and the canvas separated from the boat. She could see lights on the wall of the big ship. They were dull, but still hurt her eyes.

Allowing her eyes to adjust, she could see white walls of steel and a doorway with a light on either side of it. The door was closed. All of the people must be inside the door. Jackaleena pushed on the border of the canvas, which felt thicker than the top. Pushing upward, she was able to move it enough to get her hand and arm outside and on top of the canvas. Slowly she made her way, feeling along the top to the lashing.

It began to get very tight, the closer she came to it. She could feel the rope lashing as it zigzagged back and forth to two prongs. The canvas cover was tight enough at the lash point, and it began to cut off her circulation in her hand. With her hand growing numb, she pulled her arm back inside. With circulation restored, her hand began to burn as the blood flowed normally to her fingers. Feeling along the bottom of the boat, she found only a clean boat.

She made her way to the back of the boat, where the captain sat as they made the journey from shore to ship. Feeling along the cushioned box he sat on, she found that the cushioned board lifted. It was some type of container, with a cushioned lid on top. Slowly she moved the cushion aside and worked her fingers downward.

The sea rations she encountered were neatly stacked in rows. Not knowing what they were, she removed four of them, careful not to drop them on the floor of the boat. They were each as big as her hand. She could feel the pull tab on the top of each can, but did not know exactly what they were. Carefully stacking them on top of each other, they naturally stayed in alignment, due to the lip ridge around the top of each can.

Quietly she placed her hand under the canvas and peeked out to see the lighted area as quiet as it was before. Carefully pushing the canvas up, she was able to slide the stacked cans slowly on the edge of flat boat rail toward the tied lashing. The closer she got to the lashing, the tighter it became. When she was a short distance away, she could move the cans no further. This time, she could easily place her arm outside the canvas and feel the lashing slipknot. Exploring the slipknot, she could feel one piece of the cord sticking out by itself.

Grabbing the single piece, Jackaleena pulled gently on the cord. It did not move at first. Applying all of her strength, it began to move slowly and came free.

She pulled her hand back inside and listened intently for a while. Maybe once she unwrapped the lashing, she would be able to place her sack outside the boat and onto the floor of the ship. Once she got outside, then where was she going to go and not be seen? The first thing she would do was find a place to hide and relieve her water maker.

Feeling like she was hiding in the jungle and about to make her presence known, she moved slowly and cautiously. Slipping her arm outside the canvas, she made her way up to the stacked cans and the lashing. Grabbing the loose cord, she began to unwind the lashing from the prongs. After she had moved the cord back and forth three to four times, it came free. Immediately she grabbed the four cans and held them down so they did not fall. Then, carefully reaching up with her other hand, she lifted them off the rail and to the floor of the boat. Making her way back to the captain's sitting box, she placed the cans back into the exact spot where they were removed from. Quietly, she placed the cushioned seat board back on top of the box and crawled to her sack.

Gently holding the door with one hand, she pulled her sack out and slowly lowered the door back into its closed position. Gently pulling the door latch closed, she gathered her thoughts one last time before exiting the boat. If she was caught, they might take her back. She could feel the mighty ship moving through the sea. Maybe if she was caught, they would not want to turn the ship around to take a girl back to Benguela by the Sea. Maybe she should relieve her water maker and then crawl back into the small boat. What if they made another stop and had to use the boat again? She would be trapped in the same compartment she had just come out of. That did not seem like a position she wanted to be caught in.

No, she must get out of the boat, find a place to hide, maybe something to eat and drink, and not be seen. Surely there was such a place on this mighty ship where one girl could hide. She was not so sure about the food and water to drink.

Before she lifted the canvas, she paused. "Jesus Man, this is Jackaleena. I am going to Amerika on this ship to see what my purpose is. I do not have any water to drink or food to eat. I do not know how long it will take to get to Amerika. I ask you to help me to get to my purpose."

She thought about Margaret's prayers she overheard, and feeding the chickens a portion of her food. She thought about the boy soldiers and the roosters flying over the walls, and the snake that bit the man on the neck.

Smiling to herself, she grabbed her sack. Pushing the canvas up, she gently placed it on the floor of the ship. She prepared to slide one leg out first.

"What have we here?" a low voice asked.

Jackaleena pulled her leg back in and froze.

"Well, it must not be a bird, because I saw a leg with a sandal on the end of a foot." His voice nearly sounded like music when he spoke. "Now, I wonder what type of person is on the other end of that shoe and leg? Is it a boy? Is it a girl?" He laughed. "Maybe it is my imagination?

"You must come out now. I will not hurt you. And if I was guessing, you may be a little hungry and possibly a little thirsty. Come, now, let me see who and what you are. There is no one else here but me."

Jackaleena lifted the canvas cover. She could see his legs. Looking up, she saw a large man with some type of hat on his head. He was pushing a cart with rubber wheels. Even with her keen hearing, she did not hear him approach. Perhaps she did not notice him approach while she was preoccupied with placing the cans back in the captain's seat box. All of that did not matter now, he knew she was here.

"Well now, if it isn't a girl. Come out and let me look at you. Let us see what the night has brought us."

Jackaleena slowly worked her way out of the boat and looked up at the mighty man. He was as big as a mountain. He held out his hands, bigger than leopard paws. He smiled gently and laughed as he looked her over. "I have been expecting you."

Jackaleena looked with great surprise when he said that. "You see, the captain of the boat you just got out of told me that there was a little stowaway. He saw water on the floor of the boat when he reached in to get the ladder for the folks to climb in. He looked at the compartment you were hiding in and saw the latch unlatched. Not only that, he saw you run toward the boat. But do not worry, little one. He has only told me. I am Rufoldo Obediah. You can call me Rufus. May I ask what your name is?"

Jackaleena stared at him, mostly in awe at his sheer size. She stood speechless.

"Come, now, surely you have a name? Is it Mary? Perhaps Cindy? One of the nurses is named Cindy. I know, it is Judith. I like the name Judith."

"It's Jackaleena," she said. "My name is Jackaleena."

"Jackaleena," he repeated, "that is a wonderful name. A tribal name. I love Jackaleena," he said, making great gestures with his hands. "Now, Jackaleena, why are you on my ship? Where are you going? This ship is heading one direction, and it is away from where you just came from. Where we are going is far away."

"I go to Amerika," she said.

"America," he said. "Well, can you tell me why you are going to America? Do you have family there? What would make you get on my ship to go to America with just a sack and the clothes on your back?"

"I go to Amerika to find my purpose."

"Your purpose?" Rufus asked. "I am afraid I do not understand. What is this purpose you talk about?"

"Margaret at Benguela by the Sea pray for chickens. I see her give part of her money to Jesus Man at the church. I pray for chickens and give part of my bread to feed chickens. Jesus Man send snake to bite man that attached our village. His roosters fly over our wall to be with our chickens. They will make more chickens. Jesus Man answer my prayer. Margaret show me Jesus Man Bible words. I believe them now. She tell me I have a big purpose that Jesus Man will show me. I think my purpose is in Amerika."

"Mercy, mercy, mercy," Rufus said. "That is a mouthful of words you just said. I bet you need something to eat and drink and maybe a place to relieve yourself and take a bath? Is this true?" Jackaleena nodded. Somehow she trusted this gentle giant of a man. "Come quickly, Jackaleena, get in my clothes basket with your sack. I will cover you up and take you to a secret room when while we are moving, understand? All right, then, let's get you in this basket and covered up."

Rufus picked her up with his mighty hands and lowered her into the basket. There were already several towels and washrags on the bottom. He put her sack in beside her and pulled out three or four towels.

"I will put these on top of you, so you will not be seen. Quiet, now."

As they began to move, Rufus sang. His low voice was beautiful to listen to as he sang a song she had never heard. He would sing a little while, then hum the song, and then whistle. One of the rubber wheels would sputter off-center and the cart would vibrate for a short while and smooth up again. Jackaleena could still see the glow of the full moon on the canvas liner of the laundry cart. She could hear the quiet plow of the ship through the ocean waters as the mighty propellers pushed the ship along. The sea was smooth as glass.

Rufus stopped. "Okay, child. Let's get you to the bathroom. I will lift you out and open the door. Be very quiet and tap quietly when you are through."

Rufus dug through the towels piled on top of Jackaleena's head, smiling broadly. "Lift your arms up, child." When Jackaleena lifted her arms, Rufus scooped her up.

Jackaleena, though burning with the need to relieve her water maker, never felt safer than she did then. Who was big enough to hurt her protector? She had never seen anyone so strong and yet so gentle.

"Okay, child," he said. "Be quiet, please," as he put her down next to the door of the restroom.

He quietly opened the oblong metal door. The fetid odor that only can emit from a ship latrine engulfed her and Rufus. "I am sorry for the smell. You must breathe only through your mouth, like this. That way you will not smell. Okay? Remember, tap on the door quietly and we will continue our journey to your secret room."

Jackaleena was safely back in the laundry basket with a pile of towels on top of her, free of the burning pain she had felt since she boarded the small boat at Benguela by the Sea. Rufus pushed the cart along, singing quietly as they circled the stern of the ship, stopping a few times to throw on another towel or two left in towel bags outside doors. Slowly Rufus made his way to the bow of the ship and stopped the cart. He pulled his sash cord from his pocket and tied a hitch on the cart push rail. After testing it for strength, he tied it off to a metal clasp on the deck.

"Child, I am going only a few steps away and no one else is near. I tied the cart so it will not move."

Jackaleena could hear him walk away, and her heart began to pound. She remained very quiet.

Rufus walked slowly to his favorite spot at the front of the ship. He always felt like he was flying over the water in that spot. At this time of night, there was no other person usually awake except the captain. The first time he ventured to the front of the ship at night, the captain put a spotlight on him and called down to see what he was doing. Rufus knelt as if to pray and looked up. The captain immediately turned off the spotlight and never turned it on again for his nightly ritual. The captain could nearly perfectly time when Rufus was going to be at the front of the ship after making his towel rounds.

Rufus looked quietly at the beautiful full moon, at the many stars in the heavens that his eyes could see, and the moon's reflection on the still water. He listened to the quiet movement of the ship through the waters. "My Savior, it is I, Rufus Obedeiah. I am standing here looking at the beauty of things You made. I am thinking about the depth and countless grains of sand in the ocean floor below, all of the water in the oceans, all of the stars in the sky, and here am I. It is hard for me to comprehend Your grace on one man such as I."

Jackaleena listened quietly as Rufus prayed his unusual prayer. She lifted her head and lifted the towels so she could see. She smelled the wonderful ocean smell and felt the cool breeze on her head as the boat moved. She put a towel back on her head and kept her eyes just at the top of the cart. She could see Rufus a short distance away, his mighty frame silhouetted in the moonlight.

"I will never understand why You saved a man such as me, with all I have done, but You did. You know what I did to other men while defending my tribe. I have told all of these things to You. But somehow You already knew. You knew the extent of my unspeakable anger when in battle. I will also never understand how, from the beginning of time, when You made every speck of sand in the ocean floor, all of the waters of the ocean, all of the land upon the earth, all of the stars in the heavens and all animals, trees, and people.

"How is it that I have come to be in the possession at this time in the world and history of this small young child? Surely it is at Your will. How is it that at this point and time in the world and history that this young brave child in the basket ever got to the ship and now is in my basket? It seems to me that You intended her to be in my care, as I do not think she has anyone else to care for her except You, and now You have handed her to me. She tells me she is going to America, which is where this mighty ship is going."

Rufus laughed at the thought of the roosters and the chickens.

"My Savior, she is but only a small child, but she believes in You because You sent her roosters to make more chickens after she prayed. A simple prayer from a child that You answered and she believed in You as I do forever. So now, You have delivered to me, Rufus, this little girl that is going to America on this ship, and I must care for her. I must care for here without her being seen by others and make sure she is fed and clothed and gets to where she is going to in America. She told me she has a purpose, but I am not sure she knows what that purpose is. I think only You, my Savior, know what that purpose is. As You have put me here at this moment in time in the history of the world to take care of this child, I am asking that You please guide me on what I should do. How do I know what her purpose will be? I do not know where to take her or how she will get there."

Jackaleena could not make out all of the words Rufus said and what they meant. She heard and understood enough to begin weeping quietly. She was amazed to hear a mighty man pray in such a way to his "Savior." She could feel that he was talking to Jesus Man, but she never heard him say it.

Peace came over her. Never had the world looked more beautiful. The full moon—with Rufus's mighty body framed in the middle, he looked like a giant man in the moon. The beautiful array of endless stars. The arrangement of stars that only a master builder could make. Some in straight lines looked like a drinking cup, while others were clustered so close together they looked like a cloud. She thought about the depth of the skies and stars. *Jesus Man is truly powerful. No one is more powerful than him.* Everyone she met to get her to this laundry basket with a towel on her head, Jesus Man had sent them at the exact time she was coming by. That only meant he knew everything about her and where she was at all times. It meant that he knew about how Joao Cubala found her on her way to Benguela by the Sea, her village, the soldier boys and the snake that killed. It means that he knew before she that the big white ship would carry her to Amerika.

With this thought, she became blissfully at peace with the killing of her parents. Toto, she realized, was just a man who fooled people. She never saw him do any of the things he said he could do. Jesus Man makes people meet at the exact spot in time that he wants them to meet, and for the reason they should meet. She would have to ask Rufus why he called Jesus Man his Savior. Surely, she reasoned, I have a big purpose in Amerika.

Rufus lifted his mighty arms towards heaven. "My Savior, please help me to do my best job with this child. Already she has stolen my heart. Her mighty bravery to get on the ship makes my heart and my eyes cry. She is so little, and I have never helped a little girl child. But since You sent her here, I will do my best. But I ask again, please let me know where You want her to go and how she is to get there. When we come to port in America, she will have to claim asylum as I did. Maybe I can help her with that portion of her journey when we get there. I am sure that since You got her to me that You have already worked out who will receive her across the water in America. I hope whoever it is will be good people and take care of this little girl so she can make her purpose. I thank You for my life and that You have kept me alive to breath the air that you made, smell the ocean that you made, look at the stars and moon that You made, ride on the mighty ship carrying this precious creature that You have sent me. It seems to me she is going to have a mighty big purpose. Amen, my Savior. Amen."

Jackaleena, though overwhelmed with emotions, ducked her head into the basket and pulled the towels back over her head. She could scarcely contain her joy from listening to the prayer that Rufus prayed to his Savior.

Her stomach was growling loudly as she could hear Rufus's footsteps nearing the basket. He said nothing, only hummed. He untied the sash and folded the cord into his pocket. He began to push the cart slowly.

Jackaleena heard different sounds as Rufus made his way below deck and down long, steel corridors. The loose wheel occasionally vibrating along the way. Rufus was greeted by several people as they made their way along. Ship porters and other service workers spoke as Rufus passed them. She could smell the good smells of the galley as they passed. Cooks were busily peeling and chopping potatoes and onions, meats and other vegetables. Placing them in freshly washed bowls with covers. To the refrigerated bins went all of that.

Jackaleena's mouth began to water as the wonderful smells of the kitchen wafted through the canvas siding of the cart.

Rufus stopped and visited with one of the men in the kitchen. This man had a voice that did not sound as deep as Rufus but was kind. "Mr. Rufus need some food?" he asked, holding his stomach.

Rufus laughed mightily. "Yes, indeed, Mr. Jole," he said. "What have you got for me tonight?"

"Perhaps some bread and cooked meat? Maybe some banana or pineapple?"

"Anything sounds good to me this time of night, sir. And as you know, Rufus did not get to be this big without eating a lot of food."

"Yes, sir, Mr. Rufus. I like you. You always make me laugh with what you say. I think you make me laugh to get more food out of me," Mr. Jole chuckled. "Let me see what I can get for you, so you not go hungry."

Mr. Jole scurried around the kitchen with his potato sack, poking into food of all kinds. He put in several cans of meat, one pineapple, and a few bananas.

"I know you like my fresh-baked bread, Mr. Rufus, so I give you two loaves. I am also putting in some cold milk from our ice room. That will make the bread even better."

Rufus was rubbing his stomach and laughing. "You are going to make me fat, Mr. Jole. But I thank you, my friend. You are a good friend."

Mr. Jole handed Rufus the potato sack full of food. Shaking hands, Rufus departed, humming his song. "May God Almighty Savior watch over you and bless you, Mr. Jole," Rufus said, waving his hand.

"Yes, may he do so," said Mr. Jole.

He placed the potato sack beside Jackaleena and whispered. "Soon you can eat, child." Rufus wheeled the cart along and finally stopped. She could sense him looking both ways before he opened a door. Once inside, he pushed the cart another short distance and opened another door.

Flipping on a light switch, he peered inside the tiny servant's quarters, a seldom-used room on the second level below deck. It had a vent tube for air, a small electric fan, a small lavatory, showerhead and latrine, and cot and clothes rack. There was a small steel tray welded to the wall with a small canvas chair in front of it.

"Well, my child, you may lift your head, now. This is where you will live until we get to your purpose in America." He lifted her out of the basket and peeled the towel off her head. Her legs were still a little numb from remaining rigid in the small boat and riding in the laundry cart. Rufus lifted the food sack out of the cart.

"This is your food. Drink the milk while it is cold. Don't overeat and make yourself feel bad. Here is your bed. It looks like there are two blankets here. This is your latrine, with plenty of paper," motioning to the toilet-paper rolls on the floor. "I will see what else I can get to make your life easier while you are onboard the ship. Here are some pills you take with milk if you start to feel sick with the ship moving through the water. Do not wait to take them when you are sick. Take them before you get sick, do you understand?"

Jackaleena nodded.

"Child, no one will bother you here. You must lock the door from the inside with this hasp. I will tap on the door like this when I am here. Two short taps, stop, and two more short taps. Anything else, do not open the door. I will come by in the morning after you have had a chance to eat and sleep. You cannot go out in the daytime, only at night, with me, in the laundry cart. Understand?"

Jackaleena trusted him and nodded. He put his mighty hand over the top of her head.

"Child, we will get you to your purpose. I promise."

He reached over and kissed her on her head.

"I promise I will do that. Yes, sir. I do indeed."

CHAPTER SIXTEEN

The news of Cotton Banks's death caught me by surprise. His widow, Maude, called me at the station and told me Cotton had a massive heart attack during the night and died before the ambulance got to their home.

Maude was crying so hard she could barely speak. "We had such big retirement plans, Alfie. You know Cotton only wanted to work to make it through his twenty-fifth year." She paused. "We been married nearly thirty-seven years. He was only fifty-eight years old," she said, her voice trailing off.

I listened with everything I had while my eyes misted up. "Maude, if there is anything I can do, anything at all, you let me know and it is done." Maude blew her nose and he could hear her pulling tissues out of a box.

"I don't know. I don't really know how I can go on without Cotton. He was my everything. Cotton was a great man and a great father to our two sons. I want you to be a pallbearer, Alfie. Can you do that for me?"

"Yes, ma'am, I would be honored to do that for Cotton."

"Well, there are only five or six men he ever really talked about being his true friends, and you were one of them. You know he picked his friends very carefully, and was a good judge of people. He never took kindly to anyone lying to him or about him, Alfie. If he called you his friend, you must be a very good man."

"I don't know about that, Maude, but I try real hard. Being as this just happened, do you have any idea when the service will be?"

Maude burst into full tears. I could feel a wave of compassion and grief come over me. "They have to do an autopsy first. Seems surreal, with all of the autopsies that Cotton ordered, and now he has to have one done on him. He probably would have laughed about that. He always told me not to make a big fancy funeral, and 'just dig a hole and toss some dirt on top of me, by a good tree.' We have owned our plots at the cemetery since we was early-on married. Cotton had all of our business tied up in a neat bow, so there is not a whole lot for me to do. He paid for our turnkey funerals, caskets and all, in monthly payments. I just never believed we would actually have to use them. Cotton was a quiet man. But he could make a dollar go further than any person I ever saw. He kept up his life insurance all these years, and there is enough there where I never have to worry about anything."

She kept talking while I just listened and yes-ma'amed from time to time. She was going longer talking without coming apart and it was probably good to let her talk it out. So I just listened.

"I am sorry to go on and on, Alfie, but he—we were high school sweethearts, you know, neither he nor I ever dated another person. I could never love another man."

"No, ma'am. I understand."

"Alfie, this is Monday. I will call you on Thursday. I am kind of thinking about Saturday morning. Cotton always liked the morning time. Said God always starts a new day with a rooster crowing, birds a-singing, and cows a-grazing.

"Goodbye, Alfie. Thanks for listening."

"Goodbye, Maude," I said as I hung up the phone.

It was quite rare that I could not get a grasp quickly of the worst of situations. This was one of them. Cotton was not only a close friend, he was the JP of Spring. His testimony was going to be needed at the Jenna

Couch investigation over what he found at the lake house. That was out the window now.

I headed to the house in my service vehicle. All I really needed was my backpack and the bare necessities for a night or so. My little note to Beatrice just said I would be gone for a couple of days. As much as I was gone, I doubt she would miss me, even if Birdie was not in the driveway.

The stop by the station on my way out was mighty short and fast, staying only long enough to pop my head into the Captain's office. "Gonna take two days of vacation Captain." Captain Burris, deep in conversation on the phone, acknowledged my request with a wave of the hand.

The drive to Mount Theresa was forty minutes. It was the tallest point in the country close to Spring. It was the same mountain that I climbed while investigating the kidnapping and murder of Theresa De Lagarza. There was an all-out multi-county manhunt for the deadly Mexican bandit Gato Montez. All the reports coming in on the wire said he kidnapped her in Mexico somewhere close to the border and somehow crossed into Texas with her. County roads and highways were blocked with checkpoints for several days as the chase ensued. His last reported sighting was supposedly close to Spring, and it was reported that he had taken sanctuary on top of the mountain with his hostage.

From the peak, one could command a broad view for many miles. Dust plumes brought on by vehicular traffic down dirt roads could be seen for miles without binoculars. If one had a stockpile of ammunition, food, and water, one could stay on top of the mountain for a long period of time. Of course, one could also be shot at from a helicopter.

There was no sign of Gato Montez and his hostage when I finally made my way to the top the first time on the north face trail. If he was up there on top, he truly had the tactical advantage in daylight so it took a while to get up on top without being seen.

Theresa De LaGarza was later found on the north side of the Rio Grande six days after the manhunt started. Her head had been smashed in with a rock or a gun butt, her throat slit, her body lying naked on the bank of the river. Gato Montez vaporized into thin air, most likely back into Mexico, and was not heard about again. There were a few rumors here and there that he might have been killed, but there was no way to confirm that. Merle was always quick to spread those rumors. The juicier the better. When the Spring townsfolk heard about the death of the young Mexican woman, someone started a petition to have the mountain named after her. The petition took off like wildfire, and soon there were well over five hundred or more names on it. The matter was brought to the city council and then to the mayor. Sure enough, once the county officials signed off on it, it was done. I always found it interesting that it was not named after the mayor, as much as the man thought of himself.

Making my way southeast out of Spring, I was eyeballing the mountain in the distance all the way. The closer I got, the more it loomed. It was not a big mountain, compared to the Rockies or those in the Gila. Still, it stood quite alone and impressive on the rolling plains.

As I approached the last cattle guard, the mountain stood ahead. It amazed me how much it looked like an old volcano with a flat top. All of Birdie's gauges looked good when I stopped her to take a leak in the powdery dust on the old road.

The last mile was arduous. The two-track trail was just that. Of course, most ranch roads in this part of the country were never manicured. Ranchers seldom took time to doctor them up other than to lob cut an occasional small mesquite bush directly in the tire track. If the tree would not tear up anything under the truck, they usually centered the front tires over the bush and kept moving. The small mesquite scrub in the tire paths indicated no traffic at all for some time.

I was careful to center Birdie's front tires over the small mesquite, like the ranchers do. Though not high, they were full of long thorns that could puncture a tire. It was the same kind of mesquite thorn that Gato Montez, the Mexican bandit, was rumored to have cleaned his teeth with. He was said to keep it in his hatband when it was not stuck between his front teeth.

It did not look like there had been any vehicle activity for a long time and I was in no mood to deal with human interruptions. That went on enough in day-to-day work: people who killed each other, ran over one another, burned, raped, or cut each other beyond recognition. The one thing I did not want or need right now was more people.

Approaching the base of the mountain, I saw the steep winding trail up the north face and the scattered large boulders off the trail. Although the mountaintop was only a few hundred feet above, it was not easy to traverse. Besides being a rattlesnake haven, there had been more than a few mountain lion sightings there, mostly thought to be young males out of Mexico that were venturing out on their own when their mamas made them leave. They usually did not leave their mother's side for at least a year and a half. When they did, she could no longer protect them from the large males. Rather than stay in the area, they often ventured north to Texas, foraging on anything they could catch. Being hungry, these were of particular danger, always hitting from the back and usually the neck. A fella would not know they were got until they were got. Even though they only weighed about one hundred pounds, it was all muscle, claws, and teeth. Not many folks survived their attacks.

I parked Birdie and checked my backpack and limited supplies. Essentials were a full canteen of water and six bottles of drinking water. My little propane stove was no bigger than a coffee can. Dried food packs could be mixed with small amounts of water and heated in a tin kit. Then there were the sweet peppermints and several chocolate bars. Bags of dried fruit were a mainstay, being both light and easy to carry. My little nylon pup tent had a top vent with rain fly on top. With my Army Surplus rollup sleeping mat, blowup pillow, and fabric foil blanket, I could remain relatively comfortable for short periods of time.

As always, I checked my service revolver and gun belt, making sure the pistol cylinder was full and the gun belt had thirty rounds of ammunition in it. Besides the water, a rainproof, lined windbreaker was the second most important thing in my backpack. You can get by without food for a while, but you cannot do without water for very long. About the only smart thing my Pa ever said was: "During a rain, keep a warm hat on your head and a jacket that will keep the rain off of your back if you don't want the pneumonia."

Locking Birdie, I patted her on the hood as I swung my backpack. "Guard the trail, girl, and don't get ate by the coyotes. I will be back in a day or so. If I don't, come looking for me."

The best I could remember, the first time up took over an hour. Of course I was moving slowly hiding behind those rocks and all. It was not my desire to be shot from above by a fugitive.

The early fall was always my favorite time of year. It was a familiar saying in these parts that there is summer and then there is winter. Blistering hot summers with barely a breath of spring. The sultry hot summers rarely faded into a pleasant fall. You looked up one day and the sky was dark blue in the north, with wind and sand blowing in. I have seen it come as a dust storm, sprinkle, sleet, and snow, all in the same day. The storm turned the snow a brown tinge to it next to the cotton fields. Most of the time, the winters were long and hard. Cotton and I had investigated many black sleet deaths, with rain turning to a killer layer of thin ice on the blacktops. You could not see it until you were on it. Once you were on it, it was too late if you were traveling fast, which most folks do. The best place to be when they hit is by a nice, warm fire.

I could hear the wonderful sound of the sandhill cranes that were migrating back into the area. Shielding my eyes from under my hat brim, I paused to see if I could spot them. Finally, I was able to make out several formations coming in from the west. They were heading to fields of recently harvested hay grazer or sorghum. Cotton had always admired the tall, gray birds when they were in flight and occasionally stopped to glance them over with his binoculars. He often commented how they knew to come to this part of the world from a place as far as Siberia. The timing had to be just right, to leave Siberia before the brutal winters set in, and arrive here, where by their definition winters were mild. It always amazed him see them and the journey they just made and would continue to make for millennia.

I smiled at the birds and thought about Cotton. "Them things are not good to eat," he would always say, when they began to appear in the early fall. "One of the boys shot one, you know, and Maude chicken-fried the thing. We were able to eat the breast, but them legs was like eating a piece of sinew. You know she will cook any and all things them boys hunt. Always had. Why, she chicken-fried up some of those African guineas a fella was selling for grasshopper and insect control."

I had heard the same story many times, sitting on the side of the road with Cotton, windows down, drinking thermos coffee. As soon as the cranes flew over, out would come the same story, Cotton's jowls jiggling and his smiling, warm eyes. Alfie could imagine Maude's willingness to cook anything the boys brought in. Cotton said she drew the line on a possum or an armadillo. "Them things are nasty and the armadillos have leprosy. We are not having none of those two, so don't bring them to my house because I am not cooking them," she told the boys.

About halfway up the mountain, I stopped to rest on a flat outcrop. Birdie was easily visible sitting below to the north, holding down the fort. To the east, I caught movement. A coyote was chasing a dove fluttering on the ground. You could see the distinctive white undercarriage feathers prominent on the white-wing doves that were in the area. She was playing an age-old game of deceit. Feigning injury, she would draw the coyote away from her nesting area. She would have to be careful, as the coyote was cunning and quick. Finally the dove took to the air, with the coyote looking somewhat hapless. Undeterred, he continued in his search for food heading east. Perhaps utilizing the west sun to his advantage while traveling and hunting east. Sometimes a pile of dove feathers indicated the feinting did not work. I always wondered how the doves learned this trick to protect their young. Taking a quick sip from my canteen. I wiped the sweat off of my forehead under my hat brim.

The last half of the trek upward was not eventful, with no more rest stops. One step in front of the other, my burning calves crying out, but the workout felt good. The last fifteen feet funneled up through a crack in the top boundary of the plateau. The gap was much narrower than I recalled. Cautiously making my way upward, I pulled myself along on the cracks in the sidewall. It looked like a mighty good place for a rattlesnake to hide, but they they might not be up this high. There was a tale about some rancher finding a snake den close to the top, but that never put much faith in that.

Finally, I pulled my way to the top. The view from the top of the flat plateau was breathtaking. Remembering the stories I had heard since I was a boy about how by the Comanche used it because they could see for miles in all directions, and it was easy to defend from on top. But once you were on top, you would be in a strictly defensive position, and without plenty food, water, and ammunition, the adversary could simply wait you out. As far as I could tell, there was no wood to burn up there. It did not matter how well-provisioned you might be on top. Whoever controlled the bottom would be victorious.

Supplies could always be relayed in. On top, no such hope. There was not enough vegetation to set fire to the bottom and burn someone out on top. If you did not want to try and take them by force, the only option was to wait.

With only an hour or so of daylight left, it was time to set about getting camp set up. There was no firewood on the top of the mountain, so a fire was out of the question. It would not take long to set up my small pup tent.

The telescoping tent poles were usually easy to stick into the ground, but the ground on top was mostly rock. I made do by gathering four rocks for each corner, and placed the tent poles in the center. Once the tent was erected, I wedged a rock on top and against each corner tent-pole stake. Even though it was small, it looked like a good temporary home away from the elements. I unzipped the door and placed his backpack inside. Untying the bed mat, I laid out the small, quilted, foil blanket that Bea gave me one Christmas to take on my yearly trip to the mountains. "Don't want you freezing up there," the card said.

It had indeed been a mountain treasure I had used for many years. The nighttime temperatures in the mountains would drop into the teens, and sometimes when a front blew in it was close to zero. This foil blanket was not only durable, but it trapped your body heat between layers. You could basically sandwich yourself between it and sleep comfortably. Finally, I pulled the small blowup pillow out of its little sack. It was always amazing how quick a tent could become home and an instant refuge. The setting west sun could still be seen through the thin nylon tent wall. With the sun setting, I had about thirty minutes until it was too dark to see. The air was beginning to chill as I exited the tent and zipped it back up.

On the south side, I could still see the small lake house to the south where Jenna Couch's body was found hanged. The investigation had led me to suspect that the Spring High School cheerleaders may have been involved in her death in some way. All of their parents had agreed to allow me to interview them as a group within the next two weeks. If they were involved, as I suspected, why would they hang the Couch girl? How could high school students participate in such a crime? Looking down there was of a red-tailed hawk circling below the plateau, utilizing the last light of the day for a possible quick meal of field rat. It was always amazing, watching the birds of prey float about on the upper thermals with so little movement of their wings. I remembered the conversation with a local farmer that told me when he went to running his tandem plow on the hayfield stubble getting ready to plant wheat, there might be as many as twenty or thirty hawks on the ground, waiting and watching for him to plow up a field rat or flush out a cottontail.

He said the hawks always win because of their superior eyesight. "I imagine God might have made their eyesight like the scope on my .30-06. I ain't never seen them miss a mouse from my vantage point. Sometimes they spot 'em and flutter silently above 'em, you know. Then they tuck them wings and drop like a torpedo. It is a sight to see. Sometimes they hit them on the fly. Never seen the mouse or the rabbit win. Them hawks is awesome birds, there, Alfie. And another amazing thing, they is all kinds of hawks. I seen solid gray ones, speckled breast ones, and all kinds of colors. I used to think there was only red-tail ones, but they ain't the only uns out there. I never knew God could make so many hawks."

I followed the flight of the red-tail and watched as he began to hover. Suddenly the bird dropped and caught something on the ground. The shadows were getting to the point where you could make out the bird, wings outspread with her deadly claws clasped around some unfortunate creature.

The hawk took flight with something small in tow. Heading to feed her nestlings. It was good to get on top of a mountain. I was always able to clear my brain when I was up in the high country. This was not it but it would do for now. Sometimes, without all of the clutter I would remember things that popped out of nowhere.

Somehow remembering how I started to read the leather-bound Bible that Bea had stuck into my backpack before I left on my last mountain trip. That really made me angry that she did that. *Ever since she started going to church. She knows how I feel about those folks, with my father and all.*

I did read it a little at the campfire one night and managed to get through the first chapter of Genesis, about how God created the earth. It seemed so far out there, I just put the small Bible into my suitcase and never looked at it again.

The hawk finally flew away and I sat to watch what remained of the sunset and tried to remember the sequence of events about God creating the world in Genesis. From what I could recall, God created the heavens and the earth and the birds and animals before he created man. Why would he create animals before he created man? I had a lot more respect for the sandhill cranes and the hawk than I did for some folks. When Pa took me and ma to church as a young boy, I paid attention to the good people of the small church we attended. It was mighty easy to lose your appetite for religion, watching and listening to Pa sing in church on Sunday and beat my mama during the week. He drank away nearly all of our food money. Then God took away Patricia.

Everything that had religion attached to it seemed to be affiliated with something bad. I saw the way them good churchwomen looked at my mama, especially when she had a bruise under her eye where Pa had backhanded her in a drunken rage. Yet he would drag us to church the next morning, after coming in drunk the night before. There were many times that I would have killed him if I'd had the courage.

The autumn moon was bright and beautiful. It was as if you could reach out and touch it. The man in the moon was as vivid as I had ever seen him. I walked back to the rock outcrop and sat, looking up into the heavens and stared intently at the bright orb. The brightness of the moon lit up the landscape below. Down below, you could see the old mesquites. They were easily defined with their craggy and sprawling limbs. Some of their green foliage still clung after the first light frost a week or so before. The first big frost would kill the rest, and the wind would blow them off the limbs soon enough. Some of these big trees were old enough to have seen an Indian or two. Now their limbs were big and long. High winds sometimes split them and sent them to the ground. They were still beautiful to behold at sundown, dark against the sky like an old man hardened over time. The cedar trees cast a remarkable shadow in the light of the moon. It was in those shadows that the night hunters found their retreat. Although I could not see any wildlife, I knew they were there. The coyote and the bobcat, with their nighttime eyes, were surely already stalking their prey, especially with the better-than-average light conditions. The mighty horned owls, anxious for a tasty field mouse, had surely taken wing. With their outstanding telescopic vision, head rotation, and gliding wings, the smaller, ever-vigilant field mice were at a severe disadvantage. Tonight, the owls used the excessive moonlight to their advantage. Straying too far from the burrow could prove fatal.

I couldn't help smiling, thinking of all of the talks Cotton and I had about animals. How God created all creatures with a special tool for survival and perpetuation of the species. Each was able to deflect or eliminate the threat some of the time. Maybe a lot of the time. "Imagine if God had not made coyotes, Alfie. Can you imagine how many rodents and rabbits we would have? I know they will kill anything they can catch and deal the sheep men misery to the south. But just think about the rabbit population and all of the problems that would bring. God knew what he was a doing when he was a balancing out the food chain and so forth."

I laughed, remembering the striped lizards we would catch as young boys, only to have their tails come off and get away. Then that dim-sighted armadillo we took after, to see if one of us could catch it. When I was slowly sneaking up from behind, that thing snorted and took off bouncing to his emergency hole. Managing to grab his tail just as he went into the hole, the tail started popping like it was coming apart as the armadillo dug his claws into the side walls of the burrow. There was no pulling him out.

I told the story to Cotton on one of our breaks. The tears streamed down Cotton's face, with his jowls swinging as he laughed uncontrollably. I just he wished I could hear that laughter again.

Then, there was the one thousand legs we would try to catch, only to have them roll up in a ball and go to stinking. Possums playing dead with their teeth showing. As soon as you were safely away, up and away they would go. Cotton talked about the Amazon tree frogs that were so poisonous that if you touched them it might kill you. The local tribes learned to catch one with a leaf, and roll their darts and arrows on the back of the frog. They could kill the tree monkeys with ease with the poison darts.

Thinking about the Bible, or at least the part I read, it seemed it might be true that all animals, fish, and insects were purposely designed by a master creator. I saw it right before my eyes that each of these creatures, no matter how big or small, was given a place in the world and a way to survive. *If that were not true*, I thought, *who taught all doves to feint like they have a broken wing? Everything has a lifespan, some shorter than others.* Even though there was a lot of animals in the human race, I was still alive.

Standing up and looking at the moon, I screamed at the top of my lungs. "Why am I here? Why in this stupid crap of a world am I here? I have absolutely nothing to show for my life. Why did you give me a drunk for my Pa? Why did you take my Patricia Jean?"

Pent-up rage came all at once. Anger turned to tears. Screaming into the night, "I just work. I always work and I am really good at that, you know. There ain't nothing wrong with work neither."

The silence was deafening. The scream did not change the moon. The tears offered release but did not make me feel much better." Who is listening? The coyotes?"

"All I've got is my work. You tell me what else there is."

Wiping my eyes and nose on my shirt sleeve, I turned and walked back to the tent. Once inside, I turned on my flashlight and began digging in my backpack. I found a package of dried soup and a bottle of water. It smelled good as I watched it come to a boil in my coffee cup on the small propane grill. Gurgling and bubbling as I stirred it with a spoon, the aroma drifted up to my still-dripping nose. It made my mouth began to water as I had not eaten since morning. The small package of saltine crackers thickened up the soup a little as I slowly began to sip it. Remembering I stuck the Spring obit column in my shirt pocket, I pulled it out. There along with Old Lady Williamson's writeup was Cotton's picture, in his suit.

There were things in the write-up I never knew. Even though Cotton spoke only two or three times about religion over coffee, the words in the obituary column were amazing. About how much time he spent at church. Serving on this committee or in that capacity. Cotton definitely had a large life, outside of being the JP. Written in the obituary column was one of Cotton's favorite activities from his wife, Maude: "Cotton always enjoys Friday night date night. Especially so as I have to pay. He never can seem to get his billfold out of his pocket at the cash register. He just acts like he is trying to get it out." Cotton mentioned on many occasions about his and Maude's date nights, rarely if ever, anything intervening in that occasion.

Sometimes, when funds were short after baby food, and they had enough food to feed them for two weeks, they could afford a hamburger at Mel's. Then, come tax season, they might have a steak or a pizza, depending on the size of the refund.

"You ever take Beatrice on a date, Alfie?" Cotton used to ask.

I always just sat there and listened, and kind of looked away without answering. Cotton would smile and look away. "Alfie, she will like you for it. Even might love you for it. Every girl likes to be a-spooned and a-courted. I mean every one of 'em. Well, there are some that don't want to be a-spooned and a-courted. Them mean ones, it is usually a man that made 'em mean. Kind of like sitting on a pony and hitting him between the ears with a stick. Why, they just never forget, and they dang sure do not forgive. They just get and stay mean just for self-protection."

Cotton once told me that although they never had a large supply of money, God had always taken care of them and their family. "Why do you reckon that is, Alfie?" he would ask. "Why, before we began giving 10 percent of our income to the church, our money ran through our hands like sand through a sieve. I mean sand through a sieve."

I remembered frowning at that. "You actually give away 10 percent of your income to the church? Why in the world would you do something like that?"

Cotton looked at me with those bright and brilliant eyes. "Well, in the Bible, God said to test him on that. You know, giving 10 percent of your money, sheep, or wheat, or whatever your money is. He said to do that and your cup would surely run over. It is kind of a test, you see. The way I see it, if he can trust you with a little money, he might be more apt to let you have more of it. Sounds pretty crazy, I know. Me and Maude agreed to do just that, with whatever money came through our door."

I chuckled at him mockingly. "Well, did your cups run over?"

"Youngster, I can only say that it did and it does. A cup running over does not necessarily always mean money. It can mean seeing Maude smiling back at me in the morning on the back porch, looking at the sun come up. We are sitting there drinking a cup of her hot, percolated, rich coffee, watching the sun come up. Sniffing the fresh smells in the air, listening to the birds, and watching the cat stalk a squirrel below the oak tree. I look over to Maude and say, 'It is a good day, Missy.' She looks back and squeezes my hand and just smiles that beautiful smile of hers. It is a smile of a happy woman. A girl that has never been hit between the ears with a stick, so to speak. Seeing that smile is worth about a million dollars to me. She is free from harm. Free to be a mother and a wife without fear of a man, getting beat and so forth. You know what I mean? Don't you and Beatrice share coffee in the morning?"

Cotton seemed to know that the answer would be no, but he always moved on to the next thing without demanding an answer. He would always end with, "You know what I'm a-talking about, son?" Dropping a little seed and then moving on. Then he would reflect a little while and start up again.

"Now, I ain't a-saying there ain't been a few rivers to cross," he would say. "My gosh, we have crossed a few rivers in our time, and probably will cross a few more 'fore we finish. Like always, we just take ahold of each other's hand we take ahold of God's hand and he either leads us across or carries us. Don't know that there is a big difference. Then there is that money till. You and Bea got to save and spend your money wisely because he don't expect you to be reckless with money he allowed you to have to start with, and then go blaming him for your misfortunes. And that scripture in the Bible about the widow's mite, you know, is real powerful when it comes to poor people giving more than they can afford. Why, there is many a rich folk ain't never gave a dime to the church, excepting on Easter Sunday, when they make their uneasy pilgrimage. All dressed up in their finery for a Sunday church visit. You see, some folks in these church houses . . . they think they are a little better than most folks. So when these folks come visiting on their yearly Easter Sunday visit, they just kind of get the feeling they ain't a-welcome in the house. Some never come back. We shouldn't be makin' people a-feel that way."

The words Cotton spoke in the distant past rang out in my head like it was yesterday. Cotton's country lingo rolled off of his tongue easy, like silk, but clear as the night sky he was looking at. Cotton was always easy to listen to, with his low melodic and somewhat theatrical country voice. He smiled with his sparking eyes while his huge jowls swung. Cotton always marveled out loud about God's creation. I had heard the story a few times, but relished the memory of recalling it.

"Alfie, you ever read up on them wildie beasties over in Africa?" he asked.

I always acted like I had never been asked that question, and shook my head no.

"Well, now, they make this annual wildie beastie pilgrimage, I call it, but they call it a migration. What makes them start? Well, they are a-headin' to a big old savannah of good grasses call the Mara Mara or Maisa Mara, something like that. Now, that is all the way from Kenya and Tanzania, and that is a lot farther than crossing these here plains, you know. They get together like our buffalo used to do, before we nearly wiped them out. Then they go to traveling in somewhat of an orderly fashion, all goin' in the same direction. Now, why do you think they do that? I will tell you why. Cause God done told them to head that way. Kind of like the geese and those sandhill cranes coming in from the north every year. So they get to a-headin' all the same direction towards this beautiful savannah, just loaded with fresh, sweet grass that them wildie beasties just can't resist. Now, there is only one problem, Alfie. You know what that is? You know what is going to hold up the show? You know what is going to cause some problems for them wildie beasties? Well, I will tell you right now what that problem is. Alligators. I'm talkin' about dawg-gone big alligators. Why, they are as long as about two of them cars out there. Now, how do you think the alligators know that every year at this time them wildie beasties are goin' to be a crossing this here river. Well, I'll tell you. God told them to be there. And just like it was then and to this day, you or me can't stop it. We might get fretful about all of them wildie beasties getting attacked and et by them alligators, but they got to eat too. Now we might try and divert them and mess it up for a while, but there ain't no a-changing God's plannin'. Ain't that a marvelous thing, Alfie? That we cannot change things, only mess them up for a while.

"Why, we only live about seventy years, if we make it that long. Some shorter, some longer than others. Now, in that seventy years, how much time do we spend a-sleepin'? How much time do we spend a-workin'? Alfie, how much time do we do a-livin', a-worshiping our Creator? A-lovin' on our wives and kids? Well, I tell you, it ain't enough. Why, just take these jobs of yours and mine, they are just a means that God gave us to provide for us and our families. These animals, these wildie beast-ies, and them alligators. They ain't got no means to go earn or the need to earn money. There is only one thing that God put in them and that is survival. They got to eat to live. What else in the world do you reckon them alligators live on the rest of the time?

"Do you reckon time is relevant to most animals out here in a given day? Doing all of that plannin' and a-plottin' like we do? No, they just want to live. And there is plenty of things standin' in their way, I tell you. Why, there is wind, rain, snow, predators, vehicles movin' left and a right. Do you see what I am a-sayin', Alfie? Do you see what I am really say-ing? It ain't easy being an animal. And God knows their lives are meant to be shorter than ours. Well, maybe exceptin' them Galapagos turtles. Now, them things—God made them things to last a long time in this world. I can't imagine them a-frettin' much about anything. They just go a-swimmin' around and eatin' what God provided them to eat, and maybe tryin' not to get et by a big ol' shark or something like that."

I smiled, thinking about Cotton's melodic speech pattern. It was like listening to water trickle over a rock. Or maybe a little wind whis-tling through the pines in the fall. Nothing demanding. Nothing caustic. Nothing melodramatic. Just simple reflections that rolled off his tongue. I always felt like someone had sprinkled a little powdered sugar in my ear when I listened to Cotton talk.

It was hard not to remember the coyote and the feinting dove and the red-tailed hawk hunting late in the evening. Well into the night, I remembered Cotton's countrified words of wisdom and inspiration. For reason, all of the words and phrases came flooding back to me in vivid clarity. Maybe blaming God for every last thing that had gone wrong in his life was the easy way out. Pa spending most of the meager funds he earned on booze. Then, once good and drunk, beating his mama. Little Patricia.

It was not just God that I blamed for taking Patricia. I had always blamed Bea. I stared upat the moon and stars. "How in the world could she possibly be to blame for Patricia's death?" There was no blame, yet I had cast a wide net of blame toward God and Patricia for over twenty years. I began to weep. Great sobs overcame me with every fiber of my body until there were no tears left.

I sat for a long time on the rock perch, overlooking the sprinkling of lights in the distant, bright moon. My handkerchief was wet from all of the nose blowing. "How could Bea possibly stand me?" Hell, I am never home and she ain't been hugged for I don't know how long." She was treated her as a necessary evil that I had to put up with after the baby died. "What kind of man would abandon her to deal with the pain all by herself?"

I could never remember discussing the issue with her, for fear I would fall apart, not her. Then, like a coward, I ran away every year. Ran away to the mountains to not deal with the anniversary of that terrible day, sitting on the side of a mountain feeling sorry for myself. Poured myself into my damn work before and after my yearly trip. Coming in late from work and leaving early every day. And never a comforting word to Bea.

The grief and guilt continued to sweep over me like an ocean wave. I could hardly ever remember crying in my life other than when Patricia died. But here, alone in the moonlight and for whatever reason, now I can't seem to stop. My eyes were burning and red, but there was no one to see or care if they were, so it did not matter. Looking up at the Milky Way, the pattern of the Seven Sisters and beyond. As far as my eyes would allow me to see. "What, if anything, does someone like me have to offer the God of the universe? The maker of the universe, the world humans live in, and all that is in it? The builder of the moon, many moons, the twinkling stars, and God only knew what he built beyond the stars?"

Maybe it was just too late. I remembered Cotton saying several times: "Alfie, you know we are only made of clay. When we die and they plant us in the ground, we just turn back to dust."

I reflected the better part of the night on things that I set aside long ago. "Why had God allowed me to continue living? Me, Alfie Carter, was of no use at all to the mighty God of the universe. There was absolutely nothing I can do that will affect the outcome of anything. Well, nothing other than my investigations of other folks." And I was getting ready to wrap up his latest one on the Couch girl. There were people always killing each other, slandering and lying about each other. Other than the murdering part, some of those things I was guilty of myself. As far as the murdering I have seen, yes, I do wish that some of those guilty folks were no longer on the face of the planet, occupying space where decent folks existed. Who am I to make such an assumption? I just never had any sympathy for lying, killing murderers.

I thought about the case I was working on. The cheerleader girls who were about to be interviewed. The dead Couch girl. All of this under God's sky. But God's world keeps on a-turnin', as Cotton would say, in spite of men, not because of them. Is it possible that God had something I, Alfie Carter, could do for him while I was alive on the planet?

It seemed my relationship with Bea may be beyond repair after nearly twenty years of neglect and there was no particular way to restore any semblance of a loving and trusting relationship with her. She probably would be suspicious of my motives. Not now, not after all this time. Not after all of the things I had done to her, as far as neglect and guilt, not to speak of the things not done for her, like missing yearly anniversaries, and some birthdays, to name a few. It was always too easy to get caught up in my own life to worry about hers. A long time ago I told God "I do not need You" in a fit of rage after Patricia died. But oddly enough, right now I desperately felt the need to talk to Him.

I really did not now how to even begin a prayer but fell to my knees in anguish. My mind was completely drained and I could think of precious few words to say. "God, this is Alfie Carter," I began. "I was very wrong for blaming You and my wife Bea for everything, about Patricia and all. I am very sorry, and I am asking for forgiveness from You and from Bea— only I do not know how to ask her. I am asking You for a second chance, and for a second chance at love and a relationship with Bea. I have not been a good husband to her. More than likely I would not have been a good father to my girl, had she lived. I don't know. For whatever reason, You saw best that Bea and I not have her. I imagine You have taken good care of her in Your Heaven. I just cannot hardly stand to talk about it because it hurts so bad. But I know it probably hurt Bea worse than me but she just never lets on."

I blinked back what little tears were available and was physically and mentally drained.

My insides were not the same as before. I do not know what lay ahead only feeling for the first time that just maybe I was truly maybe a small part of God's universe. Maybe something was out there waiting that I have never seen. Before I got off my knees, I looked up toward heaven. "God, I want to thank You for Cotton. I want to thank You for his death. as crazy as that sounds. If he had not died, I would not be on this mountain, talking to You. Maybe one of Cotton's purposes in life was to tag up with me. I don't know. But I want to thank You for him."

All of my bitterness and hate seemed to vanish. All of the pent-up rage was nowhere to be found. *How had that happened?* It seemed to happen all of a sudden, when he reached out to the God of the universe. *How in the world did that happen?* Wearily, I retired to the tent. At peace, totally spent, not knowing what lay ahead. One thing for sure, I found himself missing Beatrice.

As I laid my head on the little blowup pillow, my brain could not turn off enough to sleep. "There is no way in the world that girl would go out with me now on a stupid date night," I said aloud. "No way at all! How do you ask your wife out for a date? That sounds totally stupid. And what if she says no? Then what? That would be the end of that. That girl could be as ornery as a one-eyed snake. We are not teenagers."

She would probably walk out laughing, even though she had not laughed out loud for a long time. She was mighty pretty when she laughed her snarky laugh all the way from her belly. What did she have to laugh about? *We have not been physically intimate in at least ten years or more,* he thought. *I know she tolerates me now, but I don't think she loves me and probably does not even like me anymore. Who would?*

You have only got yourself to blame, buddy. Only yourself.

I had forgotten to zip the tent fly. I sat up and zipped it from the top to the bottom in the t-pattern, my head back on the pillow, and pulled the thermal blanket Bea gave me over my shoulders. This time, I drifted off to sleep.

CHAPTER SEVENTEEN

The First Christian Church was full to capacity at Cotton's "Life Celebration," as they called it. I arrived early and was placed with the other pallbearers. We all received our instructions at the front of the church. Each pallbearer was given a white carnation for our lapels. Maude greeted each of us with a kiss on the cheek as she pinned our individual carnations on them. I marveled at her beautiful visage and calm spirit. She was not a train wreck. She was so composed and at peace.

When she was through, she stood before us. "I want to thank each of you for being here to honor Cotton. He loved and respected each of you. I am sure that all of you do not know one another. I would encourage you to get to know one another. As you can see, this will probably not be a normal service." She pointed to the instrumentalist setting up a few feet above them. There was a pedal steel guitar player, standup bass, two guitars, a piano player, a set of drums, and a mandolin. Maude looked at the musicians for a moment or two and turned back to face us, smiling with both hands on her chest next to a beautiful string of pearls. Cotton had given it to her after receiving a special bonus check for his work a few years back. She took them, but told him he should not have spent the money on her. He looked back and said, "What money? I got these oyster diving," and laughed as he placed them around her neck. She smiled, thinking back at that occasion, and shared the hilarious event with all of us. She could see some of the men wiping away tears at the thought of his selflessness.

"Gentlemen," she said, motioning to the band. "I am afraid what you see is what you get. He loved his music, you know. He could not sing a lick but he loved to try. So we are going to have music. And not your typical church music, if there is such a thing. Just hang on."

It seemed there could be no more folks fitted into the large sanctuary, with its wooden truss beams with tongue and groove pine above them. The high-angle roof was sure to make the music resonate beautifully, I thought. This was the first time I had been in a church since my childhood, other than once or twice with Bea under protest.

I turned to look at the clock on the back wall and saw Beatrice come in through the back doors and make her way to the seats behind where we were seated. She was striking in her dark blue dress, high heels, and the silver necklace her mom had given her. She had her auburn hair drawn up into a bun. It was real hard not to linger looking at her, so she would not notice. She looked beautiful. Always had. I really never knew or appreciated it until now. Since the night on the mountain, I had longed for her, but knew it probably would not happen. How would I gather enough courage to ask her out on a date?

The overflowing crowd was finally seated. The ushers had to bring in many folding chairs, to accommodate everyone. That was quite a testament to the lives this man had touched. I reallly could not think of many folks at all that had not been personally affected in a positive way from knowing Cotton.

The preacher slowly stood from his seat on the platform, carefully buttoning his suit coat as he approached the podium pulpit. Once behind the microphone, he asked the audience to please stand in honor of Cotton while he prayed. Unlike the longwinded, sanctimonious, and bloviating prayers I remembered hearing, in the times I attended church, this prayer was different. It was void of the thees and thous, but was stated simply and to the point.

"Dear Lord, thank You for this man's life, his testimony, his service to You and to his wife and family. May Your name forever be glorified. Amen."

The music was beautiful and nonstop for forty-five solid minutes. Different singers took to the stage in singles and in groups. We were somewhat stunned at the level of talent. It also was unique in the fact that these instruments were allowed in the building. It was invigorating and refreshing. Most of the music had a country flavor, especially with the crying sounds of the pedal steel guitar. The instrumentalist closed with a pedal steel guitar version of "How Great Thou Art." You could hear muffled sniffling, nose blowing, and open weeping when the pedal steel guitar player went into the chorus all by himself without the other instruments.

All of the audience seemed to start singing all at once. When they got to the last "How great Thou art," the pedal steel guitar stopped and let the sound resonate in the building. It was a marvelous thing to hear. Nearly like a million angels singing in heaven. He ended with the last "How great Thou art" with vibrato. For the first time in my life, I shed tears openly and unafraid. In fact, I saw more tears shed that day than at any time in my life. Pa had always told me that I was a pansy if I cried. So if I did cry, it was in my room, under my pillow. That was usually after he beat my mama. The deeper I got into my teen years, I simply taught myself not to cry. *What a foolish notion. There is nothing wrong with this.*

When the song was over, the audience stood and gave the band and singers a standing ovation for well over two minutes. When the clapping finally died down, the preacher stood, buttoned his open jacket, and approached the pulpit smiling.

"How in the world do I follow something like that?" he asked. "Impossible. Absolutely impossible. Anyone that knew Cotton knew that he loved music a whole lot more than a longwinded preacher. So Maude and family, friends of Cotton, I will not be longwinded."

He listed the family members, where Cotton was born, when he passed, and listed his service to the church serving in several lay capacities.

After the brief introduction, he reached into his coat pocket and pulled out a piece of folded paper. He carefully unfolded it.

"Ms. Maude and family, you have never seen or heard what I am about to read, nor has anyone in this assembly. Why? Because I watched Cotton type it in my office one day, long ago. He folded it and stapled it. He told me to lock it in my safe and never look at it until his funeral. Then, not fully trusting me, I suppose, he said, 'Preacher, gonna make you a-knock knuckles on this, a-promising what I have asked you.' So we a-knocked knuckles, as he said. Until yesterday, I truthfully forgot about it. But I did remember it. So, church, family and friends, let's see what Cotton says from heaven:

'Friends: I don't know how many friends are at this thing. I always heard if you could have one or two true friends in your lifetime, God has indeed truly blessed you.

'First, to my God. Thank You for life and for saving a man like me. I am truly not at all worthy. But, You did. Your Bible says that whoso-ever believes in You shall not perish but have everlasting life. Well sir, I definitely believe in You. Therefore, I will be spending eternity with You. How wonderful Your promise is.

'Next: my Maude. You are my girl from a long time back when we was just little chickens. Why in the world God chose me for you and you for me is beyond me. With my big old swinging jowls and all, you could have had your pick of all of the good-lookin fellas. But, for some reason, you chose me. I have never been able to figure that out.

'Maude, God must have known your areas of strength and my areas of weakness, which by the way are many. He melded the two of us like some kind of fabric, two peas in a pod with one common denominator. Kind of like one of them Navajo blankets we seen in Santa Fe. They was a-woven so tight, why you could probably pour coffee on them and it would not go through. That was like our fabric, you see.

'You did not know I knew such a big word like denominator. That denominator was Him, God. It has been quite amazing to me how it all turned out with the kids and all, don't you think? Your ability to bend, when I would not, saved us. I just did not know it at the time. Your comforting, assuring smile was always my light after a dark day, which by the way were many in my trade. You was always a telling me how smart I was when in fact, it was you, Ms. Maude, who was the smart one. God could never have given me a better mate than you. So to whoever is listening today, I love you with all my heart.

'To my boys, or should I say men: I am proud of both of you and what you have become. Continue to be good men in Christ who made you. Love your wives and your families. And keep taking those girls on those Friday night dates like I taught you. They will like you for it. Don't be bringing your mama no more armadillos. She ain't a-having it.

'And finally, to whoever is here: God gives us all a chance to believe in Him and serve Him or not. He does not force you to go down that path. No, sir, not at all. You can simply walk away. All of us are free to do what we want individually. There ain't nobody a-draggin you to God. I would invite you to come and know Jesus. His yoke is easy and his burden is light. May God bless each of you and your families.'"

The preacher smiled while foiding up the paper. He walked down from the podium and over to Maude. He handed her the paper, shaking his head. He hugged her and gently kissed her on the cheek. Walking back up the podium stairs, he paused behind the pulpit, in deep thought for a moment or two.

"I can't say I have ever preached a funeral like this, because I have not. I guess you could say that Cotton eloquently preached his own funeral, in a way, and on his terms. He preached it from his heart on a piece of paper. I would have to say that no man could have said it better and with more clarity than what you just heard. His way of wording things still amazes me, and I must say pleases me to no end. Kind of reminds me to watch snow quietly on a cold winter day. It calms your spirit. Will you all please stand and, starting with the last rows, come on by and greet Ms.

Maude and the family? I am sure they will be glad to see you. The casket is closed, by request of Cotton long ago. He told me to close that casket. 'The last thing folks want to see is me with my big hog jowls laying there a looking dead. Which I will be, but be reminded I ain't down here. I will be up there,'" the pastor said, pointing toward the heavens. He shook his head, laughing. "He was right, you know."

The folks in the church made their way around to pay their respects to Maude and the family. The pallbearers picked up the casket and slow-walked it to the waiting hearse. Each man was silent. The limousine awaited us as we stepped in and set it down. We all exchanged pleasant-ries, but the ride to the cemetery was quiet. Each man quietly reflected on the last hour or so, and each of their personal experiences with Cotton. My brain was a little blurred, emotions running high, especially after the night on the mountain. My thankfulness to God was at an all-time high. And it was all because another human being, someone I could call my closest friend, went to eternity. It did make me wonder if he had coun-seled each of these men in his own unassuming way like he did with me.

There was this strong realization that I had been given another chance at life and hope. There was no way I would not take full advantage of another chance with Beatrice. Maybe she might learn to like me again. Maybe not. There was just no way of knowing. It was in God's hands now and, unlike me, God never made a mistake. I just hoped and prayed it would work out. I guess what I had done to Bea emotionally was as bad as what my Pa did to Mama physically. I was no better than him.

There was a rather large crowd at the cemetery. All along the route, folks were stopped on the side of the road with their lights on as the long procession came by. There was even some bearded bikers at full attention with their hands saluting when the hearse came by. Their leather vests were covered in patches, but their helmets were off and stowed under their burly arms. Fierce-looking men in their sunglasses paying homage to someone they may have met along the way. The family was seated at the front of the large tent. The pallbearers solemnly carried the casket from the hearse to the tent and set it on the tethers above the grave.

The pastor asked us to please take a seat behind the family while he said a few words. Beatrice was in the third row, right behind me. When we were seated, the pastor began: "Folks, there is not a lot left for me to say. I loved this man. You loved this man. Ms. Maude, you loved him and lived with his as his able helpmate. You should be very proud. You and the boys. All of us should be proud that he was allowed to be part of our lives. Think about the fact if that was not so, and what a loss that would have been. For me, personally, a huge loss.

"This man was one of the finest God put on the earth. God took him when God was ready, didn't he? Certainly not when we were ready, because we were not. I know I was not. I wish he was here to tell me once again about them wildie beasties, you know. How many of you under this tent have ever heard Cotton tell the story of the wildie beasties? Please raise your hand."

A large number of folks lifted their hands, laughing.

"You see, to each of us that heard it, he told it for a reason. That reason is that God ordained the crossing of the wildie beasties, as he called them. They crossed at a point where them alligators big as two cars could eat their fill until the next year's crossing. Not by chance, but by providence.

"So, it is not happenstance but providence that Cotton is gone and you are here under this tent. It is not happenstance but providence that he appeared in your life. I would say in some cases, when you really needed someone like Cotton to eschew words of wisdom and comfort. Am I correct?" He could see a lot of folks nodding their head in agreement. "So, folks, let each of us take that example and go and do likewise. Not to linger, but remembering one thing Cotton told me from time to time that I will share now. He remarked from time to time over coffee, 'Pastor, we are the world's worst at condemning folks that we think need condemning. The man that stole the car, the people on the scourge of drugs with no way out. All of the things that can beset us if we ain't careful. I have done it myself in my work. What right do we have to condemn them? Well, I tell you, preacher man, we ain't got none. No, sir, we ain't got none. The thing that we need—do you a know what that thing is, Pastor? Well,

I will tell you right now what it is. That thing is compassion and prayer. Have compassion on them, pray for them. That's what they need, not my condemning. Yes, sir. That's it.'

"And folks, having known Cotton for many years, he did more compassioning and praying than he ever did condemning. If you knew him, I am sure you would agree.

"And with those final comments, I will say, 'Earth to earth, dust to dust.' Pallbearers, if you will rise and place your carnations on the top of the casket, please."

Each pallbearer stood and walked by the casket. Each man came to a halt, gently placing their carnations, and some even patted the casket. One man dropped his head on the casket and began weeping. Finally, when the last one passed, the pastor spoke: "Folks, you are now dismissed. The family requests some quiet time at the grave site before we lower the casket into the grave. Traveling mercies to each of you, and may God bless you."

CHAPTER EIGHTEEN

I tried not to be noticed as I sat a few rows from the bottom of the cement bleachers at Spring Stadium for the last of the district games. This game was critical to the next round of playoff action for the Spring Tigers. Efron Tillman had the top quarterback stats in the region and probably in the state in division 16A. It was assumed that there was probably a large group of division-one and -two scouts previewing each game he played in. It was rumored that he was being looked at by at least six division-one schools because of his strong arm and running ability. From the opening play, Efron made an end around and proceeded upfield fifteen yards. *Mercy*, I thought, *He runs just exactly like a mirror of his father*. There were several men in sports jackets with binoculars below the announcement booth, high above the stadium seats. I reckoned these were college scouts from all over. There must have been ten or twelve of them.

I slowly trained my binoculars on the cheerleading squad on the running track. Their uniforms clearly separated them from the pep squad in the bleachers. With the binoculars, I carefully studied each of their facial features. As usual, on pep rally and game days, each girl had on one yellow and one black tennis shoe. Their shoelaces were yellow and black as well. Short, white ankle socks, very short cheerleading skirt, and yellow top.

Each girl had her name in large black letters on the back of their shirt. Feigning interest in the game, I looked intently back to the field periodically, as the crowd stood and cheered wildly for the Tigers.

Swinging back to the cheerleaders, each girl had on the game face black lipstick with yellow flecks. At close range, it appeared to sparkle, when the lights hit it right. I noted all of the names Tom Orlager typed out for me at the high school that day.

Mostly I watched Britanee Phelps, the head cheerleader, the closest. Her face seemed devoid of emotion during all of the cheers. There was never a smile across her face. You could hear the reserved-seat cheer section with their foghorns, and you could see them waving their yellow and black kerchiefs. It was hard to hear the announcer over their racket.

Britanee's mama was easy to recognize. She was a hard person not to miss. Yellow and black sweatband with a ponytail. She had on a fancy yellow-and-black jumpsuit jump suit. Every time she would yell and blow her foghorn, folks in front of her would cover their ears. She appeared to be a woman undeterred by other folks' feelings. She was going to root the Tigers to victory all by herself, no matter how big of a spectacle she made of herself. Her husband stood stoically with his hands in his jacket, looking somewhat detached and forlorn. Periodically he would wave his kerchief a swirl or two and sit down. Britanee's mama never sat the entire game. She was the loudest in the cheer section, screaming routinely at the referees when a play did not go her way.

I called a meeting with Captain Burris and Judge Clovis McGee, Saturday morning after the game at 10:00 a.m. and laid out my case before them. Judge McGee listened with great intensity, never speaking, until the end. Captain Burris would shake his head in disbelief from time to time.

"Mr. Carter," the judge said, "I have watched you work for many years. Bulldog, I think they call you, isn't it? What you are proposing is a gamble that may fail. If I understand you, you are proposing a pretrial hearing, or what you are calling an evidentiary hearing, on a case you have developed. Am I correct in that assumption? You understand that no one has been

charged, you have just now culminated your thoughts and your investigation of what you say happened. Not one of these people suspect, I suppose, what you are preparing to lay out before them and their parents."

"Yes, sir, Judge. I believe I have sufficient grounds and what I believe
to be credible circumstantial evidence to bring this to trial. I know what
I think took place leading up to Jenna Couch's death, I just don't know
exactly what happened at the scene, which I believe these girls, the cheerleaders, were at when this young girl was hanged. All roads lead to one of
them, and possibly three more. I feel strongly that if I am allowed to bring
in the pieces of evidence to a hearing with a select group of folks, we will
get to the real story of what happened."

"And you would bet your badge on that, sir?" the judge said. "What if
it backfires? What if you get sued because they were not allowed counsel
at a hearing? Normally, when you lay out your case, both sides are repre-
sented by counsel."

"Judge, I can understand your hesitation. However, I have studied
these girls at the football game. Something is not right. Their mind is not
on what they are doing. I saw it firsthand. At least one of them acted very
strangely at the football game. She was the head cheerleader. What I am
saying is, let me have this evidentiary hearing on my terms, and I will take
full responsibility for the outcome. If it does not work out, I will turn in
my badge. And if they sue? Yes, sir, that will be on me as well."

"You are willing to be sued, sir?"

"I did not say I was willing, Judge, I said it would be on me as well."

The judge took a long and thoughtful look at Captain Burris.
"Captain?"

"Judge, I have worked with Mr. Carter a long time, over twenty years
now. If he tells me a crayon mark is red, it is red. I trust him. I trust his
reasoning power and his ability to analyze what he finds. He is excellent
at reading the tea leaves."

I just cringed at that statement, but said nothing, because I certainly
had not read the tea leaves correctly on Beatrice. In fact, I had stepped on
and crushed the tea leaves.

"Okay, Captain Burris, I believe you," said the judge. "If this thing falls apart, I will hold you responsible, Mr. Carter, do you understand?"

"Yes, sir, Judge. Yes, sir."

"Evidentiary hearing is therefore granted for next Wednesday at 10:00 a.m. Have a list to me tomorrow of folks you want to attend. I will look at those, and if all is in order, I will approve. I will have my clerk record the exact proceedings of the hearing, as I fully expect you may indeed get sued."

"Yes, sir, Judge, I will have the list to you tomorrow."

The judge got up and left the chambers, leaving Captain Burris and I alone.

"You better be right, Alfie."

"I am, Captain. I am."

"I will need to check out pieces of evidence to bring and a picture of the girl."

"Get what you need, Alfie, just make sure you cross every T and dot every I, or we will both be unemployed and maybe in jail. Then both of us will have our butts handed to us on a silver platter."

CHAPTER NINETEEN

Mr. Black stared stoically through the evidence room window.

"Hello, Orville! How are you?"

The blank stare back betrayed nothing. "What do you need, sir?"

"Well, Mr. Black, I have been authorized to check out some evidence."

Mr. Black's eyebrows raised and lips pinched together. "Check out evidence to review in this room?"

"No, sir, check out evidence to take from this room to a hearing."

"Well, that will be impossible. Per our procedures, you must have clearance up the chain of command to have that done. Without that written permission from the top of the chain of command, you will not be released any evidence from this room, sir. We follow the procedures around here at all times."

I slowly pulled the approval slip from my pocket and slid it into the tray under the window. Mr. Black snatched it up and quickly unfolded it. His eyes blinked as he read it through his thick glasses. He brought his gaze slowly to me as I smiled at him.

"Well, Orville, what are you gonna do? Count flies or go to swatting? I need me some evidence bags. See the ones noted on the note. That is what I need."

"I can read," he said. "Please have a seat at the designated table, and I will be with you shortly."

It was hard not to smile at Mr. Black's apparent open disdain for all things human. *You don't get any evidence out of my evidence room and take it out. No, sir. That is, not without a note, and I had one.*

Mr. Black returned a few minutes later with the plastic bags from the scene of Jenna Couch's death site: the bag containing the Marlboro cigarette butt, the second cigarette butt with black lipstick and yellow flecks on one of them, as well as the bag containing the red-and-black lead rope, number 3404 on the clasp. He had a list of forms in his hands, and was shuffling through them.

"You are required to sign several of these forms, sir, and I will remind you that you are on camera. You must use a set of these gloves I have placed in this bag, if you remove the evidence from the bag. Your superior must witness and sign off on this form each time you remove a piece of evidence from the bag. This is a set of sterilized tweezers you are required to use if you remove the cigarette butts from these individual bags. I highly recommend that you leave the evidence in the bags, sir. The rules so state that you must keep the evidence under lock and key in your possession at all times, sir, until said time they are to be reviewed. Is that clear?"

"Yes, sir, Orville, that is perfectly clear."

"It is Mr. Black, sir. I do not go by Orville. I will need to see your badge and your driver's license, sir."

"Somehow I knew you were going to ask me for them, Mr. Black," I said as I handed them to him.

Mr. Black spent at least thirty minutes filling out the paperwork, and would hold each page in front of the camera after he and I had signed it. "Please stand in front of the camera, sir, and hold the document," he said. He would then describe the date, document signed, and that I was the one who signed it. He had a return date for the evidence to be returned intact to the evidence room. This was noted as the morning after the hearing.

Finally all of the forms were complete. Mr. Black spent another ten minutes scanning over them before stating that all was in order.

"Well, that is a good thing, Mr. Black. I like to have all of my business in order," I said.

Mr. Black handed me the evidence bags and bag of gloves.

"What do you have to secure this evidence in, sir, per requirements? Lock and key?"

"I have nothing with me, but I will get a briefcase or something."

"No, sir, that will not do. You have been told the rules. Now, I can check you out one from here if you wish, of course you will have to sign a form to do so."

"Mr. Black, I have signed so many of your forms, what damage can one more possibly do?"

"Please do so, sir. Please do so."

Fifteen minutes later, the evidence was securely locked up in a police-issued briefcase and of course a picture was taken of it and the document held in front of the ever-peering camera.

"You are released to go, sir. Remember the return dates on the evidence and the evidence satchel. Remember not to lose the key, as it is the only one assigned to the satchel. Is that clear?"

"Yes, sir, Orville, it is very clear." I really could not help myself as I turned at the door and looked at Mr. Black. "Orville, you would be a lot better off if you would smile sometimes. Act like you enjoy life a little. Loosen up, man."

Mr. Black's twenty-plus years in the Corps showed. He glared back without smiling. "Yes, sir, rules are to be followed to the tee. You want evidence, you follow the rules, or you will get no evidence."

I smiled to myself as I left the room. "You can if you have a note from the Captain."

I arrived at the courthouse an hour early, to set up and gather my thoughts. My nerves were steady, and I realized that others' might not be that would be in attendance. Judge McGee had granted his list of participants at the hearing. All six cheerleaders and their parents, Captain

Burris, Samantha Divine, Turtle Vines, Tom Orlager, Rose McDonald, Jenna Couch's parents, and her grandfather Pap.

I set the briefcase on the table normally reserved for attorneys, and carefully unlocked it, then placed the bags of evidence side by side. I took out the ten-by-twelve-inch photo of Jenna Couch and moved the overhead projector to the table from the side of the hearing room. Laying it on the surface, I flipped on the projector light. The visual effect was immediate. There on the pulldown screen was the image of a young woman with blonde hair and green eyes. She had a beautiful smile. I turned off the screen and insured the picture was square in the frame.

Slowly, I took out my carefully prepared notes and reviewed them. Around 9:30 a.m., folks started to come in. First came the Couch family.

Mr. Couch said, "I had to take off at the refinery today, but I am glad to be here," as we shook hands.

Mrs. Couch nodded as I shook her hand next. "Where would you like us to sit?"

"How about that front table on the right side of the hearing room?" I said.

Pap extended his bony hand to me. He had on a clean set of clothes and had shaved. He had missed several spots on his face but looked better than the first time we met.

"How are you doing, Pap?"

"Well, son, I ain't staring up at dirt," he said, and walked up to the front and sat. "I'd rather be hunting them grackles."

Next came the cheerleaders and their families. They all arrived at the same time, as if planned. I greeted each of them and showed them where they were to be seated. All of the girls were void of expression. All walking heel to toe, they stared ahead glassy-eyed once they were seated. All sat shoulder to shoulder, holding hands. Their folks took up seats directly behind them.

Mr. Phelps looked one hundred years old. He looked like a man who never stood for much of anything, who always fell in line with Mrs. Phelps and never got out of line. His face showed much pain. Maybe he was thinking about how he let himself lose control of the reins of his house and his family. He was just a puppet and nothing more. His face said he wanted to be more but could not.

Rose McDonald appeared through the back door of the hearing room. She was radiant in a white blouse on and tailored pants. I walked to the back door and met her. "Hello, Rose. Thanks for coming."

"Anytime or anything you need, Captain," she said.

Her perfume was bold.

"Please take a seat anywhere in the hearing room," I said.

"Yes, sir, Captain, yes, sir," she said, without saluting this time.

Samantha Divine, Turtle Vines, and Tom Orlager came in together. They probably all rode in together. Samantha usually had her dark red hair pulled into a ponytail and with her ever-present gum. Today it was hanging neatly on her shoulders. She looked much older than when I interviewed her. They took a seat behind the cheerleader parents.

At 9:55, Captain Burris strode through the door in his splendid uniform. He came to the front of the hearing room and sat to the left of the cheerleaders. Judge McGee did not put up with anyone showing up tardy. His clerk was already at her position on the stenograph machine.

At exactly 10:00 a.m., Judge McGee entered the courtroom in his robe, even though this was an evidentiary hearing. Captain Burris ordered all to rise before the judge was seated.

The judge looked at the entirety of the audience, all invited by me.

"Ladies and Gentlemen, I am Judge McGee. Please be seated. We are here today for an evidentiary hearing called by one of our lead investigators, Mr. Alfie Carter. Everyone here is by invitation only and was not required to attend. I am pleased that each of you chose to come. As you can see, there is no counsel present for this hearing. The evidentiary hearing is to address some critical findings in the death of one Jenna Couch, approximately sixty days ago. Her parents are seated to my left, and to your right, up front here, along with her grandfather.

"Investigator Carter asked for and was granted this hearing based on his findings to date. Again, I thank each of you for being in attendance. I have asked my clerk, Mrs. Stevens, to record the hearing on stenograph. If anyone has objection to that, please indicate by holding up your hand now.

"Okay, I see no hands raised, so I will consider there is no objection. No one is to be sworn under oath, as this is an evidentiary hearing only. We are not asking for statements of any kind from any person in this hearing. Any statements made will be considered strictly voluntary but with merit. If anyone does not understand what I just said, please indicate by raised hand and I will repeat myself with clarity.

"Okay, there are no hands raised, so we will proceed. Investigator Carter, please proceed with your hearing."

Slowly, I stood and went to the front of the room. The high ceiling of the hearing room provided adequate acoustics. There would be no need to have to speak loudly to be heard.

"First of all, ladies and gentlemen, I want to thank each of you for attending this evidentiary hearing. The culmination of approximately sixty days of work in the field brings us to this date. The purpose of the hearing is to effectively show you what is known to be fact concerning the recent death of one Miss Jenna Couch."

At that point, I flipped on the overhead projector and Jenna's picture was shown on the pulldown screen. Mrs. Couch was visibly shaken by the photo and began to quietly weep and dab away tears. Mr. Couch and Pap sat rigidly, without visible response, but they were more than likely deeply shaken.

I left the photo on the projector while carefully canvassing the faces of each of the cheerleaders.

"This picture of Jenna was asked for by myself and given to me to use from her parents. A beautiful young girl, don't you think? This photo was taken at the beginning of this year."

"Now, before me on this table are some pieces of evidence I gathered at the scene of her death. I will walk you through what is known thus far. Please be patient as I present the data. As the Judge said earlier, no one is required to speak at any time.

"First, the recently deceased JP Cotton Banks and I were called to the scene of her death approximately sixty-two days ago at Moore's Lake, east of town in a guest cabin. Inside, we found her hanged with this rope," I said, pointing to the red-and-black lead rope. "She had apparently been standing on a stool, which we have in the evidence room but I did not bring to this hearing.

"She had apparently been burned or burned herself with a cigarette on the back of her left hand and on the middle of her left calf. While examining the scene, I recovered this Marlboro cigarette butt," holding up the plastic package holding the butt. "It is to be noted that this butt has interesting markings on it. It has what appears to be black lipstick with yellow flakes on it." As I spoke these words, I cast a slow glance around the room and past the cheerleaders. Britanee Phelps cast her eyes downward. "Ms. Couch also had on a small pinkie ring with the letter E on it when she was found deceased.

"Now, I will continue. Coming back to the rope in the other bag, it also has some distinguishing marks on it. Captain Burris, would you please come read the inscription on the brass clasp on the end?" Captain Burris buttoned his jacket as he stood, surprised he was asked such a question. I held the bag out to him and pointed at the clasp.

"It has the numbers 3404 on it," Captain Burris said.

"Thank you, Captain. The investigation took me to where this particular lead rope was purchased. The number on the rope clasp is recorded by the owner of the store that sells them, Rose McDonald's feed store. Rose is in attendance today. It turns out that the rope was purchased by Mr. Turtle Vines, the Spring High School agriculture teacher. Mr. Vines is also in attendance today. It is not uncommon for Mr. Vines to make purchases on behalf of the agriculture department, as he is in charge of all Spring School agriculture students and their animal projects. These are quite numerous.

"After interviewing Mr. Vines, it was noted that this particular lead rope was loaned out to one of the folks present in this room approximately one and a half months before the death of Jenna Couch."

Momentarily, I stopped speaking and allowed that statement to sink in. All of the cheerleaders had their heads down.

"The autopsy report indicates Jenna died by strangulation by hanging. It also indicated she was approximately two months pregnant. We took samples of blood from the deceased in both accounts and those are being held at our crime lab in Spring for further forensic testing as necessary—possibly to assist in determining who the father of the unborn child may be."

The Couch family all had their heads down.

"Now, the next thing in this hearing is from an eyewitness account the day before Ms. Couch passed away. That account would come from her grandfather, affectionately known as Pap Couch, seated in our presence today. Pap lives in a small travel trailer on the two-acre Couch property, north of town. Pap observed a certain type of vehicle come to Mr. and Mrs. Couch's home in the late evening the day before Jenna's death. Pap saw this vehicle parked under an elm tree in the yard. He has indicated that all of the folks in the vehicle were young females, dressed alike, with what appeared to be a certain type of lipstick applied to their mouths."

At that point, a visibly angry Mrs. Phelps jumped to her feet. "Are you trying to say our girls were involved with this somehow? You better have good evidence before you go to running off at the mouth like that. You have got a big bit of nerve, to think—"

"Ma'am, I will remind you that any statements made are recorded and all are voluntary."

Mrs. Phelps looked at her husband, disturbed and staring at the floor. "Ain't you going to say something, or you just going to do your normal thing and sit there like a little mouse?"

She sat down with her arms crossed and said something under her breath to the woman next to her.

"Now, I will continue. I was able to locate the vehicle described by Pap Couch, as apparently this is only one of that kind in Spring. It is a late-model, two-tone blue, large Ford Bronco with white lettering on the tires."

There were audible gasps in the hearing room. Britanee Phelps put her head in her hands. All of the other cheerleaders turned and looked at Britanee at once.

"That Bronco is owned by one of the folks attending this hearing. I have the license plate number here as well: BWG-1400, Texas plate. We have gathered samples of the syrupy mass on top of the vehicle, and it matches the samples of the elm tree at the Couch home. Pap Couch indicated they never park under this type of tree, as it emits a syrupy type of mist, if you will, that will literally stick to anything it lands on."

I stopped speaking and turned to look up at the photograph of Jenna Couch on the projector screen.

"We know a lot of things," he said, "the only thing we don't know is exactly what happened at the lake house."

Britanee Phelps slowly stood. She looked around and started to speak.

Mrs. Phelps stood and screamed, "You sit down! You sit down now!"

Britanee slowly let go of the girl's hand next to her and turned to look at her mama. "No, Mama, just please sit down. You are not going to ever tell me what to do again."

The judge spoke to Britanee. "Young lady, I want to remind you that anything you say in this hearing is without a lawyer or counsel and will in fact be recorded. You are not required to say anything without counsel. Do you understand?"

Mrs. Phelps stood and screamed, "She ain't saying nothing without a lawyer. This ain't no damn trial."

Britanee walked to the front of the room and looked at the audience, the Couch family in particular, then looking up at the photograph on the screen and back to them. "I am so sorry for Jenna's death. It was an accident. I am more than willing to testify under oath with or without a lawyer." She turned and looked at her mama. There was no shakiness in her voice. "Mama, you wanted me to always be a cheerleader. I never wanted to be one, and I am never going to be one again. Your stupid idea that we should ride in a van because we were special makes no sense. I am done with cheerleading, as of this moment. You wanted me and

Efron to be together. You wanted him to get a division-one scholarship and somehow I would go to the same school, following along like a little puppy. That allowed you to get to go and be the head whatever to fulfill your own selfish dreams.

"You never were a cheerleader and you pushed me all this time to be one so you could be one through me, I guess. I really cannot stand who we are and what we have become. We are the most vicious of the vicious. You said we were the elite, the chosen group, and therefore deserving of special treatment over all other girls.

"You were wrong. We are nothing. We are better than no one. Jenna Couch's only problem was that she was poor. She was just poor, Mama. Something we are not, or maybe we are, because of all the credit card debt you run up that Daddy has to pay for. For what, Mama? Clothes? She did not live up where we live and shop at LaVelle's like all of you do for us. Who cares? Who really cares but you?"

She pointed in a sweeping gesture at all of the cheerleader moms and Samantha Divine.

"Just look at you. You are all in your forties and you are still wearing a ponytail, for gosh sakes. Blowing your stupid foghorns and waving your stupid spirit kerchiefs. Do you think that mattered to Jenna? No, it did not. You told me yourself, Mama, you told me she had to go because she had tagged up with Efron. That was probably his ring she had on when they found her, and I bet it was his baby she was carrying. Efron was your ticket to the big time. Some division-one school with some even stupider football program that is more focused on jocks than it is on academics. Some of those guys cannot even count to one hundred without a math coach. Why don't you check into who does Efron's homework for him every night? It ain't him.

"And there you would be, at some college, head cheerleader mom, blowing your dumb foghorn, hooting and hollering with your spirit kerchief and sticking your nose in everyone's business. Trying to be the center of attention, like always. Blowing your temper when you don't get your way. Never changed since I was a little girl. Well, one thing is for sure. That ain't never gonna happen. It is over.

"We drove over to the Couch's house. Me, Shiloh, Amber, and Wiley. We told Jenna that she was gonna be let into the cheerleading squad next year if she passed the cheerleading test at the Moore lake cabin. We left the house and stopped down the road a bit and waited. She snuck out after dark and met us down the road. She trusted us." Britanee began to weep. "We went to the lake cabin and I took that rope with me. All we intended to do was scare her. We tied the rope around her neck as she stood on the stool. We told her that if she could stand the pain without screaming, she might just get to be one of us because you have got to be tough to be a cheerleader. Britanee paused and caught her breath, looking up at Jenna's picture and wiping away tears and already runny makeup.

"I lit up a Marlboro. You did not know I smoke, did you, Mama? I touched her on top of her left hand with the cigarette. She did not scream. Then we all passed the cigarette around and took a drag. I made Jenna take a drag as well. She began violently coughing, as I guess she never smoked before, being an athlete and all.

"Then, after a minute or two, when she quit coughing, I took the cigarette and touched her on the back on the left calf. It was then that her left leg buckled with the pain, I guess. She never said a word or made a noise. She just lost her balance and fell off the stool.

"We grabbed her legs but it was too late. Her neck and head were at an odd angle, like her neck was broken. We all turned and screamed and ran out the door. I guess I threw the cigarette butt down when we left, and that is where the lipstick came from we had on."

Throughout the hearing room were muffled cries and gasps.

Britanee looked at the Couches. "I am really sorry. I did not mean for it to happen. She did not deserve to die. She was a much better person than any of us will ever be. I do not know what else to say. If they put me in jail, I deserve it. For the rest of my life. I simply do not care. No person deserves to die like she did even if it was accidental. I caused it."

With that, Britanee sat in the front row, alone, looking straight ahead.

Mr. Couch stared at the picture of his daughter before rising slowly. He walked to the center of the room and looked at Britanee for a long while.

"Britanee, I am just a refinery worker. That was my only daughter. I do not hold any animosity towards any of you," he said between tears. "What you said today lifts my heart above where it has been for the last sixty days. Now I can put it to rest. She is gone, never to return, that is true. But at least now we know what really happened.

"We did not know what happened. Everybody makes mistakes. Especially when they are young. Really stupid mistakes. Some of those mistakes ruin their lives for the rest of the time they are on this earth."

Mr. Couch faced the Judge. "My daughter is gone from this world. And apparently a grandchild as well that she was carrying. That grandchild, no matter who the father was, had my blood running through its small veins.

"I am asking the court, in this hearing, not to prosecute these four girls. We are not going to press any type of charges. My daughter is gone. I don't want these fathers out here to lose their daughters. So as far as I am concerned, there will be no trial. This is it. It is over."

With that, he walked over to Britanee and held her in a long hug. She wept as he held her.

I stood slowly, looked at the parents of the cheerleaders, and walked slowly over to the Couch family.

"Judge, in light of the unexpected outcome of today's evidentiary hearing, I would like to make a couple of recommendations to the court, if I may?"

Judge McGee said, "You may indeed, Mr. Carter. Please proceed."

"Well, number one, I am strongly recommending no charges be brought against these girls, as the family refuses to bring charges.

"Number two, I respectfully ask all of the girls involved to be removed from the Spring cheerleading squad immediately and never allowed to be in that role again. Their roles can easily be fulfilled by the pep squad for the remainder of the games, and for all time, as far as that is concerned.

"Number three: I request that each of the girls on the squad involved in the death of Jenna Couch be assigned one thousand hours of community service each at the senior citizens' home, cleaning, changing sheets, mopping, cleaning bathrooms. Basically anything needed and permitted by the staff to assist in the maintenance and upkeep of those facilities.

"And lastly, for their respective families to pay for all of the funeral expenses the Couch family endured, including the cost of her grave plot. That is the least they can do. That is all, Judge."

Judge McGee looked at Jenna's picture reflectively. Slowly, he turned and faced Jenna's parents. "Do you see any reason not to impose what Mr. Carter has asked? You know charges can easily be filed."

Mr. Couch stood slowly and wiped away tears from his eyes. "Judge, we will not file charges against these girls. I have no problem with what Mr. Carter has proposed."

Judge McGee turned to the weeping cheerleader mothers. "Parents of the girls involved. Most do not get a second chance in life, after such a heinous action against another human being in a court of law. You understand that, I assume. This is a real crime with real consequences, though it was unintended, according to Ms. Phelps. However, the courts' hands are somewhat tied, as the Couch family, to their credit, does not want to press charges. I believe in the strongest terms that a human life was totally wasted, due to the actions of four girls who thought more of themselves than they did of others. Clearly not a good life precedent, I am sure you will all agree. And you," motioning to the cheerleaders' parents, "for whatever reason, pushing them to believe they are better than other girls is a travesty and you should be ashamed of yourselves. You and they have wreaked unfathomable harm and hurt to other human beings that have the same rights to be here, breathe the same air, participate in every opportunity in life that your girls have. Understand?

"Now, I am going to ask each of you to stand up that believes the requests asked for by Investigator Carter be granted by the court with immediate effect. Your actions will be noted by the court clerk, and will be enforceable by the court in light of today's results."

Each of the four girls stood, then their parents.

"Please let it be noted by the court that all of the requests asked for by the investigating officer, Mr. Carter, are agreed to and affirmed by the act of standing in this courtroom by all of the cheerleader parents, not just the four girls involved. In addition, this is enforceable by the court and will assign personnel to monitor the requirements set forth. If these requirements are not met, the young ladies assigned the requirements will be brought back before the court, and the court will make an assessment of the next steps forward. This hearing is adjourned. Mr. Carter, please see me in my chambers along with Captain Burris."

I made my way to the judge's chambers after watching the audience file out. Samantha Divine was ghostly white and clearly distraught. Her beloved cheerleaders were no more, only the lowly pep squad. Britanee sat alone in thought at the front of the hearing room. Mr. and Mrs. Couch appeared to be working their way to speak with her. Mr. and Mrs. Phelps quickly exited the hearing room, her in the lead, him following like a puppy.

When I entered the judge's chambers. Captain Burris was already seated, drinking a bottle of water. "Sit down, Mr. Carter, please," gesturing with his hand to a leather-bound chair. Collapsing in the chair, I looked at the judge. "Investigator Carter, you took a huge chance. A monstrous gamble. Yes, sir, a monstrosity of a gamble, for which we all and you especially could have paid a great price. I have to hand it to you, you played your hand craftily and without fault. I commend you. You need to be an attorney. I have attorneys that cannot do what you did today. I guess in our world, sometimes it is run a great bluff, if you will. We will never play cards together, sir. Now, you are dismissed. Please never try that again. Get out of my chambers."

I cast a parting glance at Captain Burris on my way out. The captain lifted his water bottle in a toasting fashion with a smile. "Good job, Bulldog. Take the rest of the day off."

CHAPTER TWENTY

Jackaleena could feel the low whirring of the ship's propellers as it glided along. She had never been in a boat before, much less a ship. It had been a short time since Rufus had left her locked in her room. She could smell herself and felt she needed to wash off with soap.

She stripped out of her dress and turned on the water. There were two handles. Not knowing which one was which, she turned both of them on. To her surprise, one was warm and the other was cold. She stepped under the showerhead and began to wash off and rub the white bar of soap on her body. She could not remember anything so refreshing. She scrubbed her hair well. Her head was itching badly and the soap made it feel better. She dried off with a towel on hanging on a rod on the wall. She could really smell the clothes she had taken off.

She turned on the water again and washed them with the water, then hung them to dry with the towel. She opened her pillow sack, took out the only other dress she'd brought, and put it on. At least she no longer smelled.

She sat and looked at the food that Rufus had brought from the galley. She broke off a piece of bread and ate it slowly. There was a cup in the sack. She turned on the cold water and filled it to the top. The bread tasted very good. As long as it had been since she ate, she tried to eat slowly and chew it well. She was so hungry she wanted to gulp it down, but resisted the temptation. Then she ate a banana.

When she was through, she sat on the bed. There was a comb on the sink with a mirror above it. She stood and took the comb and began to comb her hair. She heard footsteps approaching the door. She froze. Then the two taps came. Then two more light taps. "Jackaleena . . . Jackaleena," Rufus said. "It is me, Rufus. It is okay, unlock the door. Can you hear me?"

She moved to the door and unlatched the lock, peeking through the crack. "How are you doing?" he asked. He opened the door and brought his massive frame through the opening that did not seem big enough for his body. "How are you doing, young girl? Everything okay? I see you have washed yourself. Have you eaten any of your food?" Jackaleena nodded. "Good, good, good. That is wonderful. Now, you cannot come out when the sun is out, only with me at night in my basket, understand? So every night I will come by and pick you up. We will put the towels on your head." He laughed as he talked. "Just like last night when I found you. You stay under the towels, and then we go to the top deck and you will get fresh air. I call that a good plan, don't you?"

Jackaleena looked at him with her beautiful black eyes looking into his. She nodded. She quietly thanked Jesus Man for putting her with a man like Rufus. He would not hurt her. She somehow knew he would really do what he said he would do, and she could trust him. He was big enough to be a fierce protector if someone bothered her, she thought. She wished he had been in her village when the soldier boys came, and Mingas and the others. Maybe her people would still be alive.

"Okay, now, when I come by, I will give my tap-tap and then tap-tap. Then, like just now, I will say quietly that it is me, Old Rufus. Okay? Yes? I will bring you food and something to drink every day or so or, whenever you need it. We are going to be at sea for twenty days, including the days we make port calls. So, in about this many days," holding up all ten fingers and pointing to all ten toes through his sandals, "you will be in America. I do not know where you will go in America. But God does. He surely does. He just has not let me know where that is. But I bet wherever it is, it will be for your purpose, don't you think? And if he is letting you cross the ocean on a ship, it sounds like it is a pretty big purpose. Come give Rufus a hug."

He opened his mighty arms. Jackaleena, having never hugged another human being, went into his arms. He felt like a mighty beast. Strong but very gentle.

"There, my little one, come see Old Rufus. I will take care of you like a lion. Like a mighty leopard. Like a mighty elephant. Nothing is going to hurt you now, little one."

He held her for the longest time. She put her arms around him as far as she could go and held him tightly. She could feel his great muscles in his arms and chest. Unlike some of the smaller men in her village, Rufus was the fierce picture of a strong and gentle man.

"There, now. Everything is going to be just fine, little girl." He kissed her on the forehead and tapped her gently on the head. "You rest now, and I will see you when the moon is up in the sky. Be ready, you hear? Be ready. Rufus will come tap-tap-tapping." He smiled as he walked out the door. Jackaleena smiled as she quietly latched it.

She lay on the bed, trying to sleep. Her mind would not shut down long enough for her to drift off, especially in the daytime. She knew it would be a long ride to Amerika, but here she was. She felt a calm easiness about her and felt somehow free of worry. It was just a little lonely, sitting in the room, waiting for the nighttime for Rufus to come around.

Rufus made his normal daytime rounds on the ship, picking up towels in his basket during early daylight hours. He would dump the used towels and linens out of mesh bags left hanging on folks' door handles. Then he would hang the empty bags back on the door handles, repeating the exercise in the evening. The below-deck laundry crew was made up mostly of folks from Thailand. Working in the "hole," or the gut of the ship, was excruciating work. The man heading up the whole operation was simply called Mr. Royal. Under his leadership, the entire ship and its occupants were fed three times a day, linens and laundry were washed, and the ship was kept spotlessly clean. They were in charge of the ship water makers, boilers, and propulsion system. There were never complaints. The only cabin they did not clean was the one Jackaleena occupied. It was simply never used because of its unique position in the ship.

Rufus continued to pick up Jackaleena nightly, just as the sun went down every day. He always had a few towels already in the basket for her to sit on, and one or two to cover her with. He always reminded her to be very still and quiet. If she needed to cough or maybe sneeze, she would plant her face in the towels as best she could to muffle the sound. He said, "I will cough like this if you have to sneeze. That way they will only hear me, okay?" Jackaleena could time the route nearly to the minute. Even the odor of the towels was ever-present, the smell of the ocean even more prevalent when they reached the top deck. As it was dark when they reached the top deck, she would lift her head with the towels on top. She could feel the ocean breeze against her skin when the basket was positioned just right, and smell the salty odor of the ocean. She would take deep breaths, gathering in the smell. Counting her fingers, and the evening sun going down, Jackaleena counted they had been at sea ten days. Rufus told her that all of her fingers and all of her toes made the number of days they would be at sea before the ship reached Amerika. She wondered what big purpose Jesus Man had for her there. Maybe she would be taking care of a large group of chickens that people would help feed. Or maybe helping other children like her.

Rufus was heading to the front of the ship to pray, as was his nightly ritual. Jackaleena took great pleasure and reassurance in hearing the mighty man pray to Jesus Man. He always thanked Jesus Man for saving someone like him, and always asked him to help him take care of his precious cargo, Jackaleena. She knew it was coming in the prayer and always waited for it. It was a wonderful thing to hear, that someone else cared for you and would take care of you, like Joao, then Margaret at Benguela by the Sea. Someone really cared whether you were fed and where you slept at night. Not that her parents did not care, because they did. Jackaleena just sensed the ferociousness with which Rufus would defend her if something happened. She had never seen a man like this.

Dr. Ronald Lynn was out on the upper deck most nights, to absorb the night air in the long and grueling ride back to the states. His yearly tour aboard the Mercy Ship started in Luanda. He arrived there by air, as did the other doctors who paid with their own funds. The team of physicians and nurses were a hearty mix of pediatricians, Ob-gyns, cardiologists, gastroenterologists, and a smattering of general medical physicians, including a dentist from Detroit. All were geared to share their expertise in war-torn countries where the general population, children in particular, came up with the short end of the stick. The nurses that accompanied them were from all over the United States, and every now and then a nurse from Canada on her vacation. Each person generously volunteered their services for the sake of people who had nothing. Some worked in the operating rooms, emergency rooms, prenatal wards, or elsewhere in local hospitals large and small. Mortality rates among the infants were high. Malaria took a great toll on them. The doctors were always on the lookout for malaria cases and carried an abundant supply of malaria vaccines. There was no guarantees of the vaccine working or that the children or adults would live.

*   *   *

Dr. Lynn remembered seeing some of the nurses hide tears as a malnourished child was brought onto the ship or into a makeshift tent at some village. Or the child with a cleft pallet who smiled after two or three visits and corrective surgery by a skilled physician. Children that the rest of the world did not seem to know or care about. The children remembered them if they returned the next year, oftentimes reaching out to hug and hold their caretakers without letting go.

He had the financial means to have a chopper pick him up in Angola, or anywhere on the coast, and take him back to Luanda for the long international flight back to the states. Instead, it help restore his senses to ride the ship back for twenty days or so. It seemed to help cement his purpose in helping the multitude of children and adults. Twenty days on a ship certainly did not hurt his practice back home, and it was simply worth doing. He always had another Ob-gyn fill in for him while he was gone. His patients knew about it and respected him for it.

He got to visit with physicians and nurses that pursued the quest out of their love for humanity. The ride home on the ship was exhilarating. Three meals a day. Roundtable discussions on this or that patient. Coffee and tarts in the evening after supper. And then, those great evenings on the top deck, smelling the ocean breeze. Looking at the moon and stars. Strolling on the catwalks. Standing at the front of the ship, it was nearly as if you were flying. The quiet hum and thrust of the propeller. Not felt at the front of the ship as at the back. After twenty days, Dr. Lynn had to get back into the "life in United States" mode. Hurry up to get out of the house. Rushed coffee and toast, appointments and surgeries and baby deliveries. Endless reports, out-of-sight malpractice insurance rates for never-ending lawsuits. The folks they treated overseas had no lawyers, mostly just gratitude and love. Lots of love. Two weeks of long days overseas and twenty days of reflection made the rest of the year back home tolerable. He spent the next six months planning ahead for his next overseas visit with great anticipation.

He noticed the nightly ritual of the laundry man as he came onto the top deck. He watched nightly as he pushed his laundry basket to the front of the ship. He would secure it carefully with a cord out of his pocket and lock the wheels. Then he would make his way a few feet to the uttermost front of the ship close to the front gangplank. There the large, black man would kneel and lift his arms to the heavens in some type of prayer. Usually it lasted a few minutes, but sometimes he noticed it went on for a longer period of time.

Movement at the laundry basket caught his eye on at least two occasions. He noticed that the towels seem to elevate as if pulled by a hidden string. He stood and moved a short distance closer, to ensure his eyes were not deceiving him. The towels would slowly move up a few inches and remain there, and then seemingly lower of their own accord. When the nightlights on the ship and the moon were just right, he saw the reason why. There was someone in the basket. He barely made out the shape of a neck and head for a brief moment. From the size of the laundry basket it could only be a child.

Dr. Lynn suspected they might have a stowaway on their hands. They had been at sea for at least ten days. He reasoned there was no turning back now. He had no idea where or how long this person had been onboard. He knew he had to make it known to the ship captain. All of his years of college and medical school had not prepared him in the least in how to handle something like this. It could have international consequences.

First and foremost, senses aside, he had to ensure that what he saw was, in reality, a child. And if it was a child, where was he or she staying, and with whose help? Maybe the child was being smuggled in some type of child trafficking ring. Maybe folks on the ship were in on the deal. Maybe there were others.

He calmed his mind and spirit. When his heart rate had reached a normal level, he slowly made his way to the basket and large man. The man had just gotten up from his kneeling position when he saw the doctor approaching slowly.

"Nice night out," said Dr. Lynn.

"Yes, suh, yes, suh. It is a wonderful night out, Doctor. My name is Rufus Obediah. I take care of the laundry on the ship," motioning to his basket secured with sash cord. "I come up here at night to smell the fresh ocean air," he said as he took in a deep breath and exhaled. "Smells good, don't you think?"

"Yes, sir, Mr. Obediah, it does smell good. I am Dr. Lynn from the United States."

"I have seen you, suh, and am pleased to make your acquaintance."

His great and gentle hand swallowed the small hand of the doctor.

"Yes, suh, I am wonderfully glad to make your acquaintance. Well, suh, I need to be getting on about my rounds and get this laundry to the hole. These folks don't like to be held up waiting on me."

Dr. Lynn watched him untie the sash cord secured to the clevis. Carefully he held the basket with his foot while he rolled up the sash cord and put it in his pants pocket.

Dr. Lynn placed his hand on the laundry basket. Rufus looked horrified as he carefully placed his hand down and pressed on the top towel. He felt the top of Jackaleena's head.

Rufus turned his head away, knowing that things were likely going to change. "Please, suh, don't hurt my girl. She is just a little girl that I found on the ship. No one but you and me know she is even on this ship. You're not going to tell someone, are you, suh? She has a big purpose in America, I think."

Dr. Lynn carefully raised his hand. "Mr. Obediah, I will follow behind you a ways and you take me to where she is staying. Then I want the details of where she came from and how she got on this ship. I will have to let the captain know as soon as I have all of the facts, you understand?"

"Yes, suh. I guess so. As long as she does not get hurt by anyone. I will not let that happen."

"No, sir, Mr. Obediah, I can see that. I can assure you no one is going to hurt this girl. We simply cannot walk her off the ship in America without notice, you see. There are laws, international laws. We have to abide by those."

Rufus carefully unlocked the door to Jackaleena's room. He pushed the laundry basket in, with Dr. Lynn coming in behind them.

"Lock the door, Mr. Obediah," he instructed. "Now, let me see what your 'girl' looks like."

Rufus pulled the top towels off of Jackaleena's head. "You can come up now, Ms. Jackaleena. This man is not going to hurt you."

Jackaleena was concerned but not terrified, as long as Rufus was close. She raised her head from between her knees.

"Let me help you out of there, little girl." He lifted her out with ease and stood her on the floor by his side. "Well, Dr. Lynn, here she is. Jackaleena. My little girl."

Dr. Lynn witnessed the young girl in front of him. She appeared to be in excellent health, probably eleven or twelve. Her eyes bestowed what appeared to be a very high level of intelligence. Her countenance was bright and assured, for someone who was not supposed to be on the ship. "Do you understand English?" he asked.

Rufus countered, "Oh yes, suh. She can speak most English, but it—"

"Can you understand English?"

Jackaleena nodded. "I can't make all of the words," she said. "I can understand what you say."

"Thank you," said Dr. Lynn. "I guess the big question is, where did you come from, and how did you get on this ship? You know we are halfway back to America, the United States of America. Where are your mother and father?"

Jackaleena looked him in the eyes for a moment or two, reflecting on her answer. "My mother and father were killed by boy soldiers and their leader. They killed everyone in my village. They cut off all of the heads of men in my village and put them on stick posts around our communal fire ring. I start to Benguela by the Sea that takes care of boys and girls. I meet Joao on the way to Benguela by the Sea. He tell me about Jesus Man and lead me to Benguela by the Sea. The soldier boys drop from trees and kill him and cut off his head when he get me there. I run into the gates. Margaret take care of me and teach me that I am not a witch because I bleed when moon comes up this many times," she said, counting each of her fingers and toes and then her fingers again. "She teach me book tracks and words to make. She show me in her Bible about Jesus Man. They feed me and give me this to wear and one other one. They give me these to wear on my feet. "She teach me to give one fingers of my bread to the chickens and pray to Jesus Man for more chickens. Jesus Man send us roosters to make more chickens to eat and lay eggs. He also take roosters from Mingas and soldier boys to give us after I pray for more chickens.

Then he send snake that runs to bite Mingas and he die. Soldier boys kill the other two leaders and lay down their guns. Go back to their village. Do not know if their mothers and fathers are alive.

"Then I see this ship with a glass on a stick over the walls of Benguela by the Sea. I put my clothes in my pillow sack and climb down the soldier boys' ladder and run to the boat that bring the people that help the people at Benguela by the Sea. I hide in a box on the boat. They pull us up to this big boat and I hide in box until it is moon come up. Mr. Rufus found me when I was out of box and trying to get out of the boat. Margaret at Benguela by the Sea tell me Jesus Man gives everyone a purpose to be here. She tell Jesus Man has big purpose for me. I believe in Jesus Man and I do not believe in Toto the witchy man anymore. He never help our village and never come to me when I clap like this. I could see him and he never help. I cannot see Jesus Man but he came to my prayers and help me. I can feel him. Margaret tells me Jesus Man has a big purpose for me to live. I can feel that my big purpose is in Amerika. That is how I come on this big boat."

Dr. Lynn turned his head and wiped away tears. To think that this young child's parents were both killed, her entire village wiped out, was overwhelming. Yet here she was, speaking in broken English on a big purpose in America like it was just an ordinary exercise. Not only was she extraordinary in her countenance and thought and recall, she was extraordinary in bravery. She seemed to be shrouded in God's protective blanket. She had nothing but the two dresses she said she possessed that were given to her at Benguela by the Sea and the sandals on her feet. Yet here she was on a ship heading to America, unafraid of any difficulties that could and would arise from the journey. She seemed unafraid of unpredictable events. Jesus Man had a "big purpose" for her.

Dr. Lynn was quite astounded. He in his own life had never experienced anything that would come close to her dire circumstances. Where would she go, how would she survive? Who, if anyone, would take her in? How could she stay in the United States? Was she a refugee or asylum candidate? What were the international laws governing her and him when they arrived? She seem completely at peace and quite oblivious to any difficulties that might arise.

"Jackaleena, first of all," he said, "I have to inform the captain of this ship that you are here. We will make sure that you are fed and taken care of during your journey. Mr. Obediah has apparently done an outstanding job of doing so thus far. However, we are going to make sure that you are in the care of female nurses that will help take care of your needs, not that Mr. Rufus has not done so.

"Next, we will ask the captain to help us decide what is the best way to take care of you once we get to America. I do not believe there is sufficient reason to ask him to turn this mighty ship around and take you back. You have nothing to go back to, except Benguela by the Sea. It alone is not supposed to be a place that holds children forever, I would think."

Rufus stood by, looking on. "Can I say something?" he asked.

"Yes, sir, Rufus, by all means."

"You see, suh, I have been praying to God every night when I go out. That is what I was doing when you came to me. I have been praying for help in taking care of this baby girl to get to her purpose. It seems that the answer to that prayer for Old Rufus is you, Dr. Lynn. God sent her you. Maybe you can help her. She is real smart."

"Yes, Rufus. I realize she is very smart. But we have laws in our land that must be heeded. Especially when someone, in this case a child, stows away on a ship. The laws do not care if she thinks she has a big purpose. A lot of people might think that and try to get into America. In this case, as in all, we have to follow the laws of the land. I cannot guarantee what exactly will happen and will not make any promises. For right now, let's get her situated with the nurses in their berthing. There will be no more of her living by herself and going out in a laundry basket at night," he said, smiling at Jackaleena. "She can come out in open daylight like the rest of us. They will take good care of her, sir. You can stop by and see her anytime you wish."

CHAPTER TWENTY-ONE

Captain McKewn listened intently as Dr. Lynn told him about Jackaleena. "You know, Doctor Lynn, she is not our first stowaway. She is in fact the only one that has made it halfway back to America. It sounds to me like she is all right, physically and mentally, right?"

"Yes, sir, Captain. And not a care in the world. She claims that her Jesus Man has a big purpose for her, and it is in America. I cannot imagine what that might be, but I know for a fact she is not one bit afraid of anything. I have never seen someone with as much confidence. It is really quite amazing. You should meet her, sir."

"I intend to do just that, sometime today. We have her. We have to deal with her when she gets to America and follow the laws. She could possibly be heading back to Africa."

Dr. Lynn protested. "And where in Africa do you suggest we send her back to? Benguela by the Sea? A missionary outpost that struggles to feed the group of children they have? All are children of warfare, and most do not have parents or family. Jackaleena has no family, she has no village, Captain."

"I understand, doctor. I said she could possibly be heading back to Africa. I did not say how likely it was. I am thinking she is some kind of refugee, or maybe can be someone that applies for asylum. I simply don't know at this point. Anyone brave enough to do what she has done and gone through what she has gone through is a trooper. I mean a trooper. But that does not change the laws. There are thousands upon thousands of folks that want to get into the United States of America. She is just one of them."

"I understand, Captain," said Dr. Lynn. "It just seems like we can and should come up with a plan to help her."

"Doctor, rest assured," said Captain McKewn, "we will try our dead level best. I hope whatever that is, is good enough. I really do. Think about this young girl on the streets of America. Can you envision that? She has to have help. She needs a home. She needs someone to feed her, clothe her. That is, if she gets to stay. She has to be given refugee status or asylum status. If all of that works out, then where does she go? Who will take a young African girl with no schooling, who speaks broken English, and is not a citizen? Answer me that, doctor."

"Captain, I realize the road ahead is full of mystery and the unknown. I have to believe that after looking at her and talking to her, something is going on. She is absolutely convinced that her Jesus Man has a big purpose for her and she is going to find it. Perhaps we are just a means for her to find it. Somehow I feel she will find it no matter what. Even if it is in spite of us and not because of us.

"She is now moved in with her one extra dress to the nurses' berthing. They received her like a bunch of mama hens. And you know what, it did not overwhelm her. She just acted like it was probably all part of the plan. I have never seen a young lady like her. She is something to behold. She does not act like young girls in America do at her age. She has seen too much and has nothing to her name on this earth but two dresses and two pairs of sandals, of which one is on her feet. And for goodness sake, let's not forget her pillowcase knapsack.

"And most of all, she has that brain of hers. That poise. Just think of the unlimited possibilities surrounding that, Captain. Just think about that. We cannot allow her to be put back in Africa. We just cannot."

Dr. Lynn left the captain's quarters and made his way to his room. His knowledge of asylum law was limited. He just knew that when they got to the states Jackaleena would have to be brought in front of an asylum or refugee officer and probably end up in front of an immigration or asylum judge of some kind.

He was to have his evening meal with Dr. Mallord Tindell III. Dr. Mallord Tindell had a resume as long as the ship. This quiet and humble man was a highly skilled physician out of New York City, with a specialty in artificial limbs for children. He gained notoriety in the United States for finding and fitting young children with leg and arm prosthetics. His intellect was said to be past the genius level, and he did not tolerate foolery in any form. Conversations were intense and direct. There were absolutely no mind games or mental gimmicks to get him to contort to a line of thinking. He simply knew the answers before he asked the questions in nearly all cases.

Dr. Tindell listened intently over their meal as Dr. Lynn described the situation at hand. After Dr. Lynn had emphatically and nearly breathlessly told the entire story, he paused and looked at Dr. Tindell. "I do not know exactly what we are going to do, Mallord, I simply do not. I have never dealt with this before."

Dr. Tindell sipped his strong coffee quietly for a minute or two, gazing out at one of the workers in the galley. "Hard workers, wouldn't you say, Dr. Lynn?"

"Why yes, they sure are. But my questions."

"Calm down, Dr. Lynn. Before I became a doctor, my first learning in college at my father's request was to be an attorney. Well, I am an attorney. I am also a doctor. Quite a bunch of school wouldn't you say? Yes, indeed, a lot of school. Now, what you have on your hands is this: You have a child from Africa—Angola, I think you said. She was in a missionary compound, Benguela by the Sea. She made her way to the compound after her parents and her entire village were wiped out ruthlessly by a murdering bunch who opposed the government. That bunch has apparently been dealt a final blow by their own hand, or perhaps the hand of a higher being, and are no more. However, there is and certainly will be others. That civil war over there has been going on a long time and will continue. Read up on it sometime. They maliciously kill with rifles and machetes. You have seen those body wounds yourself.

"Now, this young girl is on our ship, heading to somewhere in America. The way I see it, she enters the US as a URM. That is an Unaccompanied Refugee Minor that is not over eighteen years of age. You indicate she is around eleven or perhaps twelve years of age. The program was developed to help children that are victims of civil or economic unrest. She fits both of those. If she is sent back to this type of uncertainty, where will she go? She will have to claim this status before an asylum judge. He can either rule on the spot or perhaps let her in before he makes a judgment. She cannot say, in my opinion, that her Jesus Man has a big purpose for her in America. I do not know how well that would go over.

"Next, if she passes that hurdle, it would be good to have a place she can go. Possibly a family or facility that takes in kids no matter what. A pre-committed family is always a good thing to tell a judge, I would think. In other words, she is not going to simply become a ward of the state. She would have an actual family to go to.

"Now, if I were doing an analysis of the possibilities of how many families were out there just begging to take in a stowed-away African girl that is eleven or twelve years old, those odds are not as good as your chances of winning on a slot machine in Las Vegas two times in a row. I would rank them very low, if existent at all.

"That is how I see it.

"Build her case as a URM that is coming from a war-torn nation with no end to the current civil war that is going on. To send her back would be detrimental to her existence. She has no family alive, if what she says is true. Next, where are you going to recommend to place her? To me, that is the biggest problem you have. A judge might just allow her to stay. Where is she going to go? That is your problem. She has no family in the US, no family in Africa.

"The complexity of this problem is not something they teach you in college, Dr. Lynn. Will you take her in? Will you adopt her, feed her, provide her with an education? You said she is very smart. That is good. If she is allowed into the country, she will have to be smart to survive. If she is allowed to come in to the US on the URM program, only certain states are utilizing it. Texas, your home state, is definitely one of them. They generally do not allow adoption, as they cannot prove that the child does not have parents in a foreign land. Africa, in this case. The only thing you have to go by is the child's account. Most likely she would be placed in a foster home until she became an adult."

Dr. Lynn was in deep thought as Dr. Tindell gave his simple analysis of what lay before them. His mind was racing to remember potential parents that might take her in for the long term. He had to fight for a few things in his privileged life, mostly grades. But never did he have to fight for his life. Never for his very existence.

This child had no one. She just had her conviction to come to America by any means and to simply to search for her big purpose.

Other than a few Hispanic couples, most of his clientele were Caucasian. The chances that any of them would agree to accept and adopt a refugee from Angola he judged to be small, if existent at all.

Dr. Tindell sat quietly sipping his coffee. He lowered his cup and grasped it with both hands letting the heat reach his fingers. Even though it was warm outside, the heat transfer felt good on his joints. "Ronny, I will help you any way I can, but I will warn you, this is a mountain not a molehill."

Finally, Dr. Lynn looked him in the eyes. "Dr. Tindell, if you will represent her at the asylum court when we arrive, I cannot think of anyone better. Anyone more articulate. Would you do that? I am saying here and now, if you will agree to do that, I will get her placed with a good family. What do you say?"

"You have a family that has already agreed to do this, Ronny? I need names. I need a solid commitment. Not just words. Who are they?"

Dr. Lynn looked down. "I don't know just yet. I have an idea, but I do not know. There is an orphanage in our town that takes in homeless and abused children. One of my patients works there. She tells me about them. Maybe she has an inside track to a family that would not be prejudiced toward her, due to her circumstances and ethnicity. There are some good people out there. If we can just get her in the door and into this place, maybe the rest will fall in place somehow."

"Dr. Lynn, the asylum judge sees cases all day and every day. He or she will more than likely have little patience for innuendo, desire, or that maybe you can get this done. They would want a concrete, rock-solid plan, a footprint that can be validated by the never-ending social programs and bureaucrats that run them.

"It is minutely possible that if you, a physician, agreed to 'sponsor' this child's plan, which would ultimately be to place her with adoptive parents, the judge might allow it. And that is a big 'might.' If you stepped off and did this, you would be signing up for endless paperwork and headache that might turn out to be a puff of wind. No parents and you on the hook for her well-being. Do you understand that? When we go to the judge, you have to have a plan laid out in writing to present then and there. This child may be asked to say something to the judge. She cannot just stare at him in bewilderment. It is helpful that she has high intellect and speaks broken English. That is beneficial, but it by no means guarantees anything. This will be like a miniature courtroom, if you will, and you are not an attorney. I am."

Dr. Tindell sipped his coffee and looked at the horizon for a few minutes, saying nothing, just thinking.

"Dr. Lynn, I will do it. I will do it under the circumstances I just laid out. A rock-solid, written plan before we hit the US shore. Nothing short of that."

Dr. Lynn jumped up and ran around the table, grabbing Dr. Tindell from behind with a great bear hug. "You are a very good man, Mallord. A very good man."

Dr. Mallord carefully managed not to spill his coffee. Often devoid of any type of emotion, he smiled. "You can let me go, now." Dr. Lynn looked around. There were a few folks close by, but no one seemed to notice.

"Ronny, we will give this our best shot and hope we come out victorious for your girl. It is written all over your face that you want to do it. After all of the human effort we put in trying to help those that cannot help themselves, do you think we do it to feel better about ourselves or because of our Hippocratic oath? I think it is probably both, wouldn't you say?"

"Get some rest and type me that document. I want to make sure it is your best work."

CHAPTER TWENTY-TWO

Judge Brover D. Linquist sat on the US asylum court in the port of New York City. Endless lines of people for endless days, all wanting to get into the United States of America. The land of milk and honey. The place where everyone has a job that wants one. Everyone loves one another and treats each other with respect. Just sailing by the Statue of Liberty gives inspiration to the never-ending chain of ocean crossers.

What he lacked in fundamental compassion he made up for in sharp crassness. Overweight from days of sitting with little exercise, pleurisy, and having just found out he did not get an appointment to 9th Circuit of Appeals he was counting on, his patience was running thinner than on most days. He had campaigned for the open position, one of the most sought-after in the land, other than being a Supreme Court justice. But now, he was stuck for anyone's guess as to how long he would be in this never-ending circle of people. They all started to look the same. All tired from the journey. All hopeful of their outcomes. All clutching whatever they had. All hoping for an edge, a squeak to open a door. A chance to try and improve on their awful existences in some foreign land. *Why do they think they deserve to be in the United States?* he often wondered. *Why in the world would you make the journey over land or sea to get here? What makes you think we have to take you?*

When the Mercy Ship reached port, Dr. Tindell and Dr. Lynn had spent the previous two hours with Jackaleena. She had been coddled by the nurses onboard to the extreme. They clipped and manicured her toenails and fingernails, gave her a facial, and generally hovered over her for the nine days she berthed with them. They took daily strolls on the upper deck, with each taking turns holding her hands and walking. They tried to get her to eat, as they did at every meal. Jackaleena only took out what she could eat. They noticed that she broke off a piece of her biscuit every morning and rolled it into a napkin. "Poor child, probably saving it for later," one said.

She probably was not getting enough to eat. But still, Jackaleena only took out what she would eat and never said what the biscuit was for. She would pray quietly every evening as she unrolled her biscuit piece. "Jesus Man, this is Jackaleena. I pray for chickens and give my one finger's biscuit to the chickens. You answered my prayer and gave us roosters. I am giving this to the fish in the water every day. I pray to ask you to help me find my big purpose." During the walks with the nurses, she would ask to look over the side while holding the handrail. When they were not looking, she would cast her biscuit piece to the sea.

Dr. Lynn and Dr. Tindell did not really coach Jackaleena on what to say, to a great extent. Dr. Tindell told her to look the judge in the eyes at all times, and to speak when spoken to, not before. He would do most of the talking.

Once their luggage was taken off the ship, they each held Jackaleena's hands as they approached Customs. Past Customs, both could see the asylum court area with an increasingly long line. There were probably thirty people standing outside the doors.

"Well, Ronny, there it is. Good to go?"

"Yes, sir, I am good to go," he said.

The folks checking passports and visas were moderately surprised to see two physicians with a young black girl in tow.

"Passport, please," one said as Jackaleena came through.

Dr. Tindell replied immediately. "Sir, she is with Dr. Lynn and myself. Physicians on the Mercy Ship just returning from Africa."

"Is she here for medical attention, doctor?"

"No, sir, she is here to apply for asylum. She has no living family and is in our care."

"Sir, you will immediately report to the asylum officer of the court. Take her to the uniformed officer there by the court, and he will take it from there. Best of luck, sir."

Jackaleena never said a word during the three-hour wait to appear before the Judge. She had to be escorted to the restroom by Dr. Lynn, standing outside while Dr. Tindell held her place in line.

Judge Linquist studied them over his glasses as they walked the short distance from the entry doors to his bench: two Caucasian men holding hands with a young black girl. *This should be very interesting*, he reasoned. *I thought I had seen everything.*

"State your names, please," he said.

"I am Dr. Tindell, and this is Dr. Lynn."

"What is your business today, sirs?"

Dr. Tindell carefully removed the hand-typed letter out of his lapel pocket. He looked at Dr. Lynn and Jackaleena before handing it to the judge.

"This will state our case, sir."

Judge Linquist opened the letter, looking over his glasses at Dr. Tindell. The only part of his position that he liked was having nearly this supernatural power over people standing below him. They could do nothing without his approval.

He read slowly and intently. Finally, after about ten minutes, he laid the letter down, carefully smoothing out the folded seams with his index finger.

"Who wrote this?" he asked.

Dr. Lynn looked up at him, never releasing his grip on Jackaleena's hand.

"I did, sir," he said. "I wrote it."

Judge Linquist looked hard at him. "Does she speak?" he said.

"Yes, sir, she speaks broken English, but she does speak."

"What happened to your parents?" asked the judge, looking at Jackaleena.

Slowly and intently she looked into the judge's eyes. "The boy soldiers and their leader, Mingas, kill them. They cut off the men's heads and put them on posts at our communal fire. They kill the women. There is no one left but me. I go to Benguela by the Sea and they take care of me. The big white boat with red cross come to help the children. I get on the little boat that they take up to the big boat to come to Amerika. The women that take care of me are from Amerika."

The Judge looked at her intently. "Are you afraid to go back?"

Jackaleena looked at him carefully before answering. "If I go back, I have no peoples. I have no home. My village is no more. Benguela by the Sea take in children of war. They have not much to feed. There will be other attacks on Benguela by the Sea. Just like when I was there. The soldier boys attack us."

"So, Doctor Lynn, you are saying that this young lady is wanting to come in under the URM program, which Texas participates in. The church-affiliated operations, of which there are two, place these children normally in a foster home surrounded by a great many rules. You are saying in this letter, if I read it correctly, that you will provide 'guardianship' over this child until she is permanently adopted, and if not, you are liable for her and all that that means until she reaches the age of eighteen? Is that what you are saying?"

Dr. Lynn looked down at Jackaleena and then back up to the Judge. "Yes, sir, that is exactly what I am saying. I would like to make the application today, if you will grant it."

Judge Linquist stood. "I will be back in five minutes." He walked through the back chamber doors of the courtroom. Dr. Tindell looked at Dr. Lynn, shrugging in an unknowing fashion.

Judge Linquist finally made his way back through the chamber doors and took his seat in his great, black chair.

"I have sat at this bench for over seven long years now. I have seen just about everything there is to see, and seen everything tried there is to try to get into the country. Religious persecution, physical persecution, and the like."

He took out his handkerchief and blew his nose. Slowly he took off his glasses and dabbed his already red eyes.

"Yes, sir, I can say I have seen it all. But I will tell you one thing. I have never seen two doctors come in from Africa aboard a Mercy Ship holding the hands of a young African girl and one of them offering to take care of her. Unheard of. And her. Why, she stands there tall. Undefeated. Parents killed. Whole village killed. She told me that with conviction. She is telling the truth. I can tell.

"It is the position of the court in this case that she be granted URM status. Her application will be made out today before you depart. You, sir," pointing to Dr. Lynn, "are appointed as her guardian under the provisions of the letter you have put before me. When and if she is placed for adoption, she and the adoptive parents will appear before the court. If she is not adopted, you sir will appear before the court. In this case, I am putting a one-year timeline on adoption so her fate will not linger. She can get on with her life. She will also begin the normal process of applying for citizenship, if she desires, and that will be laid out in the court order as well.

"She is hereby granted URM status and is allowed entry into the United States of America. Welcome, young lady."

Dr. Lynn stood there, speechless. He scooped up Jackaleena and hugged her. He kissed her on the forehead as he danced in a circle. He put her back down and hugged Dr. Tindell, dancing in a circle.

"We did it. We did it." He ran around the room and back to Jackaleena, grabbing her hand.

The judge looked down from his bench. "Doctor, we do have other folks that want to come before me. You are now dismissed."

"Yes, sir, Judge. You bet, Judge."

CHAPTER TWENTY-THREE

I came home early on Friday afternoon, wanting to be there before Beatrice came in from work and mostly to just get my thoughts together. There was absolutely nothing to lose by asking her out on a date. Imagine asking your wife out for a date after over twenty years of marriage. What if she said no? She had every right in the world to say no. I had decided that if she said no, I would simply try again on another night.

Sitting in my easy chair, I waited. The two hours passed slowly, and I finally heard her car enter the driveway. It kind of felt like a high school kid asking a girl out for the first time. My palms were sweaty and I could not keep my heart from pounding out of my chest as she entered the door.

"Hey," she said. "You get off early today?"

"Well, I did get off a little early."

"What was the occasion? Captain Burris figure he is working you too hard?"

"That is not it at all," I said as I eased out of the chair.

"Alfie, is there something wrong?" Her beautiful eyes rose in slight alarm.

Walking slowly to her, I held out both of my hands. She looked down and carefully placed her hands in mine. "What is wrong, Alfie? Is something going on?"

"Bea, I don't really know how to begin."

She looked intensely at my eyes for a sign of what was going on.

"Go on," she said.

"Bea, you are beautiful. You are the most precious thing I have on this earth. I want to say I am sorry for the way I have treated you for the last twenty years. Especially since we lost Patricia."

Bea looked down and let her grip go, retreating to a bar stool. She began to weep.

"I ran out on you because I could not handle the grief myself. I never even thought of you and what you were going through. I am asking forgiveness."

Tears came in rivers down Bea's elegant face. She stood and hugged me hard and kissed me with all her might. "Of course I forgive you. I love you."

"Bea, I know I have not said it much at all. I really love you. I really do love you a lot. I don't just like you, I love you. I hope you not only love me, I hope you like me too."

"Alfie Carter, of course I like you and love you. I respect you, too."

"You have gone to church every Sunday, and I have not gone since, well, for a long time. When Cotton died, something changed me. God changed me. I really cannot explain it any better than that. I am changed. I don't think like I did before. I do not look at folks like I did before. Can you understand that? That night on the mountain, something happened to me up there when Cotton died. I just kind of came apart at the seams and well, I prayed to God for forgiveness. I accused you and God for everything."

"Alfie, I have prayed for you and us for a long time. Nearly as long as I can remember," she said, dabbing her eyes with a tissue. "I won't say I had given up, but I was just kind of running on empty. I love you so much. I never stopped loving you. I know how bad it hurt you with Patricia and all. It hurt me real deep, really deep. I was her mama and never got to see her. That hurt me real bad, Alfie. That was a long time ago. We have a long way to go hopefully. Maybe it is time to put it to rest."

"Bea, I never been to the grave after I buried her. I just can't."

She placed her fingers over my lips and just looked in my eyes. She shook her head ever so slightly. Then she kissed me tenderly on the lips.

"Bea, there's one more thing I have to ask you. I want to ask you out on a date tonight."

"A date? You, Alfie Carter, want to take me, Bea Carter, on a date?"

"I am afraid that is what I want."

She grabbed my shoulders and jumped up, wrapping her legs around my waist. She kissed me mightily, nearly pulling my lips off my face. I cried as I could taste her salty tears.

"I have not been asked out on a date since high school. You were the one that asked me. Of course I will go out on a date with you. Where are you taking me?"

"Well, I have not thought that through just yet, because I did not know if you would go."

"Well, you better decide pretty fast, mister, because we are leaving when I freshen up a bit, and I am real hungry. You better have more than twenty dollars." She set her feet back on the floor and held my hands. "Alfie, God has answered my prayers. I finally got my Alfie back. I have something I want to talk to you about as well. We will talk about it over supper. And I do not want to go to Merle's Café. He is the gossip of the town, probably the universe."

"Okay, it will not be at Merle's. We will go get a pizza. I have enough money ratholed back for a pizza."

The mood was light all the way to the pizzeria downtown. A new establishment, it was getting high marks around the police station and the boys. Good food, fast service, and comfortable booths.

Bea ate like a horse.

"For a small person, you can sure put away the pizza."

"Yes I can, and don't be trying to steal one of my pieces," she laughed. "Alfie, let's take a drive to someplace private."

"Bea, we are a little old to go parking, don't you think? I am an officer of the law, you know."

"Well, we can do a little parking if you wish, but there is just too many ears in here."

"Okay, Bea. We will go parking. I hope we do not get arrested. Think of how that would look in the paper."

I guided the car with the headlights up to Turner Point, outside of town.

"Been a long while since we been up here, little girl. I am talking a long time. About twenty years, plus or minus."

She kissed me mightily. Looking intently into my eyes, she reached out and took my hand and put it over her heart. "That is our life blood pumping. Can you feel it?" she asked.

"I do indeed, that is pretty wild."

"I have something I want to talk to you about, Alfie. Something that is very important to me and I hope will be important to you as well." She took my hands in hers. "Alfie, I mentioned maybe adopting a child one time before you left for the mountains. You remember that? It was just a thought then. Well, there is this little girl I want you to meet that came to our orphanage recently. Are you against something like that?"

"Why, no, Bea, what am I meeting this little girl for?"

"Well, she is a very smart little girl. I mean really smart and wonderful. She arrived at the orphanage a short time ago. Brought in by my doctor, Dr. Lynn. Do you remember him? He was my doctor when Patricia died."

"Yes, I do remember him. Been quite a while."

"Well, Dr. Lynn brought her in with another doctor from Africa. Her family and village were slaughtered by a group of guerrilla fighters. She stowed away on a mercy ship to get to America by herself. By herself, Alfie. Can you believe that?"

I shook my head in acknowledgement. "Brave little cuss, I would say. So why do you want me to meet this girl? What does she need?"

"Alfie, I love you with everything I have. I am past having children and do not care to do so. But this little girl needs a home. I want her to live with us. I want us to be her parents. Maybe adopt her."

I stared out the window for a good while. "Bea, I am not sure God wants me to be a father. Especially after what I have done, the way I have behaved."

"You will make the best father that ever was, Alfie. You just have to trust in God and let Him do the rest. Will you at least meet her? You don't have to commit right now. Just let me introduce you to her. Maybe get permission to bring her home for the weekend, or something. If you do not think it will work, we will not do it. I will just tell her she will get to come home with us for the weekend as a reward for her English efforts, or something like that. How does that sound? But I am warning you now, cowboy, she is going to win your heart."

"Well, this Friday night date certainly did not turn out like I was a thinking, as Cotton would have said. But it sure turned out interesting. Yes, Bea, I will agree to meet this girl. How old is she?"

"I think she is about maybe twelve years old. You will like her. I just know it."

"Well, we will see about that. We will just see about that."

"Now, let's do some parking, cowboy."

CHAPTER TWENTY-FOUR

Dr. Lynn agreed to allow Jackaleena to come to the Carters' for the weekend.

"How did Alfie take it when you asked him, Bea?" he asked. "As I recall, he was not in a good state of mind when you lost your child many years ago. What has it been now, close to twenty years?"

She turned her head away.

"I am so sorry, Bea, I did not mean to dredge up old, bad memories."

"It is okay, Dr. Lynn. Perfectly okay. I am doing better these days. I never talked to Alfie about the way I felt. I guess we just dealt with it in our own ways. He would take off to the mountains every year while I stayed home and cried the whole time he was gone. Pretty sad, in its own way, but that is what happened. Anyway, I really hope this meeting with Jackaleena goes well. She has stolen my heart and I want that little girl."

"Well, to be quite honest, I have had you specifically in mind from the time we got off the ship. I saw the connection when you and her were first introduced at the orphanage the day I brought her in. It was Alfie I worried and still worry about. I am not sure how he will take to adopting a child."

"Well Dr. Lynn, we just won't know until she gets there, will we? How does Jackaleena do in a car?"

"She walked from her village to Benguela by the Sea, stowed away in the small boat to the Mercy Ship, rode it across the ocean. Flew with me from Houston, Texas, then home. Rode in a car to my home and then to the orphanage. She will be okay on the car ride from here to your home."

I was behind the barn with my cowboy hat and leather gloves on when Bea pulled into the driveway. I could make out the small black girl getting out of the vehicle. She was not short or tall. Kind of in-between. Bea took her by the hand and led her into the house.

Bea poured her a glass of water from the fridge. She was sipping the water and looking around when I cracked the back door open.

"Well, I see we have a guest," I said. "Bea, who is that you have with you?" as I took off my hat.

"Alfie, this is Jackaleena. Jackaleena, this is Mr. Alfie Carter. He is my husband."

Jackaleena walked toward me. I just stood there, surprised to be approached by a young black girl whom I had never laid eyes on before.

"Hello, Mr. Alfie. I am Jackaleena," she said. She reached out her hand and touched mine. "I am pleased to make your meeting."

"Well, I am pleased to make your meeting, too. Would you like to go outside with me for a little while? I am lopping down some small mesquite bushes in the back and raking brush. Big thorns, you know and not good on—well, they are just not good to have around."

"Yes, I go with you," she said.

I turned and showed a look of concern to Bea as I closed the door. Bea put her hands to her face and looked out the window as she watched them head toward the back. She was quite small when compared to Alfie, but did not linger behind him while walking to the back. She was taking two steps to his one but managed to keep up.

"Now, this is a mesquite thorn," I said, picking up a broken branch from the pile and pointing out the green thorn. "They are worse than a bite by a snake. You ever seen a snakebite, Jackaleena?"

She said nothing, just nodded.

"Well, I tell you, these things are worse, I believe. Especially in the knee when you are on a horse. Be very careful when I cut them. Just pick them up easily like this and place them on the pile for me, okay?"

She nodded as he began to lop the remaining bushes.

The job took an hour. I lopped the mesquite bushes with my newly sharpened loppers and Jackaleena picked the branches up carefully and placed them on the pile.

"Well," I said, taking off my gloves. "Looks like we got this job done. Are you tired?" I looked at her carefully. "Jackaleena, you have a cut on your arm. It is bleeding a bit. Let me look at that." I took her hand and looked at her left arm. There was a large scratch undoubtedly put there by a mesquite thorn as she was dragging the branch.

"Mr. Alfie, you have one on your arm, too." She pointed to a bleeding scratch on my arm above the glove line. She held her arm up to mine. "Look, you are Milano, I am darker. Jesus Man give us all the same color blood. It is red. See. All blood I ever see is red."

I had to turn away as the tears came to my eyes. Never in my life had I ever seen something like that. A small girl from Africa, different skin tone than me and showing me that all blood is red. I turned around and looked at her.

"Yes, Jackaleena. Skins are all shades of different colors. But all blood is red. I never quite thought of it like that, but it is true. How about we go get a glass of Bea's lemonade? Ever had any lemonade?"

"No, Mr. Alfie. I have no lemonade."

"Well now, let's go get some. How about you take hold of my hand so no bears get you?"

"Mr. Alfie, what is bears?"

CHAPTER TWENTY-FIVE

The formal adoption process was put into place for Beatrice and I to adopt Jackaleena. I fell head-over-heels in love with her and did not want to spend a lot of time apart from her. Her high aptitude and thirst for knowledge were some of the highest hurdles for Bea and I had to jump. We could never keep enough books for her to read and on any subject matter. She not only read them, sometimes ten or more a month, she absorbed every letter, every syllable, and every phrase of every page. It was as if she had a photographic memory. We had never seen such a gifted child. Once she was formally adopted, she would take our last name and over time would become a US citizen.

I found her reading one day in the late afternoon. Strangely, Bea was not at home when I arrived home from work. This was never the case.

"Jackaleena, where is Mrs. Bea?"

"She goes to see dead baby, I think. Maybe she need you very much."

I had not been to the graveyard since Patricia was buried over twenty years ago. I felt very uncertain.

"Mr. Alfie, maybe she need you very much I think. Let us go to dead baby place. We have one of those in Benguela by the Sea. It is where Joao is below the ground."

I pulled up to the graveyard slowly. The memory of how I had handled the owner of the graveyard years before came flooding back.

"Mr. Alfie," Jackaleena said as she touched his hand. "Mrs. Bea, she need you I think. Let us walk."

I could scarcely remember which section of the graveyard Patricia was buried but finally spotted Bea's car, parked behind some cedar trees lining the roadway under the Garden of Gethsamane sign. There were small cherubs on each side of the sign with wings.

I parked the car and could see Beatrice lying on a blue blanket on Patricia's grave. It was the same blanket she had made for Patricia before she was born. She was facedown and crying quietly. There was box of tissues by her head. She did not hear or acknowledge Jackaleena and I when we approached. Jackaleena looked up at me and pointed at Bea.

"Bea, it's me. It's Alfie." She turned her red, swollen eyes toward me. She saw Jackaleena standing to the side. "Bea, I am here. I am finally here. You never have to face this alone again. I promise."

"Oh, Alfie," she said. "I am sorry. I am sorry I could never give you a child. I failed."

"No, ma'am. You did not fail. I have a child, she stands right there." I motioned Jackaleena to come forward. I wrapped my arms around both of them. "Bea, Patricia is gone. Jesus is taking care of her. We will see her again someday. We all have each other now."

Jackaleena stood away from both of them.

"Mr. Alfie and Mrs. Bea. Jesus Man send me. I have a big purpose. My purpose is you, Mr. Alfie," as she grabbed his hand. "Mrs Bea, my purpose is you," as she grabbed her hand. "Your baby died long time ago and is with Jesus Man. If she could come back, she may not want to, I think. I think my father and mother are dead. I hope they are with Jesus Man. If they are and could come back, I think they not come back.

"I think we live today and not think too much about yesterday. Let us walk to the car and let us go home. Together."

CHAPTER TWENTY-SIX

Judge Parker looked worn out.

"That is the most incredulous and intriguing story I have ever heard in my life, Ms. Carter," he said. "The very fact that you are an attorney working in my court is unfathomable to me after what you have told me. Your courage and determination are somewhat breathtaking and the most commendable thing I have ever heard of in my lifetime about any human being. But you have told me nothing about how you ascertained your schooling and your law degree, the bar exam and the rest. That journey, I am sure, was full of potholes and hurdles but just look at you. I mean just look at you. I am honored to be working with you to say the least."

Jackie looked at him closely. "Judge, it has been a long day. We have a very busy day tomorrow. Yes, it was a remarkable journey and it continues today. But that is another story for another day."

ABOUT THE AUTHOR

©Alaina Eubank

BJ Mayo was born in an oil field town in Texas. He spent the first few years of his life living in a company field camp twenty-five miles from the closest town. His career in the energy industry took him to various points in Texas, New Mexico, Colorado, Utah, Louisiana, Bangladesh, Australia, and Angola West Africa.

He and his wife were high school sweethearts and have been married for forty-six years with two grown children. They live on a working farm near San Angelo, Texas.